The Augur: Indigo

Lauren Jiggetts

Published by Lauren Jiggetts, 2021.

THE AUGUR: INDIGO

First edition. May 13, 2021.

ISBN: 978-1737153313

Written by Lauren Jiggetts.

This is dedicated to my Makers, who know naught of my future nor of the reason I even draw breath. I was told you would not have brought me here to endure what is needed to maintain this life. It was said that, if you had known, you would have spared me from the world you now understand to exist. To this, I am thankful you had not. For I carry your light in me, and your decision was not made in vain. As we are human, so too are our ambitions.

1

The restaurant was crowded.

Regardless of how often I enacted this practice, I still would get anxious. I worried it would be the day I begged for. When that day came, I would be done. I didn't even fully understand why because I had no reason to wonder anymore. I had been doing this for years. I could say most of my life, I guess. I couldn't really remember when I wasn't doing it. Even as I sat here, staring into his eyes, I felt my heart pounding. I asked myself; what if it didn't work?

"This is a nice spot," he said, scanning the establishment. "They must have really good service."

I hadn't taken anyone here yet. It was a fairly new location and its name could easily sound like someone sneezing. Classical music played faintly amid the chattering patrons. The overhead lighting was soft, allowing the flames from candles set at the center of our table to glow brighter. The table itself appeared to be authentic wood. Gleaming silverware, wrapped in a cream-colored cloth napkin held closed by a silver ring, was arranged on white porcelain plates with elegant floral and vine patterned edges. There were two sets of empty drinking glasses and a pair of wine glasses. I imagined they hand polished everything.

"Yes," I agreed. I leaned forward to point at a random meal on the menu. I could hardly read the calligraphy font. "The food is also really good. I like this."

"Oh, nice." He eyed it briefly. "I think I'll try it, then."

He raised his gaze to me and we locked eyes. He shifted in his seat, clearing his throat quietly. He gave a weak smile as he tried to avert his eyes, yet he couldn't seem to look away.

"Should we order now?" I asked, smiling sweetly.

"Yea," he replied, almost in a whisper, "I think we should."

My smile grew wider as I called for the waiter. I ordered two of the meal on the menu and an expensive red wine.

"Ah, Cabernet Sauvignon," the waiter smugly presented when I stumbled over the brand's pronunciation. He filled a set of our glasses with water. "Yes, that one is a favorite. Imported directly from France..."

Though I did savor the wine, the food was unremarkable. He offered to pay for dinner. He said he enjoyed it and would like to return one day. I nearly made a comment on this, but smiled instead and pushed the plate away as he requested the check. I needed to finally take him to bed. I had been indulging him long enough. Tonight, was the night. It had to be.

We reserved a room at a luxury hotel for the night to spend more time together. I'd been interested in trying this particular hotel for some time. Once we arrived in the room, I located the mini fridge and set my purse on top before I picked up one of the drink glasses to use. I removed a small vial from my purse and poured its contents inside. I twirled around to face him and saw he was already in the bed.

He was naked, lying on his back. His name was Gregory. At least, I think that was the name he told me. He may have said it was Jeffrey. He was tall, with dark chocolate skin. The muscles in his left arm rippled as he stroked himself. His broad nose curved strong above his voluptuous lips. He grinned eagerly and his teeth were almost sparkling.

I stood there and watched for a few seconds as he pleased himself before I started to undress. I seductively let my blouse drop to the floor. As I bit my lower lip, I peeled the skin tight jeans off my body and I felt my heart beat quickening. I slowly walked over to him while unclasping my bra. I climbed onto the bed once it dropped to the floor and, while still wearing my panties, I sat on top of him to take over his stroking.

He licked his lips and placed both hands behind his head. He stared into my eyes, lust oozing through his pores.

"Close your eyes," I ordered.

"I can't," he answered, and reached out to grab me. He pulled me close as he sat up to kiss my bare chest. He cupped my breast and began sucking my nipple. He flicked it with his tongue gently, then grasped my face to give me a kiss so fervid, I could almost taste it.

I sighed in satisfaction before pulling away and pushed him back onto the bed.

"Close your eyes," I repeated, sternly.

He hesitated, then did as I instructed.

I removed my panties and leisurely pulled out my tampon to mount him. I caressed his member, lightly pressing my lips onto the tip for a kiss. I ran my tongue along his shaft and then positioned to slide it inside of me.

"Mmmm," he moaned deeply. His eyes remained closed. Grunting in appreciation, he grabbed my hips. "Mmhmm... Ride me, girl... like that..."

I moved my hips to the rhythm he created with his arm motion. I started to bounce with gradual intensity which caused the bed to creak as it rocked. I watched his expressions change from mild to concentrated enjoyment and I felt increased pressure below which indicated he was close to the pinnacle. I swiftly slid off of him. I wrapped my lips around it and he ejaculated into my mouth.

"Ah, fuck!" he yelled, his body tensing while he sat up. His eyes snapped open. They trembled and rolled back as he fainted.

I got up from the bed and immediately spit his semen into the glass. I checked the mini fridge and discovered it contained a minibar. I had already purchased a small bottle of liquor that dwelled in my purse, but decided to use the vodka from it to fill the rest of the glass. I swirled the glass around a little, took a lungful of air, then poured the drink down my throat. I scowled at the taste, and swallowed several more times before I set down the glass to return to him. As soon as I sat down on top of his unresponsive body, I used my blood to draw my master's symbol onto his chest with an unsteady hand. I closed my eyes, raised my hands above my head, and mouthed the incantation.

The temperature in the room escalated. A shadow crept around me, crawling across the floor. It made its way up the sides of the bed and climbed into my mouth. It held me in place as it entered me.

I was restrained for almost ten minutes, undergoing the pain from the shadow. I felt it discharge from my body and I was freed from paralysis. I fell over, gasping for air. I whimpered and clutched my abdomen.

"Please, Lord," I whispered, tearfully. "Please save me from this... Please..."

I would beg for His help. I pleaded for Him to alleviate my burden, but I was unable to refuse performing these deeds.

Once I entered the bathroom, I stood at the sink and stared in the mirror at my tired face. My brown skin was dull and desiccated, with prominent wrinkles. I had dark circles around my eyes and my lips were harshly cracked. The salon style I received that morning had reverted and my gray hair was scraggly, and rough. I mopped away my tears before I took a shower. The water ran over me for what felt like an hour. Upon leaving the bathroom, I saw the room was pitch black. I cautiously stepped from the bathroom and my heart palpitated as I hastily went to the light switch by the exit. I held my breath.

Is this the day? I thought, fearful. *Will I finally see an end to this?*

I prayed for the day, but I also dreaded it. With my eyes closed, I flipped on the lights. I reopened my eyes one at a time and exhaled with immense relief.

His body was gone.

I promptly got dressed, then gathered all of our belongings. I requested a pickup through a ride sharing app that arrived about eight minutes later. I urgently fled out of the room and exited the hotel through a side entrance. As the driver advanced toward my apartment, I grew progressively woozy. I was fighting to stay conscious when we reached my complex and strained to climb the stairs, tripping over my own feet. Upon entering my place, I headed straight for my bedroom. The fatigue overpowered me and I fell forward on to the bed.

~~ * ~~

My eyes sluggishly opened to bright rays of sunshine. I turned over on my back and the room whirled slightly. My head ached something fierce. I rolled with less exertion to my side to bring my legs over the edge of the bed. As I sat up, I slipped my feet into my house shoes. I shut my eyes tight and rubbed my forehead. My skin felt coarse and worn. I opened my eyes to view that my nails had grown almost three inches.

"Ugh," I griped.

I inspected my feet and realized my toenails were close to puncturing holes through my slippers. I removed them and with a short glimpse out of my window, I went to the bathroom. I splashed water on my face and observed myself. My hair grew an extra few inches. I grabbed scissors from the medicine cabinet and began chopping off the additional growth. I watched the matted clumps fall to the floor and noticed a vivid red stain between my legs.

I need to shower, I thought.

I scooped up my hair to drop it into the trash. I twisted the knob on my shower and the water sputtered out as I heard a knocking noise behind the grimy tiled wall. After my shower, I promptly trimmed my finger and toenails. I examined my face in the mirror again to make sure I washed away any residual makeup.

"I assume last night went smoothly?"

I peered to my left and saw my cat sitting in the doorway. I continued checking my face. She stretched and began to lick her paw.

"Is that a yes?" she asked, noting my silence.

I narrowed my eyes and I exhaled in frustration, trying to ignore her.

"Oh, come on," she said. "Don't give me that look! You enjoy this."

"I hate this!" I suddenly yelled, pounding the sink. "I fucking... hate it!"

"Then stop. You don't have to do it anymore."

"Oh, can I? Can I really stop?" I glared at her. I was so filled with rage, but I couldn't bring myself to attack her. "How do I stop?"

She stared at me, impassive. She said nothing and I could swear her eyes were laughing at me.

"Well?" I hounded. "How do I stop? Huh? Kill you??"

She snickered, purred and rubbed against my leg. "Oh, you can't try."

"God give me strength..." I knelt down and stroked her chin. "Fuck you."

She was right. I couldn't even attempt to harm her. I only had my thoughts. They told me I wanted her dead every waking moment. She purred louder as I pet behind her ears and down her back.

"I'm hungry," she said, casually trotting to the kitchen.

I don't give a fuck.

"I'll get you breakfast," I replied, "give me a fucking second..."

I reentered my room and saw the time on my phone displayed six minutes past eight A.M. I would need to head to my job soon. Before fixing my cat a meal, I decided to prepare for work. I got dressed in a salmon colored frilly blouse and a charcoal gray pencil skirt with dark brown stockings. I slid on black heels, brushed my teeth and applied more makeup in the bathroom after tying my hair as best I could. Satisfied with what I had done, I went to the kitchen.

"Finally!" my cat shouted impatiently. She sat on the kitchen table with an empty bowl in front of her. "You were taking forever. It doesn't look like you did much to yourself. Are you wearing makeup? It looks hideous."

I wouldn't protest, as she was accurate again. My makeup didn't accentuate my appearance in any way. I bit my tongue and pulled steak from the refrigerator.

"Can you move a little faster?" she quipped. "I know you can move faster."

"Lord, help me," I whispered, gazing at the ceiling. I started cooking the steak on the stove. "Help me with this demon. It holds me hostage—-"

My back was to her, so I didn't see what she was doing. In an instant, her tail wrapped around my neck. The brown fur stood up and felt like needles as she tightened her grip. She rotated me around to face her.

"Your Lord can't help you," she growled. "You hold yourself hostage, remember? You don't really want to stop..."

I grabbed at her tail, gasping for air. I struggled to breathe as she pulled me towards the table, causing my feet to drag across the floor. I tried to speak but nothing would come out. Spots appeared in my eyes and my heart hammered on my rib cage.

"Hmm," she purred, and released my neck. "My steak is burning."

I finally drew breath, coughing and hacking. I spun around to yank the pan off the burner. I shivered as I made my way to the table and dropped the steak into her bowl.

"What are you doing?" she demanded, repulsed. She elevated the bowl with her tail to throw the steak onto the floor. "Make me a new one, how I like it. I need to see blood."

How long will I have to do this? Why can't I be free?

I fought back tears while going to the refrigerator. My mind slinked into memories I had predominantly suppressed. I began to remember how I met her. This wasn't the first time she told me she needed blood.

$$\sim\sim * \sim\sim$$

I can hardly remember much about my childhood, but I remembered the events that surrounded my very first menstrual cycle.

"It means you're becoming a woman," my mother told me. "Means you need to be grown now."

"Yes," my father chimed in. "You're a woman and have to act like it."

Those were the words he told me almost every night.

I was an only child, but I felt as if my mother never had time for me. I scarcely saw her before sunset. When I did see her, I couldn't tell her what I really wanted to. She had little confidence in my feelings and often called me dramatic.

"Stop acting like somebody killed your dog!" she said one night. "You don't know enough about life to know about suffering."

I wanted to tell her about what my father was doing to me, but I was afraid she would blame me for it.

"Leave that girl alone," my father regularly defended me by telling her. "She just needs some guidance..."

We were in the living room. My mother and father sat on the couch and I had come from my room to observe what they were watching on the television.

My mother huffed at my father's words and sipped her drink. He took the cigarette she was holding and put it to his lips.

"Give me back my cigarette!" she exclaimed, flinging her arm in his direction.

He jerked away in time for her to miss.

"Take it back," he teased, and started smoking it.

She cackled heartily, long and hoarse. She brought her glass to her lips and once she discovered it was empty, she held it out to me as a signal for me to refill it. She leaned in and grasped my wrist when I took it from her.

"Don't go taking some for yourself," she disparaged, "because I know you do."

I didn't actually sneak any drinks, but she firmly believed I did. I found it challenging to talk to her when she was in this state. I nodded in reply and she let me go.

She sat back and propped her heavy feet up on the coffee table. "Hurry up, then!"

I scampered to the kitchen to get her favorite drink. It was a dark liquor, and she loved it. I sometimes felt she loved it more than anything else in the world, especially me. I pulled the bottle from the cabinet beside the refrigerator and my father appeared next to me as I closed it. Alarmed, I almost dropped the bottle.

"Daddy!" I shrieked, startled. "You scared me—-"

"Shhh..." he cut in and abetted as I filled my mother's glass. "You don't need to do that, baby. She's asleep."

"Oh, I'll put this back then..." I opened the bottle again.

"No, have some." He picked up the glass and put it to my lower lip. "Drink."

I hesitated. I didn't want my mother's accusation about me drinking her liquor to be true.

"Just a little..." my father prodded. "She won't even know."

I shyly opened my mouth and he tilted the glass. The bitter liquid burned on its way down. I cringed at the unpleasant sensation.

He chortled, amused by my reaction. "There, not too much..."

He caressed my face, and neck, then leaned in to kiss me. He tasted foul.

I held my breath and closed my eyes while he forced his lips on mine. I felt his hands slide under my arms and he hoisted me onto the counter.

"Please," I begged quietly, "Please..."

"Shh, shh, sshhhh..." He pressed his finger against my lips and it smelled like smoke. "It's ok. I will never hurt you..."

I grew increasingly frightened. "Momma..."

"She's asleep. She won't wake up for a while... I promise."

"No, I..."

He kissed me again, shoving his hand between my thighs. He tenderly rubbed before gliding his hand underneath the elastic waistband of my shorts. He forced his hand down between my legs to massage me.

"Wet..." he sighed in delight, breathing heavily. He pulled his hand out and his fingers were red. "You're bleeding..."

"I'm -—I'm sorry!" I blurted out. "I don't feel good, Daddy, I should lie down!"

"It's ok, baby..."

"Please, don't be mad at me... I'm becoming a woman. You said so..." I could hear my heart pounding.

"Shh, it's alright. It's just a little blood." He stuck his fingers into his mouth and sucked them. He unhurriedly pulled them back out while staring into my eyes. "A little blood never hurt nobody."

I was shocked and immediately climbed down from the counter. I wanted to run. I also didn't want him to be upset with me for disobeying.

He tugged my waistband and proceeded to lower my shorts. As he brought them down to my ankles, he kissed my hips. He pulled down my panties and stood up.

"Turn around," he ordered. "Turn around and bend over."

I cautiously did as I was told, repressing my sobs.

~~ * ~~

My father developed a habit that lasted months. One day, my mother fell ill. She was too sick to go to work or do any household chores. My father relied heavily on me to assist during her illness. He confided in me his worries about my mother's health and frequently spent evenings in bed with me. He thanked me countless times for how much I comforted him.

My mother was sick for over three weeks. When he came to me this evening, it was probably close to midnight. He was coming to me like he had done every night before.

The bedroom door quietly swung open as he tiptoed inside. Upon shutting the door, he snuck over to my bed and sat down. The mattress creaked faintly.

My skin started to heat up, perspiration forming in my palms. My chest thumped and I tried to act as if I was still asleep. I almost jumped when I felt his hand rest on my hip.

"Are you awake?" he asked, his voice just above a whisper.

I kept my eyes closed and didn't respond. I hoped he would decide to let me sleep. I hoped this every time.

"Are you awake?" he repeated, a little louder. He slipped my covers off. He began to breathe heavily as he glided his hand along my thigh. He lifted my nightgown to expose my skin.

I shut my eyes tighter and prayed for him to change his mind.

There was no movement for several seconds. His hand moved to my panties and he started to pull them off. He wasn't going to leave me alone.

"I know you're awake," he said. "Let your daddy spend some time with you..."

He made it sound so supportive when he used that term. He made me feel like I wasn't being a good daughter if I refused. He climbed on top of me and turned me onto my back.

I opened my eyes as he removed his pants.

"There you are," he whispered, and kissed me. He softly pushed my legs apart to insert himself.

I squirmed as I tolerated discomfort from his actions. I watched while he closed his eyes and began rocking over me. The bed squeaked in response to the activity. Bubbles of sweat formed on his head. He growled gently and periodically gave me a sloppy kiss on my neck. I hoped he wouldn't be long this time. I bowed my head to peek at my door when I saw a sliver of light appear under it. I thought of warning him, but the feeling quickly passed.

The door smoothly opened and my mother's shadow loomed in the entranceway.

"What the FUCK?!" she screamed. "What the fuck are you DOING?!!"

My father was jumping to his feet as she hobbled over to the bed.

"Estie, baby," he sputtered, apologetically. "I—-"

"Shut your fucking mouth, James!" She held her chest, wheezing. "Just, shut UP!"

He adjusted himself, blood staining his hands and crotch. He retrieved his pants to pull them on.

"Jesus Christ!" she wailed. She pointed a shaking finger to the door. "Get out... Now!"

He hung his head and exited into the hall. My mother followed him without acknowledging me, closing my door behind her. There was shouting. A door slammed, then everything was quiet.

I waited in bed silently for my door to open again, but it didn't. I got up and stared at the door, petrified to leave. I couldn't hear anything.

More time passed, and I still heard nothing. I took a deep breath and opened my door. I peered out warily into the dark hallway. Down to the right, light glowed from the bottom of my parents' bedroom door. There were shadows passing back and forth.

I advanced toward it and could hear what sounded like fighting. I froze as the noise increased. There was scuffling and crashing. I started moving backward, when I felt a breeze on the back of my neck. A chill crawled up and down my spine. Hot air blew into my right ear. I flinched and spun around to look in my room. I switched on the light nervously, but saw nothing. I felt the hot air again on the back of my neck that caused me to twirl around back to the hall.

"Mrowr..."

I slowly peeked over my shoulder to find a cat sitting on my bed. I was surprised and approached it.

"How did you get here, kitty?" I asked it. I reached out to pet its head. "Did you sneak in a window...?"

It brushed against my hand, purring.

I giggled and patted its head. "Hello, pretty kitty..."

It suddenly glanced up at me with a penetrating gaze.

"Your mother is dying," it said in a calm, female voice. "Right now."

"Huh?" I gasped and bounded back. I tried to process what I just heard.

"I said, your mother," she replied. "She is dying. She will die if you don't help her."

"You're... you talk..." I managed to form a sentence, astonished.

"Yes, and I am telling you that your mother is dying. You're next if you don't know what's good for you."

I eyed the door.

"He's not coming yet," she assured me. "He's currently planning how to tell you what happened. It's going to be a lie."

"No..." I shook my head. Tears welled up in my eyes. "I don't believe you... How are you talking? None of this is real..."

"Stop trying to understand everything, you don't have time."

"My Daddy would never hurt me. He loves me..."

"He will kill your mother." She leapt from my bed. "He will be here soon. I can help you get away."

"You're not REAL!" I cried and ran to the door.

My father stepped in from the dark hall, stopping me in my tracks. His shirt was torn at the collar. There were scratches on his neck and the left side of his face. It seemed like my mother may have fought him.

"Daddy?" I sniffled. "Where's Momma?"

He stood there, breathing erratically. His forehead was damp and his eyes were glassy. He shook his head.

"What, what's wrong?" I choked out. "Where's Momma?!"

He entered the room and lunged at me.

"Aaah!!" I quickly dodged him and bolted out. I turned left to run towards the living room and tripped over the coffee table upon arriving. Landing on one knee, I began crawling to the couch to hide behind it. I attempted to control my breathing so I would stay quiet.

The floor boards creaked from the hall. The sounds grew closer until they were just on the other side of the couch.

"Let me help you," the talking cat said. She was behind the couch with me. "You don't have to die."

The creaking moved away and back down the hallway.

"He's going to find you," she persisted. "He won't let you live."

I shut my eyes and attempted to pay no attention to her voice.

"Cats don't talk..." I whispered to myself.

Unexpectedly, the couch lifted from the floor. My father shoved it aside, exposing my hidden spot.

"Daddy, no!" I yelled. I scrambled to my feet and ran down the hallway to my parents' room. I busted through the door and closed it behind me. After locking it, I searched for my mother.

She was lying on her back in the bed, her eyes wide and staring blankly at the ceiling. One of her hands hung off the side of the bed, quaking. She wore one slipper and her feet here twitching. The table lamp was on the floor beside the nightstand, its base in pieces.

As I stepped closer, the sound of battering stunned me. I heard the bedroom door rattle as my father tried to gain access. The banging strengthened.

$$\sim\sim \, ^* \, \sim\sim$$

I was snapped from my reminiscence by the rapid banging on my front door. I closed the fridge without removing another slab of meat and dragged my feet to answer.

"My steak!" my cat hissed.

When I arrived at the door, I checked the peephole.

It was my landlord, Harriett. She was a middle-aged woman, probably in her late forties. She had a unibrow and wore her hair in a messy bun. Large framed glasses sat on the tip of her nose, which she pushed up with her middle finger before she balled her hand into a fist to beat my door again.

I jerked the door open just as she swung for another round.

"Oh, good morning!" she chirped. She grinned, revealing her gapped front teeth. "I wasn't sure if you got off to work already..."

"No," I responded. "I'm just about to go—-"

"Can I come in?" She stepped inside, making her question rhetorical.

"Ok..."

"I won't take long." She was in the kitchen, probing around. "It's just... I got word you have a pet..."

"A pet?" I replied, uncertainly. I narrowed my eyes and followed her.

"Yea... you see, when I rented to you, I made it clear no pets. Ever." She left the kitchen and walked down to my bedroom.

I was right on her heels.

"I... I don't have a pet..." I said. "Who said I have a pet...?"

I can't get kicked out of here... I thought, apprehension increasing. *I don't have a new place yet!*

"Someone heard a cat meowing or something last night," she answered. She was determined to prove this. She stood in the doorway of my bedroom and turned around. "And it's not the first time, either. So, where is it? You signed an agreement. If you have a pet, I need to charge you a penalty. You've been here for five months, so that's eight seventy-five."

"What?! How's that?!" My face grew hot. "I don't have a fucking cat!"

Her eyebrows hiked and she stared at me, appalled. She legitimately wanted me to pay the fine. "No need for foul language, ma'am. If you have a pet, you pay the penalty and remove it. There's no special treatment and no deals here."

As I heard her call me 'ma'am', I felt very old. How I felt was probably nothing compared to how I appeared.

I took several breaths. "There's no cat, and no pets here. I need to go to work. Unless you have something else, I prefer you leave..."

"Ma'am, I am doing you a courtesy by asking you about the pet—-"

"I don't have a pet, and now I'm leaving. Check whatever the FUCK you want, and see yourself the FUCK OUT!" I grabbed my purse from the living room couch before stomping out of the apartment.

2

I was fifteen minutes early to my job. I usually was there before anyone else arrived and would spend time in a stall of the restroom because the office was full of open space. I favored the ability to close the door for privacy. I wanted to quit working, but I needed the money. How else could I afford to live?

I sat on the toilet, biting my nails. They had grown a little since I cut them earlier in the morning. I was replaying the conversation I had with Harriett over in my mind. I wondered who heard a cat and why they reported me. If my cat made noise every time I sacrificed, what drove them to tell Harriett now? Were they fed up? I patted my hair, curious if it was still neatly tucked in the style.

"Did you see his post last night?" an animated feminine voice pierced the restroom's tranquility.

"Yes, I did," another responded excitedly. "He's so sexy. I wish I knew him for real. We would be at his parties instead of here…"

"Honey, I will be. I have an idea that'll get me noticed, you watch."

I recognized the voices as Tiffany and Stella. They were two young, very attractive black women in their late twenties. They started working here after me, maybe two or three months ago. They came to work to mostly ogle themselves and gossip. Tiffany was hired first and referred her friend, Stella.

"Yea?" Stella asked, inquisitive. "Let me in on it, will you? I do NOT wanna be here for the rest of my life."

"Who does that?" Tiffany replied, laughing.

The answer was inaudible. The walls seemed to vibrate as they giggled loudly.

"I can definitely see that!" Stella said. "When you said she was old as dirt, you weren't lying."

"She's fucking old as shit," Tiffany agreed.

"She kinda stinks too..."

"What?? No..."

"Yes, girl."

The sink turned on.

"Like what?" Tiffany dribbled with anticipation.

"Cat piss."

I stood up and opened the stall door.

They were situated in front of the full-length mirror by the sinks, admiring themselves. Stella stood directly in front of the mirror, blowing kisses at herself. She began rubbing her finger along her bright red lips. She spied me through her reflection and stopped. Tiffany was posing for a selfie with her back to me. She hadn't noticed me behind her and snapped a photo.

"Cat piss?!" Tiffany repeated, and held her phone higher to get a better angle. She spun around when she saw me in the background of the shot.

They both stared in silence.

"You bitches should get back to work," I barked, heart pounding through my chest. "This isn't your house, so get the fuck on."

"Who are you talking to?" Stella interrogated, visibly offended. She turned toward me.

"You, bitch." I went to the sink to wash my hands. "Get back to work. I have no problem reminding Gary he should fire the both of you this month. That should help you move on."

As if on cue, Gary's head appeared through the door of the restroom. He was a white man, average height and build with brown eyes and light brown hair that was peppered with a little gray. He was the Office Director.

"Knock, knock," he said, smiling warmly as he stepped inside. He nodded at the two women and then looked at me. "I need you. I need your expertise."

I wasn't working at this place for very long, just over seven months. It was an employment agency named Faculty Climate Solutions. It basically was an office space full of desks. The main goal of employees was to attract candidates to place into positions they were most likely unqualified for. The clients would transmit a request for specific applicants and if the person was not considered a 'good fit', a new person would be offered in their place for a nominal rate. The applicants were clearly incompetent. It was ridiculous, but I didn't feel bad for any client who kept using their services. If they wanted to continue funding this operation, I'd say let them.

Gary liked to have me reveal the hopefuls. He especially favored this when there were a large group of them to interview. He would ask for my 'expertise', which was my ability to sense a person's desire for work. This was precise and I hadn't been mistaken about a person's intentions. One time or another he even had me assess a few clients for the same reason. He would determine whether to pursue them for business based on what I observed.

I nodded and left the restroom with him. We went into the interview room.

The interview room was small. It was crammed with ten folding chairs and one desk. Two of the chairs were at the desk and the remaining eight were in the center facing toward the door. All eight of the chairs were filled.

"Whoa, full house," I muttered.

"Yes, full house," Gary affirmed, grinning. "I'm hoping we get at least four, ok?"

Four? I thought as I surveyed the group. *This bunch looks useless.*

One particular individual gave me prompt uncertainties. Upon first glance, he gave the inkling he was somewhat out of place. His skin was mahogany, or closer to espresso, and clean shaven. His eyes were black with serious, thick eyebrows. His lips were plump and had a subtle sheen to them. He had a medium afro fade haircut and he was dressed lavishly. He wore a sky-blue dress shirt that must have been tailored. It clung to his arms and hugged his chest. He obviously worked out. A navy-blue tie lay on the shirt's button seam. He had on a silver watch. His slacks were steel gray, pressed, and the creases neat. He wore shiny, chestnut brown wing tip style dress shoes. He clasped his large hands together in his lap, fingernails clean and trimmed. His posture was relaxed as he sat in the uncomfortable folding chair.

"Ahem," Gary cleared his throat to get everyone's attention, including mine. "Good morning everyone. Welcome to Faculty Climate Solutions. My name is Gary. We will be interviewing you all one at a time and I ask that, once you are called, please have a seat here..."

He waved his hand toward the folding chair at the desk. "After the interview," he continued, "you will return to your original spot..."

I watched each of them as he spoke and saw a couple of them smirking. I wanted to roll my eyes. I wished to leave the room and march over to Stella's desk so I could slap her in her smug face. The thought caused me to smile in amusement. My vision drifted to the man with the navy-blue tie and I realized he was staring at me. My smile dissolved.

Has he been staring at me the whole time? I'm not even the one talking. Is he staring because he's trying to figure out what makes my skin so dry?

I instantly became self-conscious and immediately veered my sight to the woman sitting beside him. Shortly after, my gaze reverted back to him. I found he was still staring and it was difficult for me to deviate again. I developed a warm sensation in my chest.

I heard Gary call me. I tore my eyes away and saw the woman who sat next to the blue-tie man was at the desk. I didn't even notice she had gotten up.

"Hi," she said. She cleared her throat and put her hands on her knees. She was unsettled and had no interest in being here.

"Skills..." Gary was reading her résumé. "Effective Time Management... Tell me about that."

I put my hands behind my back and observed her as she responded to the interview questions. She hoped to get a job, but didn't care what the position actually was that Gary mentioned to her. I looked over at the man even though I tried hard not to. I wanted to get a sense of his feelings.

He was engrossed in his phone. He didn't appear to have any expectations from the interview.

Gary called each of the interviewees up and eventually there were just two left.

"Ok, next..." Gary announced, gaining my awareness. "Uh... Nefter... T-—thu... moss... ee..."

"Thutmose," a voice corrected from the group. "Nefer Thutmose."

The man with the dark blue tie stood up and casually made his way to the chair. He practically coasted into the seat as he smiled at me.

Nefer Thutmose... I noticed his broad shoulders. *There's no way he is going to work here. He has something about him that doesn't sit right.*

I couldn't explain what it was, but he gave me a strange feeling. I began to feel the tepid impression from before as he peered at me. It travelled down between my legs and I was overwhelmed with calming delectation. I stumbled back to the wall for support.

"You ok?" Nefer asked me, genuinely concerned. He stood up.

"Yes," I sharply replied. I recovered my footing. "Please continue."

Gary glimpsed at me, equally worried and confused.

"Please... continue..." I repeated, hoping they would ignore what just occurred.

"Alright, Nefer," Gary said, "thank you for coming."

Nefer returned to the seat and said, "Yes, sir, thank you."

He smiled at me again, but I swiftly glanced away.

"So, how did you hear about us...?" Gary questioned.

"I was referred here by a friend," he answered. He was telling the truth as he spoke. "She thinks it would be a good place to work."

I examined his face and focused on the pronoun he used.

She? How many 'she's' work here? There's Ally, Lindsey, Cecilia... Francine... is he talking about Tiffany or Stella? It better not be those two dumb bitches...

"Oh, I'm glad to hear," Gary nodded his head in praise.

"Who referred you?" I blurted out.

"Sekima," he responded, gazing into my eyes.

The feelings I experienced resumed, and steadily grew stronger. They streamed through my chest, went between my thighs and my knees began to shake. I swallowed hard and adjusted my posture.

"Excuse me..." I mumbled. I pulled the door open to leave the room.

"Doris?" Gary called after me.

I virtually ran to my desk that was just outside the room and sat down. Panting heavily, I pulled a tissue out and blotted my forehead.

Oh Lord, what was that? Did he do that to me?

A sharp pain surged through my abdomen. I stood up and made my way to the restroom.

"Doris?" Gary's voice called again from the interview room and I didn't respond.

I slammed the restroom stall door closed before sitting on the toilet. I bit my nails and bounced my leg, taking long, steady breaths. I closed my eyes as I tried to calm down.

"Doris."

My eyes flew open to see Gary's feet beyond the stall door.

"Gary," I answered. "Why are you in here?"

"Doris, you ran off. Are you alright?"

"Yes."

"Well, I am done with the applicants. Come to my office to review."

"Yes, ok."

He maintained standing there.

"I think you should go, Gary," I said. "This is the women's restroom."

"Just come to my office when you finish." His feet disappeared.

I heaved a sigh and went to his office.

It was across from the interview room. It was the only other room with a door and it had windows. Three massive windows sat directly behind his L-shaped desk. Accenting the windows were pewter curtains being held back by golden tassels. There were bookshelves lining the two walls on either side of his desk. The shelves housed some books, statues, and other decorative pieces. Potted faux plants were scattered throughout the shelves. A dark blue globe that was most likely marble sat on a center shelf. One shelf had a small group of animal figurines. At the center of the room was a burgundy round rug. A single armchair sat at an angle facing his desk.

Gary was at his desk, motioning for me to come in.

I sat down in the armchair.

"So..." he said. "What do you think? How many can we use?"

"Well..." I replied, shrugging.

"Doris, don't tell me none of them are good!" He was unconvinced.

"Gary..." I shook my head.

"None?!" He shoved papers around on his desk. He held up some résumés to show me. "Not even... these? They had very good answers..."

"None of them, Gary." I shrugged again.

Not even the one named Nefer... Especially not him.

"But, these three are good. I can feel it!" He assuredly shook the papers.

"I haven't been wrong on this, Gary—-"

"Yet!" He held his index finger up triumphantly.

"Yet..." I echoed. "And I am not wrong now. None are going to work out."

I had an image of Nefer's stare burned in my brain. I thought about the feelings that formed from it.

"Ok," Gary said. He gathered the papers to place into a pile.

I caught a peep of the time from a clock on one of the lower shelves. "Gary, I need to get home now."

"Of course, sure. Go, go."

I nodded and headed for the door.

"Doris," Gary probably said my name a thousand times today.

I looked over my shoulder and glanced at him from the corner of my eye.

"Thanks," he said graciously. "If you don't feel well, you should take the day tomorrow."

I exited his office considering the idea.

3

The loud alarm of my phone ended my pleasant slumber. As it blared, I refused to move and shut it off.

I should have put my phone on silent, I thought and groaned in disappointment.

I threw my arm out to grab my phone from the nightstand but I accidentally knocked it onto the floor where its robotic song persisted.

"Ugh!" I yelled, exasperated. I pulled the pillow over my head to drown out the sounds and was able to drift back to sleep.

Several seconds later, my ringtone blasted. My sleep was ruined.

I slithered out of the bed and landed on my butt next to my phone. I checked to see who was calling me. I saw it was just after nine A.M. I grumbled, debating whether to answer the call.

"Hello...?" I said, huffing into the phone.

"Doris," Gary replied on the other end. "I know I said take the day..."

"Yes, you did." I pinched the bridge of my nose. "And I am."

"Yes, you are." There was a long pause.

"Yes. I am." I closed my eyes tightly.

"Doris, I hired the three from yesterday."

Wow. I rolled my eyes. *He didn't believe me? At least It won't be like Charleston...*

"Ok," I said.

"So... I need to get them on board and through orientation."

"Ok..." I rolled my eyes again.

"Today."

I waited for him to say more, but he didn't.

"Gary, I'm hanging up now. This is my day off." I dropped my arm and swiped to end the call.

"Dori—" Gary's sentence was cut short.

I tossed the phone on my bed and crawled back into it with the intent of getting back to sleep. I wasn't going to get a chance.

The phone rang again.

All those other training managers should get it done!

I reluctantly answered.

"Yea?" I asked.

"Doris, please," Gary implored. "If you come in, please take tomorrow and Monday. Please."

"Fine." I hung up.

~~ * ~~

I entered the office not long after the phone call. I drudged passed the desks of staff typing away on their computers and went to Gary's office.

"Alright, I'm here," I broadcasted as I walked in.

He was leaning against his desk with his arms crossed, his attention on the person in the armchair.

"Ah, Doris," he said happily. He gestured towards the chair. "Please meet our new Client Relations Associate."

"Hi," the woman said. She cleared her throat, bashfully. "I'm Margaret. Or, Maggie for short."

She was the woman that sat next to Nefer during the interviews. She, and all the others, were not worth the trouble.

"Hello, Margaret..." I forced a smile. "Let's get you set up to start working..."

"Doris," Gary came over to me. "I had her put through orientation with Lindsey... She just needs you to do the paperwork with her and the training."

She hasn't signed any paperwork. Great...

"I see..." I waved for her to follow me. "Off to my desk, then. It won't take too long."

We went to my desk right outside the office. I grabbed a chair for her from a nearby unoccupied desk and placed it at mine. I began printing all the paperwork she needed to review and complete.

"This seems like a nice place to work," Margaret said as she sat down. She was only mildly serious. She didn't care much for the office.

"Yup," I replied. I clicked away at files on the computer.

"Gary seems nice," she added, but this word was a slim interpretation of her interest.

"Sure, yea."

"Is he married?"

I glanced at her as I pressed to print the final documents. I retrieved them from the printer at the other end of the office and positioned them down in front of her with a pen.

"I'm kidding," she said, smiling awkwardly. Her eyes shot to Gary's office.

No, you're not.

"Ok." I pointed to the papers. "Fill those out. Sign and date where indicated. Read the handbook and return the acknowledgment to me."

"Got it." She picked up the pen.

"Doris!" Gary hollered from inside his office.

"Here," I replied and stood by my desk.

"Doris, you ready for newbie number two?" He was in his doorway. "Can we use the desk there? It's empty. Here, Nefer, have a seat at the desk there."

Of course, he chose Nefer. My heart began to race. *Damn you, Gary.*

Nefer emerged from Gary's office and I pondered how I hadn't perceived he was in there. He was wearing a peach colored short sleeve collared shirt and khakis. He sat down at the uninhabited desk.

"Good morning, Doris," he greeted. My name rolled out of his mouth, smooth as silk.

"Yes, morning," I responded, slightly pleased by his manners. I dropped into my chair to print out more paperwork. My hands were perspiring.

"Morning," Margaret said. "Nefer?"

"Yea, good morning," he replied.

"Nice to meet you." She meant every word.

"Likewise, Miss...?"

"Oh! Um, Margaret." She blushed, jumping up from the chair to hold out her hand to him. "Or, Maggie for short..."

"Ok, then." He shook her hand firmly. "Maggie."

She giggled like a schoolgirl and I grimaced. She smoothed her hair and returned to her seat.

I stood up and plodded over to the printer. To avoid getting the papers wet from my hands, I held them loosely. As I arrived back to my desk, they slipped from my grip and scattered across the floor.

Shit! I cursed myself and knelt down.

"Allow me," Nefer offered.

Before I could object, he had swept the documents up into his hands and sat down.

I watched him organize them, fixated on his arms. My heart thudded on my ribcage. Pulsing began down below just before a cramp developed in my stomach. I turned to my desk for balance and moved to sit down.

This feels so good, but awful. I took a few deep breaths. *I can't stand this all day...*

"I'm done!" Margaret proclaimed, clapping her hands together. "Am I done?"

I blinked slowly and stared at her. I could sense her interest in being here had increased.

"I think I'm finished too," Nefer agreed.

"Ok," I finally said. "Let me set you up with the online training..."

I demonstrated how to log in and complete the training. I showed Nefer first and then Margaret. When I directed Margaret, I used my computer. I gazed at Nefer, and saw he was watching me rather than doing the training.

His eyes looked straight through mine.

I struggled to pull my eyes away but I failed. I feebly fought the emotions heightening. They swelled uncontrollably and travelled across my body. I was overcome with extreme satisfaction and a blissful sigh escaped my lips. I jumped up from my chair.

"Finish your training courses," I choked out. I absconded to the bathroom.

What is he doing to me? I frantically bit my nails as I stood in the stall. *It feels... so good. Is he a demon? Oh Lord, please tell me he isn't here to lead me further astray.... I'm not strong enough for this...*

Someone entered the restroom. The clicking of heels alerted me that thankfully it wasn't Gary. Lately, he was attached to me like a leash.

I recaptured my composure and opened the stall to leave.

"Are you ok?" the woman who walked in asked.

"Yes, I'm fine," I responded and hastily left. I lumbered to my desk and a sudden pain shot through my head. It throbbed aggressively as I heard ringing in my ears.

"Doris?" Gary called, coming from his office. "Are you... alright?"

"I—-" I started to answer with I was fine again, when my legs turned to jelly and I dropped to the floor. "Shit..."

I fell, just great...

"I'm calling an ambulance," Gary said.

"No!" I protested. "No, I just slipped..."

I hoisted myself up, huffing and puffing.

Nefer appeared beside me, and tried to take my hand.

I rejected it and clambered to my feet.

"Doris, maybe you should go home," Gary said, alarmed. "I think the new recruits are good to go."

"I'm leaving," I replied, massaging my temple. "I'll be back Tuesday."

"Yes, ma'am," Gary authorized. "Get out of here. Did you drive?"

I nodded, and snatched my purse from my desk. "I'm going now—-"

"As first objective for our new recruit, Nefer will make sure you get home—-" Gary began.

"Absolutely not." I whirled around and headed for the exit. "Goodbye."

The pain in my head subsided while I used the elevator. I walked slowly to my car. It was a champagne colored four-door sedan and the model year was possibly nineteen ninety-nine or two thousand. I unlocked the door and had to tug hard since it would stick. My car started with a squeaky whine. It shook briefly as I switched from Park to Drive. My headache expanded, causing me to stomp the brake and revert back to Park.

"Something bothering you?" my cat's voice wafted from the front passenger seat.

I turned and saw her loafing. I snuffled in aggravation.

"Oh, that's no way to greet your one and only friend," she pouted superficially. She began to lick her paws.

"What are you doing here?" I asked as I leaned back to close my eyes.

"I'm hungry and you didn't leave me anything to eat. I think you need to go to the store."

"You're a demon." I shrugged before I opened my eyes. "Can't you just get it all yourself? I don't get it..."

She placed her paw on my right arm and dug her claws into it. "Why should I, when I have you? Get me food. Now."

I cowered, biting my bottom lip in anguish. I could see blood trickle down my arm. I felt like her claws were cutting off my circulation. I put my left hand on the steering wheel and gritted my teeth. "Fine... Let me drive, please..."

She retracted her nails, then vaulted to the backseat. "Hurry up and get enough steak to fill the fridge."

I drove to the grocery store and went expressly to the meat section. As I stood and stared at the countered display case of meat cuts, I imagined fresh blood leaking from them.

Steak and blood are what she wants, I thought. *Steak and blood are always what she wants...*

"Which would you like?" the woman behind the counter queried. "We have a special going for our flank steaks. Only nine ninety-nine per pound with your club card."

"Yes," I responded. "I would like to have flank steaks..."

I made my way to the frozen foods section after putting at least a dozen steaks in my cart. I turned the corner to enter the ice cream aisle since I was craving something sweet. I identified Nefer standing just a few feet away, holding a tub of ice cream.

What the fuck. Is he following me? No, no, I don't need this!

It was as if he heard my thoughts because he looked up and directly at me.

"Doris?" he said.

I steered my cart in the opposite direction and rushed to the registers. When I got in line behind a man who had a cart filled to the brim, I counted each item the cashier swiped across the scanner and silently asked him to go faster. I watched over my shoulder and expected to see Nefer join the line.

The cashier was finished and began to scan my items.

"Oooh, a meat party!" he said, as he scanned them. "Taking advantage of the sale, nice!"

I checked behind myself again, ignoring his dull joke and phony praise.

"Do you have a club card?" he requested when I didn't respond.

I dangled my keys up for him and then paid for it with cash. At my car, I hurriedly piled the bags into my trunk.

"Can I help you with that?" Nefer stood by the cart and started to reach in.

"I got it!" I snarled, speedily pulling out the remainder of the bags. I snatched a bag that he caught falling from my hands before he could peek inside.

"Ok, you got it." He watched me throw everything in and slam the trunk shut. "What about getting it all to your place—-"

"I'm good." I shoved the cart away. "Really, I'm fine."

"I just wanna help..." He was sincere.

"I know..." I got in my car and started it up.

"Invite him home," my cat purred from the backseat.

Invite him home? It's too early for that. Unless...

"Do you know him?" I asked her.

"Not at all. He just... looks delicious... very suitable..."

On the drive home, my mind raced with thoughts of who this man could be. My cat said she didn't know him, so maybe he wasn't a demon but I wanted to know more about him. I was afraid it was a trick. I met a large amount of men and none of them gave me any sensation remotely close to what I had felt the past couple of days. At my apartment I carried the steaks in a folding wheel cart up to the third floor. I saw Harriett walking to my door and was instantly aggravated.

She stopped when she saw me coming.

"Good evening!" she said, relieved. "I'm glad I got here when you are home! Let's go in."

I opened the door and headed to the kitchen to put away my purchases without waiting for her. I had a clock in my kitchen and the time displayed seven thirty P.M. I hadn't a clue why she was here so late. I didn't call her.

"So," she started. "Doris. I am here to discuss your pet issue..."

"I don't have a pet," I curtly replied. I stuffed the meats into the fridge and some into the freezer.

"Yes, you do. I found evidence of this and you must pay the fine as well as remove the pet immediately. I can take a check or money order. If you need a payment plan, I can roll it into your rent as ten percent increments..."

I scoffed. "I'm not paying anything, because I don't have a pet."

"Either you pay the fine, or you will be in violation of your lease." She dug in her pocket to pull out some papers.

"Where's your evidence?"

"I tried to be civil with you. Here is notice that your lease is being terminated. You are to vacate this apartment in fourteen days. If you refuse, I will call the authorities. I have legal right." She dropped the papers on my kitchen table and walked out. "Have a good evening."

4

I tossed and turned most of the night. My dreams were nonexistent. I sat up in my bed, then reached for my phone. It was two fourteen A.M.

Vacate this apartment in fourteen days, I thought.

My stomach growled.

"Sounds like I'm not the only one hungry," my cat said. She was somewhere in my room.

I groused and wished she would disappear.

"Don't you want to eat?" Her eyes glowed a golden hue at the foot of my bed. "I sure do. You just bought some juicy steak..."

I threw the covers aside and slowly went to the kitchen. I prepared her a steak prior to getting dressed in blue jeans and a green t-shirt. My stomach rumbled again while I brushed my hair, so I decided to go to a twenty-four-hour diner. I wanted breakfast.

The diner was mostly empty. There was a small group of people who were loud and possibly drunk. A couple of others were scattered in booths, sitting alone.

I chose a booth that had the most distance between me and everyone else.

"Good morning," the waiter greeted lazily and placed a menu in front of me. "What can I get you to drink? I recommend coffee, but we also have soft drinks and tea..."

"Yes," I answered. "Coffee, please. I would also like to order."

I ordered their French toast platter and handed over the menu. The waiter left and checked on the group that seemed to be getting louder. I pulled my phone out. I wanted to search for any upcoming events. I felt a presence beside me and supposed it was the waiter with my coffee.

"I thought that was you," Nefer said. "Doris."

I froze, my heart skipping a beat. I steadily peered up at him and saw his grin before I glanced at my phone again. "What the hell... are you following me??"

"No, actually." He laughed and sat down. "I think you're following ME."

This conceited asshole...

"Why... the fuck would I do that...?" I carefully put my phone face down on the table.

"No idea, which is why I'm here to ask."

My hands began to sweat. I felt my skin heat up and I trembled. I didn't want to look at him.

"I'm not following you," I replied. "I don't know what makes you think I want you around. And I don't care. I'm trying to enjoy a meal, so you should find someplace else to be."

I gazed at the table with the group of drunkards and saw they were gone. I noticed we were the only people seated to dine.

"Hmm..." He leaned back in the seat. "You've been showing up where ever I am. That's what makes me think you're following me."

"You're just full of yourself, huh? Is that it?" I gazed up at him even though I aimed to avoid it.

He stared at me without saying a word and a wave of arousal raged through me like a wildfire. It erupted between my legs and I felt pulsing. I was losing control and I whimpered. I gasped.

"What the fuck are you doing to me?!" I yelled. I shoved myself up from the booth.

"No, don't leave." He immediately leaned forward and grabbed my hand.

Our eyes met once more. It's hard to describe what happened. It was as if I fell into a trance. I was fixed in place and my mind felt like it was transported to another location.

~~ * ~~

I was outside. The air was blistering and the daytime sun scorching. I stood beside a clay building with a thatched roof that appeared to be a house. Upon minor exploration of the area, I saw there were several similar structures bordering an open area. I heard music as people danced facing the center. They were dark skinned, wearing minimal clothing. Their bare skin had various patterns painted in white. I began walking through the crowd to see what was in the middle. As the music grew louder, it reverberated through me and made me want to dance.

A small group of musicians were seated on the ground beating drums, playing the flute, shaking gourds, and clanging bells. Two people danced and sang nearby, wearing more clothing than everyone else. They also were wearing masks. They resembled animals but I wasn't certain exactly which ones. One mask had antlers, and the other had large teeth. They were dancing around a man lying down on a bed of flowers. His arms were crossed over his chest and he wore only a loin cloth. His skin was also painted with white designs. Petals of assorted colors rested on his forehead and chest. His eyes were closed. His face had white painted on the cheeks. The man was Nefer.

Suddenly, his body began jolting. The two singers stopped singing and started chanting loudly. The musicians sped their tempo, then all except the drummers abruptly ceased playing. The drumming intensified in volume. There was a momentary flash in the sky. A ball of light no larger than a baseball floated down to land on Nefer's chest. It flattened and spread across his body. While the chanting continued, it was barely audible over the drums. The light soaked into Nefer's skin and disappeared.

The sound of screaming pierced through the drumming and chanting. People were running around, entering the buildings to abandon the area. The two dancers quickly ran to Nefer to support him standing up. The musicians dropped their instruments to flee.

I turned around in time to see a spear soar in the air just before it struck me in my stomach. I grabbed the pole as the unbearable pain flooded through me and dropped to my knees. I saw men charging from the tree line into the village. They wore masks and armor that were made from bones and attacked the fleeing villagers. As I fell over onto the ground, one of the men yanked the spear out of me on his way by. I felt a tugging sensation and closed my eyes.

~~ * ~~

I was restored with a shock, gasping in disbelief. A headache flared as I observed my location. I was sitting on the floor of the diner.

Nefer cradled my face and supported my back.

"What—-" I stuttered, mystified. "Wha—-t... the fuck..."

"Doris," Nefer replied. He began to pull me to my feet. "Let me take you home..."

"No, no..." I tried to wrench away, but I didn't have the power. "Don't... touch me..."

I leaned against his chest while he lifted me into his arms. I detected a floral fragrance.

"Where did you park?" he inquired. He carried me out of the diner.

"My-—I... pur..." I closed my eyes. The pain was dizzying.

"I got your stuff and I see your car."

"I've called an ambulance!" a voice yelled from behind us.

Nefer set me down beside the passenger door and ushered me in. "We're fine, thank you!"

He shut the door after I slowly climbed into the seat. I couldn't stay awake. It wasn't clear how long we were in the car, but it felt like hours before we made a permanent stop. Nefer helped me out of the car and I didn't recognize where we were. I caught glimpses of houses cluttered together while he scooped me into his arms. We were parked in front of one house that he was carrying me inside of.

"Where...?" I groggily asked.

"I'm gonna put you down in the bed," Nefer answered.

He's taking me to his place... I began to panic. My head fell back and I blacked out.

~~ * ~~

A strong aroma of food filled my nose, smelling of cooked meat and baked goods. They stirred me from my sleep and I became increasingly aware of the environment. Daylight peeked through unfamiliar vinyl blinds. I was not at my apartment.

Nefer... I thought. *He did something to me.*

I was lying on a king-sized bed in a bedroom with olive-green colored walls. A dresser stood in one corner with a TV on top and a closet beside it. The walls weren't decorated, but there was a single piece of art hanging by the closed bedroom door. It seemed to be an abstract painting of a man and woman hugging in various shades of blue.

I lethargically got up and noted my headache hadn't dispersed. The odor of food blew into my face when I opened the door to leave. Upon stepping out into the short hallway, I saw a door on opposing sides of the hall. Ahead of me was a stairwell that I went over to and raised my eyes to the ceiling. I put my hands together.

Please, let this be a sign that I'm not being fooled... I prayed silently. *Lord, I want to do right by you...*

I descended the U-shaped stairwell to the lower level. I followed the scents to a kitchen through an archway at the right of the stairs.

The walls were bright orange and made the room almost appear to glow. The cabinets were white and the counters were a light gray marble style. A small round table with matching chairs sat to the left. Nefer was at the stove, faced away from me.

"I was wondering how long it would take you to come down," he said, without turning.

"Take me home," I responded.

He laughed. "I don't wanna burn my food here. It'll have to wait."

"You did something to me at the diner, and now you've kidnapped me. I'm not interested in what you want."

He carried on cooking at the stove without replying. He went and set a large platter onto the small table that had French toast, sausage, home fries, eggs, and fruits.

I wordlessly slid into one of the chairs. My stomach was ready to eat itself.

I'm so fucking hungry, I don't even care if I look like a wild animal eating this...

I heard Nefer chuckle.

"You know," he said, "don't take this the wrong way, but you sound like my ex-wife."

"Ok..." I sensed he wasn't trying to offend me, nor did I suspect he suggested habitual abduction. I grabbed a sausage and stuffed it into my mouth. "I won't."

"Would you like a plate? And utensils...?" He pulled a dish from an upper cabinet.

I picked up a slice of French toast. I bit into it, sighing heavily with exultation. "No. What I would like..." A piece of toast fell out of my mouth. "... is for you to take me home. You did something to me and I don't want any part of it."

I wasn't being straightforward, but I was scared.

He set the plate on the counter and sat down in the other chair. He took a melon slice, looking puzzled.

"I didn't do anything to you," he replied honestly and bit the fruit.

"Bullshit." I rose and started tautly rummaging through drawers. "Where's your forks?"

He stood up and opened a drawer I hadn't searched yet to pull out a fork.

"I really don't know what happened, but..." he said as he came over to me and held the fork up. "I felt something."

I wrapped my hand around the fork, but he didn't let it go.

"I felt something really... good," he continued. His excitement was rising. "And I know you felt something too."

I stared at the fork. I urged myself not to look into his eyes. Failing to abstain from the appeal, I deliberately peered up and the sensations grew inside of me. I felt the warmth pour down.

"And..." he added, "I'm feeling it now."

This must be a trick! Why would he want anything to do with me? He's the devil, come to take me...

"Stop," I murmured. My chest thumped, my skin was hot and my palms were dripping. "Stop playing with me..."

"I'm not," he said softly. He took the fork and placed it on the counter.

"You're blind." My breath labored, the motivation was building and flooding through my body. I wasn't certain why I told him this.

"I'm not," he repeated. "I see you."

I wanted him to kiss me.

The doorbell rang, interrupting the moment. He glanced at the doorway, which released me from his captivating stare.

"Excuse me," he said, and stepped out.

A piercing pain jetted through my midsection and I clutched my stomach. I sat down at the table to take several breaths, inhaling through my nose and exhaling from my mouth. I heard a woman's voice coming from the other room followed by footsteps heading in my direction.

"Oh," the woman said from the entrance. "I didn't realize you had company."

I twisted around to see a tall, athletically built woman with chocolate skin. She had black hair, styled in cornrows with decorative beads braided in and a gorgeous afro at the rear. She wore a soft pink camisole that looked to be made from silk. It wasn't body-hugging, but tight enough to see her perky chest. She was braless. Black form fitting jeans revealed her curvaceous hips and thighs. Matching pink sandals adorned her pedicured feet.

Nefer entered the kitchen by slipping past the woman.

"Yea, I do," he replied. "Uh, this is Doris."

"Ah," Her full lips curved into a smirk while raising her eyebrows. "Yes, Doris..."

I was unable to sense the emotion behind her reaction. I couldn't distinguish her desire at all. As a matter of fact, I couldn't sense anything from her. With Nefer, I could at least sense his intentions when he spoke.

"Doris," Nefer said, "this is my ex-wife, Sekima."

She calmly walked to the platter and picked up a grape. "Hello, Doris."

"Hello," I responded, uneasy.

"Hmm, all this food for you?" She took another grape to pop in her mouth. "How special..."

She sounded sardonic.

"Sekima," Nefer called, gesturing toward the exit, "I gotta take her home now. So, if you could get that thing you wanted...? I'm leaving shortly."

I noted his decision to take me home after his disinterest mere moments earlier.

"Rushing me out, Nefer, my dear?" she tested. "Did I interrupt something?"

I would hope to say yes.

She peered down her nose at me, as if she waited for me to answer. She didn't seem to be wearing any makeup and her skin was immaculate.

"No," I answered, edgy. "I just need to get home..."

I knew this was too good to be true. A handsome black man, who's single with no issues? I'm not staying here to be part of some love triangle...

"I won't be but a moment." Sekima sauntered to the door. "I left something upstairs."

I don't need an explanation...

She glimpsed at me on her way out. "Good to see you, Doris..."

I questioned whether we had met previously. I came to the deduction that wasn't probable because I would have remembered her. I found her features striking.

Nefer trailed behind her.

I leapt up from the table once they both were out of sight. Grabbing another piece of French toast, I left the kitchen and entered the living room beyond the stairs. I made a beeline for the front door without hesitation. Outside, a modest gust of wind hit my face and instantly replaced the stifling air I felt inside. I saw my car in the single car driveway. I quickly reviewed the area.

The dark blue house sat within a cluster of other different colored houses. Across the street was a strip of storefronts and beside it stood a tiny white church. There were more houses grouped together a little farther down. They were so close, they almost connected.

I jogged to my car and peeped in the window. I saw my purse and keys sitting on the passenger seat so I pulled the door open to grab them. I was relieved but equally disappointed that my things were exposed to possible theft.

"Not even a goodbye?" Nefer asked, mildly insulted. He was standing at his door.

"I... need to go," I answered, without making eye contact. I went to the driver's side. "Thanks..."

I hustled into my car. I didn't know where I was, and pulled out my phone for navigation. I saw the time was three thirty-seven P.M. It would take me just under an hour to return home. I started the car and drove away.

"Hmm, late night tryst..." my cat purred.

"What the fuck," I said, recoiling. "Leave me alone right now."

"I left you alone. Look what you did. You let a man kidnap you. No man should subdue you." She hurdled into the front seat.

"He did NOT subdue me. I was really tired and something drained me. He just... was there..." I grasped the steering wheel tightly.

"Who are you lying to? Certainly not me." She laughed, mischievously. "So, when do we have to move out? In thirteen days now, right? I presume the next place we go allows pets..."

5

I arrived back to my apartment just twenty minutes ahead of five in the evening. Once inside, I immediately went to take a shower. I thought about the strange vision I had and couldn't really remember it by this point and only recalled the subsequent events that occurred.

Who is that man? I thought. *He says he didn't do anything to me. He wasn't lying, but how can I believe him? If he's like my cat, he could be misleading me. I can't stop thinking about how it felt...*

I shuddered as I recollected the enthralling emotions I experienced from his stare. After I completed my shower, I decided to watch a little television. I turned on the evening news that started at five.

The newscaster was reporting the latest developments in a lawsuit that involved a local resident and a prominent construction company.

"--—stating racism," the woman was saying. "He accuses the established construction company of not only being aware of the discrimination, but also supporting it. Mr. Brown, a former employee, alleges he was a constant victim of verbal abuse. They ridiculed his name, threatened his livelihood, including the act of placing a noose on his desk..."

I shook my head in dissatisfaction.

"Foolish," my cat said, frigidly. She climbed on the couch and curled into a ball.

At the bottom of the screen, a headline ribbon scrolled. One headline read: *'Video goes viral of tap-dancing cat named Flap-Heel Fluffy.* Another read: *County P.D. loses over five hundred followers after posting their enforcement of the Anti-profanity Law.'*

Discrimination... Lord, will we ever rise above?

It spurred a memory from my childhood.

~~ * ~~

It was a year or so after my father was gone. My mother felt much better most days. She told me she didn't have many episodes of seizures, but she often didn't know when they happened. She said she could only tell when she lost instances of time and hurt herself mysteriously.

The cat stayed with me every day. She became my diary and listened to everything. Since she helped me to save my mother, I felt I owed her. She hadn't instructed me on how I would compensate her. She didn't ask me for anything.

It was a typical school day. I walked through the hallway as the final bell rang and I wanted to stop at my locker before I left for the bus. As I stood at the locker removing a notebook, it suddenly slammed.

Samantha, who was a grade above me, had her hand on the door. She prevented me from reopening it.

"Move," I ordered, glaring at her.

"Just wanted to tell you I won't miss you," she replied, smiling evilly. "I'm leaving this school before all you niggers ruin my education."

"What did you say?"

"My daddy is moving me to a real school and it's gonna have real teachers that care about America. He said they keep it pure and don't let filth in."

"Get out of here!" I was furious.

"I am, didn't you hear me?" She narrowed her eyes, her grin widening. "My daddy says it's a segredagation academy and they teach us how to protect ourselves against you filthy porch monkeys."

"Get out of my face!" I shoved her.

"Don't touch me, you dirty nigger!" She shoved me back. "That's why your daddy left you. Because you're a dumb, dirty nigger and will never be as good as us! Your daddy hates you and your nappy nigger hair!"

She tried to grab my hair in emphasis but I jerked away. I impulsively balled my hand into a fist and punched her in the face.

The students nearby were alerted and stopped to observe. Someone started shouting that there was a fight.

"Look!" they hollered. "A fight! They're fighting!"

Bolstered by the attention, I couldn't allow Samantha to recover. I swung again and hit her in the shoulder as she cowered.

"Ow!" she screamed. She flailed her arm and attempted to grab my hair again.

I dodged and kicked her shin. I raised my hand to hit her once more when I felt someone hold my wrist. I turned and saw our principal, Mr. Sandsman. He dragged me to the office where I was punished and my mother called. I was removed from school for the year.

My mother angrily lectured me the entire walk home. She was exhausted by the time we arrived, but that didn't stop her from yelling at me. She fell onto the couch and dropped her purse on the coffee table. She commanded me to pour her a drink.

"Martin Luther King Jr. would turn in his grave if he saw how you been behaving!" she scolded. She grunted as she leaned toward her purse to pull out cigarettes. "For centuries our people suffered, just to get a chance in this white man's world. And you go and do some shit like this! Lord Jesus, don't you know they can't take your smarts away from you? Do you know what Affirmative Action is?"

I shook my head, unaware. I brought her drink and put it on the coffee table.

"Every day is a struggle for us!" She lit the cigarette and took a puff. "It is our God given right to be treated as equal, and Lord above, we will fight for it! He watches over us even when they try to break our spirit! Don't let them break your spirit. You're smart! They won't change here no time soon. Get that education. Get out of this place and see the world, baby..."

"I'm sorry, mama," I said, tears welling.

"I need you to learn your rights, baby." She was breathing heavily as she smoked. "Get that education! They can never take that away from you..."

"I'm sorry," I repeated. "Samantha... she said that Daddy left us because we're dumb niggers..."

"So what?? She ain't nobody!" She respired hoarsely. She began to reach for the drink. "My sweet baby. This is a big world. You need to -—t—-"

Prior to finishing her sentence, her body became stiff. She fell back against the couch and her limbs began thrashing wildly.

"Mama?!" Panicking, I ran to her side. I tried to prevent her flailing by restraining her shoulders. "Mama, please!"

Her body continued shaking violently, her eyes frozen open.

"Help me!" I yelped for my cat. "She won't stop! It's real bad!"

Blood was spilling from my mother's mouth.

I gasped. "She's bleeding! Please! Help me!"

"She's very far gone..." my cat said when she finally appeared. She hopped to the coffee table. "If you get me fresh blood now, we may save her..."

"Please, just do what you did before! I can give you something from the fridge. Just save Momma!" I was frightened of what could happen if we wasted another minute.

"No." She stared at my mother. "I need blood. Blood from your sacrifice will fulfill this..."

"We don't have time! You said she only needed one to fix her!" I maintained my effort to hold her still.

"Yes, it would only take one to save her..."

The movement stopped. She stared vacantly ahead with her mouth gaped open. Her tongue was bleeding profusely.

I rubbed some of the blood from her face and shook her gently. "Mama, it's ok. It's over..."

She didn't move or respond. Her eyes looked lifeless.

I dropped to my knees and bawled as I shook her legs. I knew she wasn't breathing.

"You didn't help me!" I wailed and turned to the coffee table.

My cat was gone.

I was stunned with discouraging sentiments. I didn't know what to do. I had no relatives in the area. I was just expelled from school. Something inside of me told me to run if I wanted any hope of finding my way. Wiping my tears, I shot to my feet and dug into my mother's purse to collect all her cash. I sprinted to my room with my backpack to dump its articles onto my bed and replaced them with clothes along with a few other items. Upon my return to the living room, I smelled burning on my way out of the house.

The news continued buzzing. They spoke about entertainment, local crime, and more entertainment before the program finished up.

I began channel surfing and saw a commercial advertising cat food.

"Disgusting," my cat said, repulsed. "Processed, imitation, and just no real blood in it."

I dropped the remote and began searching on my phone for upcoming events. I found one that was scheduled for next weekend, on Saturday.

It was presented as a nightlife event and was called the Devil's Playpen. As a costume party, its theme was defined as bringing out one's 'inner naughty devil'. It invited everyone to wear masks. There was a contest and live performances. The event was to occur from nine thirty P.M. to three A.M.

Hmm, I thought, *Halloween is this month... Costume party will be an easy choice.*

I pondered what I would wear.

There was hammering on the door.

I didn't expect any company and definitely didn't want to see my landlord. I laggardly got up and looked through the peephole.

A man dressed in a green shirt with a tiny pizza on the chest stood at my door holding a large pizza box, a liter of soda, and a paper bag. He knocked again.

I didn't order food.

The door across the hall opened and a short young woman appeared in the doorway. She had a man wearing glasses standing directly behind her, peeking over her head. He was light skinned, with dreadlocks down to his shoulders. His mustache was tidily trimmed and he had a goatee. His pink and pronounced lips looked soft.

"Over here," the woman called. "We ordered that."

The delivery man spun around and proceeded to hand her the food.

I observed their interaction and she was visibly irritated with the man in the apartment when he returned to the couch to listlessly pick up his game controller.

"Uh, help please?" she criticized while kicking the door closed.

"Are you enjoying watching people go about their day?" my cat asked, haughty. "Hurry up and make me food. Since you forced me to watch that ridiculous commercial on purpose..."

I made my way to the kitchen and thought about going to the mall in the morning. I saw an ad on a pop-up shop selling costumes for low prices.

~~ * * * * * ~~

6

On Saturday morning, I woke up around ten A.M. and got set to head to the mall. It was packed and this reminded me why I rarely went. I didn't enjoy the company of large crowds and I especially wasn't one to keep up with fashion trends.

This outlet mall was part of a chain. It received renovations around seven years ago. A new security system was installed and some cosmetic items were added, like a fancy fountain at the main entrance and more paved sidewalks. There were also upgrades to the parking lot. The spaces were more forgiving with room and the rows were numbered.

I located the pop-up costume shop outside a store that primarily sold women's undergarments. There wasn't a crowd of people at the vendor, which was a relief. It was a kiosk with merchandise on three of its four sides. A female cashier leaned against the counter of the fourth side and was casually scrolling on her phone. She didn't acknowledge me when I walked by to view what was available. After scanning the items on display, I discovered a glittering dark bluish-purple long-sleeved leotard and a black mask that covered the upper half of the face with small devil horns. It was clear the quality wasn't exactly pristine, but it would serve the purpose just the same. There were wigs displayed on Styrofoam mannequin heads. I chose a long black curly one, then I went to the cashier who hadn't moved from her perch. I placed my selections onto the counter in front of her.

Initially, she didn't move. She gazed at the items and up at me. She then began inspecting what I put down.

"Oh," she said, pessimistic. "I... this may not fit you right..."

"What's that supposed to mean?" I replied, wary. I knew what she was implying. "It says 'one size fits most'. And it's stretchy."

"Well, yea..." she started to scan the tags. "What I mean is... it may not LOOK how you think it will look..."

I was growing more defensive. "And how would it look?"

"I'm sorry." She attempted to defuse the situation with a false apology. She computed the sale in the register. "I don't mean to be rude. Your total is nineteen ninety-seven."

I gave her a twenty-dollar bill and grabbed the shopping bag. Without waiting for change or a receipt, I left. I wasn't more than a few feet away when I looked over my shoulder at her. She was holding her phone up in my direction.

Is she recording me?

I entered the store nearby to buy pantyhose. I was getting hungry and decided to head to the food court. I had a taste for something barbecued and knew there was a restaurant called BBQ Legs, Wings, and Other Things. It didn't take long for me to place my order of a barbecued rib platter since the line was short. Just as I was pulling out cash to pay, someone reached around me and gave the cashier a credit card. The cashier waited in charging it, but the owner encouraged him to continue.

"It's fine, go ahead," Nefer assured the man.

Shit. My heart began its typical reaction. *Now I know he's following me! He's everywhere!*

I picked up my food and hastened to the nearest table to drop my tray on it. As soon as Nefer stepped within range, I raised my hand to halt his advance.

"I have already made it clear that you need to back off," I said. I refrained from looking him directly in the face. "Stop... following me..."

"Well, hello," he replied, submissive. "Nice to see you again, Doris. I was just gonna get me some barbecue myself."

Overlooking his comment as he walked away, I sat down and ate silently. I was halfway through my food when Nefer returned to sit across from me with a tray. I dropped the biscuit I was eating and placed my hands evenly on the table. I was struggling to stay relaxed.

"Leave me alone," I told him, eyeing my food. "I can't say it any other way! That is all I want, for you to leave me alone."

I was stern, and strived to convince him as well as myself that this was fact.

"I hear you, Doris," Nefer answered. "I do. And, I try. But I can't. Everywhere I go, you're there and I gotta talk to you."

I apprehensively tapped the table. I knew he meant it. I wished my heart would stop pounding so fiercely. I wanted to dry the sweat on my hands, but there was no way to do it inconspicuously. I didn't need him to know how uneasy I was. I was terrified to look in his eyes. I wasn't equipped to encounter what it did to me again. I swallowed laboriously.

"Why?" I finally questioned. I stared at my half-eaten biscuit.

Is he the devil? How is he just a man? I'm not ready to feel those feelings again... Why is he after me? He's being candid, but is it an illusion?

"I can't really explain why," he divulged. He slid his hands along the table to mine.

I instinctively removed them and took the chance to wipe away moisture with my pant legs. "Don't do that."

"Why not?" he asked, baffled.

"I don't want you to, isn't that enough?"

"It would be. If it were true."

I wrestled with myself on how to reply. I craved the sensations despite my fear of their force. It was tough to admit to him. The possibility that he was here to trap me was too great in my mind. Although, I couldn't decide whether being open would help.

If I tell him the reality of it, will that make him end his pursuit? I already told him to stop...

"I'll take your silence as my answer," he said when I failed to respond.

"When you touched me..." I began. My mouth was parched. "I saw something. I fainted... I don't want to feel that..."

By now, the vision I witnessed was too degraded to remember. I had memory of pain in my stomach and of being frightened. I was incompetent at recalling any specific details.

"I saw something too," he agreed, reflectively.

His recognition stirred my gnawing dread.

"What do you remember...?" I prodded.

"Not sure. I just remember seeing something..."

Although I enquired about what he may have educed, all I could think about was how it felt when he and I locked eyes. I was curious as to what would happen if he touched me another time. If it was as impactful, I didn't intend to find out at the mall. I was so absorbed in my thoughts that I hadn't noticed he asked me a question.

"Huh?" I replied, disoriented.

"Are you gonna finish that?" he queried. He pointed at my biscuit. "You're staring at it like you're waiting for it to jump up and dance."

I absently looked up at him, but rapidly shut my eyes to avoid his entanglement.

He laughed quietly in fascination. His laugh provoked me, and so did his interest.

"What are you laughing at?" Vexed, I opened my eyes and picked up the cold biscuit.

"You." He collected his things and went to the trash can. He came back and bent over to scoop my shopping bags from the floor.

"Excuse me, that's mine." I grabbed them first and pulled them out of reach.

"Sorry, I just figured we were done here."

"'We'?" I put the bags under my arm as I went and discarded my food.

"Can we finish talking?" He stood beside me at the trash can.

"We're done with that too."

He held a torn piece of napkin between two fingers in front of me. "At least take my number."

I timidly accepted it.

"Don't be afraid of me," he said. "I wanna know what this is. I know about as much as you."

Don't go looking in his eyes... don't look...

"Goodbye," I muttered, and hurried out of the mall.

The remainder of that day I slept excessively and recounted my contact with Nefer. I imagined various scenarios where I could have said everything I was actually thinking. I grew steadily inquisitive towards why he and I met. My cat was flippant to the unusual effects his eye sight had on me and accused me of destructively playing with my food.

"I understand making them buy you meals sometimes," she was saying, provocatively, "A girl's gotta eat... Why string this one along? At least get him prepared for the offering..."

I despised the process she referred to. Should Nefer become chosen, it wasn't my judgment to make and I wasn't alerted until the time came. I didn't even enjoy the routine. I had coerced men to financially support me in the past, but over time I grew to regret it. I ultimately discontinued asking for more than food and lodging.

I cleaned my apartment and searched for a new place to live on Sunday. It wasn't an easy task to search for an apartment that matched the rent I paid. I planned to stay in the area and the rates available were almost double the cost. I gave up and resolved I would try again later.

On Monday, I probably looked at Nefer's number a hundred times over. I did laundry and found the piece of paper in my pocket. I considered texting him.

There must be a reason why he has come into my life now, I thought. *I can't deny there is something going on. What if he is here to rescue me? What would happen if I stopped resisting him?*

I shivered as a chill went through me. I returned from the community laundry room and stood in my tiny living room, staring at the paper again.

"I feel like you haven't been showing me much affection lately..." my cat moped as she lounged on the couch. "You just throw me a slab of meat and leave. I miss the petting and the love..."

There was never any of that...

I took that as her way of saying she wanted a steak, so I gave her what she asked for. After fixing her food, I resumed my search for an apartment while lying on my bed. I finally found a prospective place and reserved a tour for three P.M. The paper with Nefer's number was in my hand.

If I call, what will I even say? I debated what the harm was. *Fuck it...*

His number was essentially memorized. I composed a new message with him as the recipient.

'*Hi, this is Doris,*' I wrote and paused.

Lord, if this is an answer to my prayers, please give me a sign...

I pressed send.

Within seconds, he replied with '*Hey Doris. How's your day?*'

I contemplated his inquiry, then wrote '*Fine. You?*'

'*I'm at work, but not bad.*'

I had forgotten my day off was during regular business hours of the office.

'Can we meet after I'm off? I get off at four.' He texted ahead of my response.

With escalating anxiety, I dropped my phone onto the bed and went to take a shower. I prepared to head to my appointment by getting dressed in a blue and orange striped shirt with a pair of dark green slacks. Once I was organized, I reentered to my room. Nefer's request was waiting. Grappling with how to answer, I chose honesty.

'I have an appointment,' I entered, then added *'But I guess after.'*

When hitting send I soon wished I hadn't suggested anything.

'Let's meet at the diner,' he answered. *'You know the one?'*

Yes, I know the one...

I vacillated before I typed my response. *'Ok.'*

As I left my apartment, I met Harriett at my door.

"Harriett..." I said, displeased.

"Hello!" she greeted, full of energy. "I am catching you when you're either coming or going!"

She laughed, thoroughly elated by her sense of timing.

"Yes, I'm going." I slammed my door shut and headed for the stairs.

"Oh! But I need a second of your time..."

"I will be out in ten days, don't worry." I didn't stop to entertain her. I quickly got in my car and saw my cat through the rearview mirror in the back seat.

"Hmm," she mused. "She is determined to get your money..."

I arrived at the apartment complex in twenty-seven minutes. It was immediately clear that the area was cleaner than my current place. The property's landscape was well kept. The buildings themselves could have recently been built or possibly modernized. I found the unit where my tour was to start. It was on the second floor. The door was open and I cautiously walked inside.

"Hello...?" I called from the short hallway at the entrance.

"Hello!" a man replied. "Come in!"

I entered the apartment and found the man standing in the middle of the moderate sized living room space.

"Hi, I'm Ken!" He smiled and shook my hand firmly, but he wasn't excited to see me. "You must be Doris!"

"Hello, Ken..."

He showed me around the one-bedroom apartment. It was a nice sized unit, with a balcony and a washer/dryer combination inside the apartment. The kitchen, which was in the living room space, had an island with the sink built into it, a gas stove, and a dishwasher. That feature wasn't exactly appealing, because I didn't make dirty dishes. I didn't cook, my plates were paper, my cups and utensils were plastic disposables. I ordered food or typically ate out. There was a microwave, which I did find useful. The bedroom had a walk-in closet that also led directly into the bathroom. During the tour, Ken described the amenities. They had a basketball court and a small playground. Their pool was indoor, the fitness room was open twenty-four hours, and they hosted events often at their leasing office that doubled as a community center. His tour was informative, but his mind was elsewhere. He was teeming with discomfort.

"That's everything here!" he said at the end of the tour, feigning enthusiasm. We stood by the leasing office. "If you have a car, we provide one parking pass and one visitor pass. Any additional passes can be purchased."

"What's your pet policy...?" I asked. "Your website said you allow pets."

"Yes, we do." He opened the door to the office. "There is a one-time fee per pet. This doesn't include service animals. Do you... have pets...?"

"Just one."

"Oh, ok." He was relieved. "Please come inside so we can go over everything and get you into your new place!"

"Oh, I actually... How many spaces do you have? Is that model the only one...?"

He let the door close. "We have other styles if you would like to take a look. We would have to schedule a separate appointment, though. I have another tour soon..."

"No, it's not that. I just need to... get my affairs in order..." I doubted I could afford the rent. I noticed the amount he mentioned throughout the tour didn't match the website.

"I understand. Please reach out when you are ready." He handed me a business card before entering the office. "I can't guarantee availability, but we also have a waiting list."

I sat in my car, staring at the apartment complex.

Maybe if I stop ordering food and going out to eat, I thought, *I could save a lot of money... I can't wait until my loan is paid off. Feels like I'm paying rent twice a month...*

I owed double-digit thousands on my student loan. I was six years into it.

"I like it," my cat said. "Very clean."

My phone displayed the time as four eleven P.M. I was supposed to meet Nefer. I drove to the diner and when I arrived, I didn't go inside. The place looked busy.

While in my car, I watched people walk in and out of the diner. I saw them through the large windows relishing their meals, laughing as they stuffed their faces. I could feel them all pampering their vast appetites. I studied one couple who had a group of servers singing Happy Birthday to a woman. It was obvious since they wore party hats and held a colorful cake with sparkling candles on top. The woman was delighted and liberally cut a piece for herself after she blew out the candles. My head was beginning to hurt. I didn't want to go in and meet Nefer.

"You've taken your obsession with watching people to a new level," my cat pestered. She laughed and licked herself. "When you go in, can you bring me their biggest steak? Blue rare please..."

"Fuck this," I muttered. As I grabbed my key to start the ignition, there was a knock on the window. I turned to see Nefer waving and I looked away. "Shit..."

"Hey there," he said. "You coming in?"

I shoved the door open and banged it shut.

"You're not gonna roll down the windows for your cat?" he queried.

"Huh?" I answered, astounded.

"Your cat." He pointed to my car. "For air?"

My cat meowed innocently as I rolled down the windows slightly for her. I expected her to react to him being able to see her, but she didn't do anything abnormal. She stared at us quietly.

How can he see you? I glared at her. *You know him and won't tell me. You love torturing me! Is he here to join your game?*

My heart was beating vigorously. I considered climbing into my car and driving away. I slammed the door, turned and walked into the diner.

"Would you like a booth or a table?" the woman at the check in counter asked.

Nefer looked to me for an answer.

"Booth," I replied, indifferent.

"Ok, it will be fifteen minutes."

We sat in the waiting area uncomfortably still. The world around was full of noise, but it almost went unheard since my brain screamed for me to escape.

"Work was interesting," Nefer eventually said, breaking the silence between us. "Gary is unique."

"Yes," I agreed, laughing. I rubbed my sweaty hands together.

The fifteen minutes we were told seemed to be more like an hour. I checked my phone. Forty minutes had already passed. I sighed.

"Maybe we should just order to go?" he suggested upon noticing my impatience.

"Go where?" I retorted, but I didn't want an answer.

"I guess the car." He shrugged and laughed. He was serious.

I wringed my hands.

"Relax, we won't do that." He placed his hand on mine and I was thoughtless to avoid him.

A wave of heat hit me and flowed through my body. A throbbing sensation began between my legs. I felt like he was stroking my body below and it caused me to flinch. The feeling compounded and I exhaled heavily with gratification. I instantly panicked from the sudden rush of pleasures. I pulled away from him as severe pain emerged in my stomach. Clutching it, I shut my eyes. His hand touched my chin, then his lips pressed against mine tenderly. The pain in my abdomen dwindled. He applied more force and I was progressively feeling overwhelmed. I became dizzy.

I was unprepared for him to pull away, which caused my head to fall forward onto his chest. I inhaled and his scent filled my nose. It was intoxicating.

"Let me take you home," he whispered in my ear. His warm breath tickled me.

What is this? Please, God, save me...

"Excuse me," the woman at the counter called, "Sir, ma'am, the booth is ready for you."

Nefer thanked her as I ploddingly regained my equanimity. I rose from the seat and shadowed the waitress to the booth. She placed menus in front of us and asked for our drink orders.

"Water," we responded in unison.

"Ok, great." She nodded and looked at Nefer. "Do you need a minute, or do you already know what you want...?"

"Yea, we need more time," he answered, shrugging.

"Alright, I'll get your waters." She beamed at him then scurried off.

I gulped as my chest panged with trepidation. Placing my elbow on the table, I closed my eyes and kneaded my forehead.

"I feel like..." I began suspiciously, "I... it's like you KNOW what you are doing to me. And you want to make me feel this way..."

I had no way of distinguishing anything beyond his profound interest in me. He hadn't said nor acted contrarily to what he was feeling so far. However, I had a cat that made me sacrifice men. This meant he could be a similar supernatural creature sent to ensnare me.

I opened my eyes when he didn't reply. Through my peripheral, I spotted him looking at me.

Does he want that? I feel like a doll! I feel like...

The way I felt was exactly what my victims underwent once I lured them to their ensuing deaths. I was sure of it and this made me contrite.

"Grr!" I lamented, and shielded my face with my hands. "Why are you playing with me??"

"I'm not," he scrupulously contended. "I meant it when I said it before, and I mean it now. I'm not trying to play with you. I..."

"Are you ready to order?" The waitress was back.

I removed my hands and looked at the menu, reacting preoccupied, "Uhh..."

"Sure," Nefer said, "I'll have the... Swiss burger with fries. Doris...?"

Doris, what??? I don't fucking know what I want at all right now...

"The... chicken parmigiana..." I read aloud the first item I saw.

"Perfect." She took our menus. "Would you like anything else besides water?"

I noticed the glass she set down and shook my head as I guzzled.

"We're fine, thanks." By now, Nefer had finished half of his water.

"I'll fill that up..." She emphatically took his glass and left again.

"What do you really want, then?" I probed when she was gone. I irascibly rapped the table with my index finger.

He chuckled and leaned forward.

"This isn't funny to me." Incited, I crossed my legs.

Distressingly, I thirsted for the vibrations he sent through me and I failed to find the humor in what he was forcing me to feel. I had never physically suffered what my prey underwent, but I was no stranger to being controlled. My cat moderated my life. I catered to her ferocity; I fed her need for blood and lustful ventures. Over the years, I had managed to reduce the amount of sacrifices to one per cycle. I lost a great deal of myself to her. I knew she was stealing a piece of my soul with each man I gave to her.

"I..." he said.

The waitress came with a full glass of water. "The food is on the way."

"Thank you..." I mumbled.

Neither of us spoke again until the food arrived.

"Excuse me," Nefer beckoned. "Can we get to-go boxes? And the check."

Why did I come here...?

"Oh! Uh... Ok..." She was disappointed. She placed our food on the table, then retrieved boxes and the check.

He quickly handed her his credit card and she was gone.

"Wait," I tried to catch her and give her money but she didn't hear me.

"It's alright," Nefer said.

I didn't want him to buy me anything else. We packed up our meals and the waitress thanked us for coming when she gave Nefer his card back with the receipt. I arose to leave.

"Where are you going?" he asked.

"Home..." I replied.

"Come to my place." He got up and barred my exit.

I shook my head.

"We can't have a conversation here." He gestured to the congested restaurant. "We need to be alone."

"Oh, you want to get me alone." I was developing a headache.

"Don't you?" He anticipated.

I pursed my lips.

"How about, I follow you, and we go back to your place. Since you don't wanna come to mine." He wasn't being deceptive.

Are my senses broken? They can't be, I sensed the waitress. She was all but drooling over him.

"I want to leave," I answered, harshly, "move."

He turned sideways and let me pass.

I stopped upon getting by him. Out of the blue, I changed my mind. "I.... don't live far..."

I didn't make eye contact. After grabbing my food from the table, I left out of the diner and into the night. I tossed my food inside my car and watched him get into a dark colored coupe as I started the engine. Sweating abundantly, I headed back to my apartment.

What am I doing??

"Uh, I don't see steak in here..." My cat had ripped open the top of the meal box.

My hands ached because I was gripping the steering wheel so tight. I yanked the box from under her when I parked. At my apartment, I struggled to remain calm while waiting for him to get out of his car and come up the stairs. He coolly walked up and we went to my door. I steadied myself to open it and grew more nervous when we went inside. I couldn't trust my feelings, even though they assured me he had no devious intentions.

I waved for him to enter first when the door swung open. He slowly went in. As he made his way to sit on the couch, I put my food in the fridge and my purse on the kitchen table. I returned to the living room to see him at one end of the couch so I sat on the opposite end. I felt his eyes on me.

"Do you leave your cat in the car often?" he asked after a minute or two.

"No," I replied. "She... comes and goes..."

My right leg began to bounce. I felt fresh wetness forming in my palms.

"Can you just ask what you want to ask?" I instructed. "This is awkward enough as it is."

"If you relax, it won't be." He moved closer and placed his right arm on the couch behind me.

"How can I relax? Doesn't it bother you that this happens between us? It hurts my head."

"I'm more... curious than anything." He inched closer. "I wanna know what this is."

Yea, curious and horny. I could feel his attraction rousing.

"Let's be honest here," I said, looking out the corner of my eye, "I am not... You're too..."

What I wanted to say wouldn't come out. I lost where my thought was going.

"I'm too what?" His left hand slid onto my thigh.

Heat radiated from his touch, flowed through my body, and ignited ardor between my legs. I sharply inhaled and clenched up. I wasn't sure how to reply.

He's too gorgeous, he's too friendly, too good to be true. He doesn't know what I have. He doesn't know what he's getting into...

"I see your mind working in there," he said. He caressed my thigh. "What do you wanna say?"

I respired deeply, realizing I was holding my breath.

"You only met me last week," I responded, after taking a second breath. "These feelings are not normal. You feel it but act like it's something you're used to. And we saw a vision, the same vision. You haven't said anything about it..."

He removed his hand.

"When we touched..." I went on, "that wasn't normal. And I don't know about you... but I lose control of myself around you—-"

I stopped short of full disclosure. I didn't even know why I said all I had by this point.

"I feel how you feel," he answered.

"You feel how I feel? You seem pretty in control to me."

"I feel you losing control."

I was speechless.

"I feel your desire," he added. "I feel your body's reactions. I feel your curiosity. And I also feel your fear."

I stared at the floor. "Who are you...? WHAT, are you...?"

"I'm a man." He laughed, regaled by my amazement. "The question is who, or what, are YOU? You do this to me."

I considered his statement because it was a rational supposition. I peered up into his eyes with the specific goal of telling him I was possessed by a demon. I fought hard against the feelings that manifested.

"I..." I was only able to utter one word before the sensations crashed through me.

"I don't wanna hurt you," he said. He leaned in and placed his hand on my face to kiss me delicately.

My body exploded from the contact. Submitting to the magnetism, I closed my eyes and kissed him back.

His kiss grew with passion while he pressed against me, moving his hands along my sides. I felt the room swaying. I began leaning back onto the couch and he kissed my neck as his hands slid down to go under my shirt. His warm hands touched my stomach, then continued up to fondle my breasts. The feelings were becoming too much. I grabbed hold of his hand that he glided down into my pants.

As he stroked me between my legs, a sensual moan slipped from my lips just before I was out cold.

7

I woke up gasping frantically for air and clutched my chest. My heart was thumping and my head was pulsing viciously.

"Ugh..." I mumbled, trying to adjust to the darkness. I was in my bed. I fumbled around for my phone, but couldn't find it and remembered it was in my purse. I was still wearing my clothes that I went out in, without my shoes. I sat up methodically.

Nefer is here, I thought. I recalled the urges I was subjected to. I could still feel his lips on me. I had a dull ache between my legs. *Oh, God, what did he do to me...? Did we...?*

"Are you going to kick that man out?" my cat insisted. She was at my bedroom door, her eyes glowing. "This sleepover needs to end."

I crept out of my room and into the kitchen to get my phone. It was three oh 'seven A.M. I snuck to the living room and could indistinctly see that Nefer was sleeping on the couch. Electing not to disturb him, I retreated to the kitchen to eat my food from the night before.

Just then, an alarm bell chimed in the living room. There was movement from the couch and the kitchen light turned on.

"Morning," Nefer greeted, his voice gravelly.

"Hi," I murmured, diffident. I put my food into the microwave to reheat.

"So... last night..." He stepped closer. "You fell asleep on me."

I grabbed my microwaved food and sat at the table. As I started to dig into it, he sat at the table with me.

"I passed out," I said. I spun my fork around to gather some spaghetti.

He leaned back in the chair as he rubbed his face. "Did I hurt you?"

I shook my head. "No... but what would you have done to hurt me...?"

"I stopped as soon as you, well, I guess, passed out. I put you in your bed. That's all."

Soothed by his rectitude, I resumed twirling my fork.

"We can try again..." he started.

"You should go," I dropped the fork.

"Ok, of course. I'll see you... at work." He stood up and leaned over to kiss my forehead.

I closed my eyes, aiming to remain stoic. I yearned to have him kiss me like he did earlier. I didn't open my eyes again until I heard the door upon his exit. I ate my food and got back in bed for a little rest ahead of going to work.

$$\sim\sim\,^*\sim\sim$$

At the office, I was exhausted. I dragged my feet to my desk and saw Nefer was already at the formerly vacant desk by mine. I didn't see Margaret anywhere. As I was sitting down to boot up my computer, Gary called from his office.

"Doris!" he exclaimed, and emerged to stand by my desk. "I hope you are well rested!"

Fuck no.

"Yup," I answered. "Am I doing orientation for anyone new?"

"Oh, no, and two of our newest recruits are no longer with us already! Guess you were right about them. You only met Margaret, but we had another named Ben. He was a no show." He chuckled. "Well, I need to finish my meeting. We will talk in a bit."

He disappeared into his office and closed the door.

"Doris?" Nefer said, marginally confounded. He was clicking a mouse. "I think I need help with this."

I went to see what he was trying to do. "What."

"This mouse won't click on the training class. Is this the right thing?" He madly clicked the mouse.

"Stop that." I forgetfully grasped his hand to take it away. I felt a strong pull on my chest. I halted as the familiar feeling of being removed resurfaced.

I blinked and squinted against the blaring light. Once again, I was outside. A raging sun beat down on my skin. I raised my arm to shield from the glare and saw I was dressed in white garments. I was wearing a long white dress with a mix of sheer and solid fabrics. The ground below was sand. I was in a desert.

The sandy hills expanded in all directions. Wind blew roughly, causing swirly clouds of dust to form.

Unexpectedly, there was a huge clattering sound that came from behind me. The ground shook dynamically and I staggered as I turned to view what caused the noise.

Bright lights formed in the sky. They grew grander and morphed into beams that plummeted to the ground. The terrain continued quaking and increased with each beam that landed. I fell to my hands and knees, noticing droplets of blood drip to the ground by my hands. My nose was bleeding. A piercing pain bombarded my head and coursed to my stomach. I grabbed it and realized I was pregnant.

One of the large beams plunged down possibly thirty feet from me. Its force pushed me back to a seated position once it hit the ground. The concentrated light seemed to drill into earth. A dark shape swelled inside the ray and took the form of a person. It withdrew from the shaft of light and meticulously moved towards me.

I couldn't focus my vision to determine who or what the entity was approaching me. I could only assume it was a person because of the shape.

As it drew closer, two eyes glowed white. It stopped midway between its arrival point and where I sat, holding out its palms.

I climbed to my feet, prompted to go forward. I took a couple of steps.

A third eye opened in its forehead, glowing bright gold. It looked to smolder with fire. Its stare blazed through me, driving me to stop. The being advanced on me and its palms faced me the entire time. I was immobilized and the temperature was rising quickly. I couldn't see it clearly, no matter how close it got. Once it was finally in front of me, its hands were on my stomach.

I gasped, then screamed as I burst into flames.

I came back to reality and it felt like I was still on fire. I hunched over the desk, gripping the edge tightly with my eyes shut. I opened them one at a time, noticing the office was unusually quiet. I looked around at the occupants to find they were staring at me.

Oh...

"Doris," Nefer said discreetly. He was sitting at the desk, his hand on mine. "Are you alright?"

I swallowed hard and shoved myself towards my desk to sit down.

I'm not on fire... I am NOT on fire...

Gary's door opened and he came out, followed by another person.

"Doris," Gary said, "I want to introduce you to the CEO of Faculty Climate Solutions, Sekima Harris."

"Good morning, Doris," Sekima said. She held out her hand. "I personally thank you for all the success you have brought to the company over these months."

Sekima... The ex???

I clumsily got to my feet to give her a handshake.

"Uh, you're welcome," I replied, prudent.

"Gary has nothing but wonderful things to say about you." She smiled, as we continued to shake hands. "I look forward to all we will accomplish in a year's time."

She wore an azure blazer and pencil skirt with a floral-patterned teal blouse and strappy heels.

"Sure...yea..." I smiled halfheartedly.

She gave me the impression she was talking about the ability Gary liked to call my 'expertise'. It was hard to tell, since her feelings were masked.

She's hiding something. Does she have a demon? Maybe SHE is playing a game with me... Is this some twisted form of entertainment...?

I never encountered a person who didn't show their emotions. I was unnerved by her. My head throbbed and I couldn't assess our interaction.

"Doris," Gary said, "Sekima and I are going to lunch. I have my cell if you need me."

I nodded as I sat back down at my desk. My mind was focused elsewhere.

Sekima waved at me and looked at Nefer. "Have a good day."

As she and Gary left the office, I stared at my computer in an attempt to replay the vision I had. It was vanishing fast. I had an image of a shadow with three eyes; two white and one gold. That part didn't fade away.

"Doris," Nefer said again. "Are you ok?"

"Stop asking me that," I snapped. "I'm fine."

"It's just... you screamed. Before... when you were gone."

"I screamed...?" I glanced in his direction.

"Not that loud, but loud enough..." He looked over his shoulder then turned back to me. "It got the office's attention."

I peered over at the other desks and some were still gawking at me.

"Oh, excuse me for disturbing their very important work." I sneered.

He stood up and came towards me.

"Don't touch me." I was becoming irate.

"Hi, Nefer." Stella and Tiffany strolled up, smiling. The lust was apparent in the way they moved.

Oh, these bitches...

I should have projected I'd see them. They often emanated their licentious goals, and loved to blather about them. Nefer was a premier target, which deepened my exasperation.

"Hello, ladies," he greeted as he returned to the desk and sat down.

The women took position at the desk to commence conversation. Stella's plunging shirt left nothing to the imagination and her skirt was a clear dress code violation. Tiffany was a little more conservative with her attire, but that was most likely because she had less prominent assets.

"You like working here so far?" Stella asked. She was overzealously courteous.

"It's not bad." He calmly leaned back in the chair and crossed his arms. "You two been here long?"

"Not really," Tiffany responded, indolent.

"You like it?"

"Uh... it's a job. So, no." She sniggered and looked at Stella to lead the discussion on the path they surely sought to go.

"Enough about work." Stella caught the hint. "There's this Halloween party on Saturday and I think you should come."

"Halloween party, huh?" He smirked and glimpsed at me, which made me look away. "Where at?"

"Up in the city. You should come." She was almost begging. She threw her straight, long black hair over her shoulder. "We have an extra ticket... I can send you the link...?"

"What's the party called? I may get my own ticket." He pulled out his phone.

"Here..." She arrogantly snatched his phone while he was using it. "Let me just do this... There. Now you have to come."

She placed it on the desk, endeavoring to be seductive.

"We'll be there," Tiffany chimed in as they turned to leave. "Pink costumes... Pink masks..."

"Pink everything..." Stella brazenly grinned and winked. They nudged each other, giggling.

"Ok." He watched them with mild fascination as they walked away.

I tried to ignore the feeling that developed from his response to the banter. I focused on what I envisioned. The thought of burning alive was etched in my skull. I also thought of the life form's eyes and how unbearable the fire was. The memory of the pain was slipping away, I could feel it. The image of my surroundings diminished with it, but the scorching eyes lingered. I was entranced as I ruminated and Gary had returned.

"Doris," he alerted me as he walked past into his office, "please come in so we can talk."

Nefer observed me go in and I met his gaze. I abruptly turned my head to avoid getting caught.

"Close the door, please," Gary directed. He went to his computer and began typing. "Sekima really likes you."

I shut the door. As I sat down, I thanked him. I knew he was proud of this information, but I could care less. I was increasingly suspicious of her.

"I'm sure you are wondering what the new employee is here to do." He stopped typing.

I'm more so wondering what he's doing to me...

"I didn't get an introduction really," I replied. An image of my fall flashed through my mind.

"Margaret and Ben were supposed to be in Client Relations. Nefer is Hiring Manager."

"Hiring Manager...?" I tried to process. "I'm the Hiring Manager."

"You are the Hiring Manager," he agreed. His computer chimed from an email receipt. He started typing again. "For these next two weeks, please train him on all that you do. Assign courses he needs to complete, that sort of thing..."

"Ok..." I clasped my hands together, irresolute. "Is... the office expanding...?"

"Uhh... No..." He steadily clicked his mouse and resumed typing. "But we are opening a new office soon."

"Oh, ok. I see..."

"I'm trying to offer you a promotion." He finished typing and tipped back in his chair.

"Oh, I..." I shifted in the seat. "To, uh... what position...?"

"Office Director. Here at this office."

"But... so, are you going to the new office, Gary?"

"That's the plan!" He stood up and came around the desk to prop up against it. "Will you accept? If you need time to think, we can discuss this tomorrow."

Promotion? I don't need to think about making more money....

"No, I mean, yes, I will accept." I felt encouraged. "I don't need time to think."

"Excellent!" He clenched his fist like he scored a victory. He was thrilled.

I smiled. "Thank you. For... this opportunity. You can count on me."

"I have full confidence that is true." He nodded as he clapped his hands together. "So, work closely with Nefer. We will touch base on Monday."

"Yes, sir." I stood up, aware the conversation had concluded.

He shook my hand and closed his door once I was out of his office. I returned to my desk.

I'm going to be boss? I grinned, and began printing paperwork for Nefer. *Does that mean I get to fire the useless people in this office? I know who will be the first to go...*

I gave Nefer documents to sign and ordered him to complete them. He obliged.

"Ahem," he cleared his throat as he went through the forms. "So... Doris..."

I sighed. "Yes..."

"When can we be alone again?"

"Uh..." It was hard to answer.

"I wanna talk about... what happened earlier," he said.

I reflected on what he perceived. I tried to remember what I even beheld. I couldn't be sure, except that there were three eyes on a ghostly figure. I considered his meaning about what happened earlier. Did he mean the vision or did he want to talk about how he made me feel? I was growing aroused from the memory. The sensations were potent and I hungered to feel them again. I kept in mind he said he felt what I felt.

Does he feel my desire right now...?

I refrained from making eye contact. I had the notion he was feeling it, and he was watching me. I could tell him anything, but he would just listen to my body's language.

No point in saying the opposite of how I feel...

I was uncomfortable with the fact that he knew how I felt.

At least he can't read my mind...

"I don't know..." I ended up responding. "I don't know if I'm ready to."

I glanced at him and he looked deep in thought. I cogitated what I wanted to say.

"Maybe..." I supplemented. "Maybe... this weekend. Sunday..."

"I can come by after church," he said.

Church... Lord knows I haven't been there in years...

"Ok." I nodded. "I don't want to talk any more about this. We can focus on work while we're at work, please."

"Yes, ma'am."

I winced. "Finish that paperwork... I need to train you on your position over the next couple of weeks."

"Doing it now."

8

The week went by and work wasn't anything out of the ordinary. As I trained Nefer, we didn't really make much contact beyond verbal and I did my best to avoid spending extra time with him by keeping our interactions strictly professional. Even though he knew how I felt, I didn't express my feelings out loud.

Outside of work, we would text but I was short with my answers. I had emphasized that I didn't want to talk about anything until Sunday. It made my days easier to manage and I didn't have to concern myself with being compromised by how he affected my emotions.

Today was Saturday. I had become fixated on the point that I would be ascertaining my next sacrifice at the Halloween party. I was only a few short days from when my menstrual cycle was to begin.

In my bedroom, I groomed to attend the party and examined myself in front of the full-length mirror by my dresser.

"Will Nefer be there...?" my cat was quizzical.

"Well," I replied as I stuffed my damaged hair into a stocking cap, "If it's the party he was invited to, then possibly..."

"I'm sure you like that possibility."

I did. In actuality, I did a great deal and this annoyed me.

"Hmmm," my cat hummed, solicitous, "you may get your wish..."

"Do you know anything about him?" I watched her spread out on my bed. "You wouldn't tell me, would you..."

"I don't know what you mean." She skipped off my bed.

"Is he like me...?"

"Like you, how...? Are you asking if he has a pet?"

"If that's what you call yourself..."

She laughed and sat beside me. "Yes, I am your pet... I am here because you will it. You called me here. Here I shall remain."

I didn't call her at all. I didn't ask for a demon.

I stared at my reflection. I surveyed my wrinkled skin, my under-eye bags and saggy jowls. Overall, my skin was exceedingly dehydrated. I ran a finger along my severely chapped lips.

How did he kiss these? I gawped in repugnance.

My phone buzzed on my bed. When I picked it up, I saw the time was seven twenty-three P.M. as I checked my new message. It was from Nefer.

'I don't know if I can wait another day before seeing you,' he wrote.

I smiled, tempted to declare my mutual feelings.

'You better not be sitting outside my apartment,' I teased.

'LOL.'

I started to reply that tomorrow would come soon enough.

'I thought about it,' he sent while I was midsentence.

I changed my response. *'Should I be regretting that I showed you where I live?'*

After I didn't receive his reply for several seconds, I tossed my phone on the bed and went to take a shower. I then laid my outfit on the bed as I checked my phone intermittently for his text. I wondered if my reply was taken literally. I mulled over what I sent while I applied makeup, using dark shades for my eyes and lips.

"I think that's as good as it will get," my cat said, studying me smear on lipstick. "You're wearing a mask, right?"

She mocked me, and she knew my preparation was unnecessary. The man to be chosen this evening didn't depend on how alluring I was.

I look like I'm auditioning for a cheesy superhero movie, I thought as I scrutinized myself. I put the mask in my purse and pulled out a small bottle of vodka to drink. I checked my phone once more.

"You will know your chosen," my cat edified. "As you have known all others. Follow the light. Your chosen will be revealed."

Equivalent to all others, I hoped this was the last one. I left the apartment.

$$\sim\sim * \sim\sim$$

The party took place at a warehouse. The exterior was appropriately decorated with faux cobwebs, blood, and insects. There were skeletons, a motorized witch stirring a cauldron, various carved pumpkins, and images of ghosts. The warehouse's loading bay door was slightly ajar. Fake smoke seeped from the opening and a mannequin made up as a zombie was on the ground posed like it was crawling out. Beside the loading bay was a regular door. This appeared to be the entrance. A line of people had formed by the time I arrived at ten thirty-nine P.M.

As I sat in my car, I withdrew another miniature bottle of vodka from my purse and ingested it. I took a deep breath, watching the people enter the building. They were wearing all types of costumes. One man was dressed like a baby angel. When he turned around, I saw he was wearing a green devil horned mask. I pulled my mask from my purse and put it on.

"Here we go..." I muttered.

"Your cycle will begin in four days," my cat said from the back seat.

"I know," I countered. I was feeling the liquor to some degree.

Her tail wrapped around my neck. "You forget who you are talking to..."

I held my hands up in surrender, causing her to let go of me. I was on the verge of tears as I shoved my door open and headed to the line.

The night air carried some heat. At the door, two men were managing entry. They both wore a red devil mask. One of the men was in a red dress suit checking I.D.'s and scanning tickets. The other man's shirt indicated he was security. He was giving directions to the people after they checked in. The man in the red suit checked my I.D. and stared for several seconds, bewildered. He stamped my wrinkly hand after scanning my ticket. The bouncer pointed through the door and told me to go straight ahead to get to the party.

"You get one free drink at the bar to the left!" he was yelling over the booming music. "All other drinks tonight are five dollars! Have fun!"

The music amplified as I made my way into the warehouse. The walls were covered in cobwebs and fake spiders. Just like the bouncer said, the bar was to the left. A blonde-haired woman, in a red cat suit and also wearing a red devil mask, ambled up to hand me a tiny cup from her tray. She casually waved toward the bar when I received it, then walked toward the people who entered behind me.

I thanked her just before slurping it up in one gulp. It was clearly watered down. I walked beyond the bar to observe the people dancing under strobe lights to the music's rapid tempo. Their carnal energy was powerful. As I scanned the dancers, the men in my proximity began to emit a pale purplish-blue glow from their bodies.

The music's volume lowered. The strobe lighting changed to solid white light and then dimmed.

"Good evening everyone!" a man's voice shouted through speakers from my right, atop a stage. "Welcome to the Devil's Playpen!"

The crowd cheered, hollered, and hooted.

"Our first performance of the night is about to start!" he said, enthusiastically. He waited for the racket to die down again. "Please give a warm welcome to the fiery duo, Mina and Nina!"

The audience roared again as two half-naked women wearing golden devil masks stepped onto the stage. They swung chains with balls of fire on the ends and they began to dance.

I skulked around the edge of the crowd during their presentation, searching for my chosen. I noticed one man with a brighter glow that flashed like a beacon. My heart pulsated robustly.

He had his back to me, watching the women dance. He wore a shaggy wig that resembled a lion's mane. His black shirt was sleeveless, his arms painted with stripes and furry bracelets were on his wrists. He had on animal print leggings.

I placed my hand on his shoulder when I reached him to get his attention.

When he turned to face me, I saw he was wearing a golden lion mask with horns on it. Our eyes met and he fell into a trance. The bright glow of his skin dissipated as his eyes flashed a deep blue. He was chosen; destined to be sacrificed.

"Go to the city park at six P.M. in four days," I whispered. "Tell no one where you are going. Wait at the fountain. I will meet you."

He nodded in acceptance, as my voice was the only thing he could hear. I blinked to sever contact and he turned back to watch the stage. Soon after, the performance was over. I clapped along with the rest of the crowd.

~~ * ~~

The next morning, I lay in bed staring at the ceiling. It was about eight thirty. Nefer hadn't texted me since my last message. I felt driven to text him again but withheld the action. I didn't want to come off as desperate. I questioned if it would even be considered desperation by him.

Is he still coming over...? I thought.

"You have identified the sacrifice," my cat said, sitting at the foot of my bed. "Wonderful."

Maybe for you... I sighed, weakly.

"Am I doing this until I die?" I asked. I checked my phone.

"Short answer? Yes." She laughed spitefully.

"Grrr!" I was infuriated by her and by how often I had checked my messages. I went to the bathroom.

"Since you're up," my cat called from the kitchen, "it's best you get that steak ready for me. I'm feeling hungry..."

I made her steak and saw the eviction notice on the kitchen table.

Oh shit, I need to move out. I picked up the papers to skim them. *Did Nefer see this when he was here...?*

Since I needed to be out by Thursday, I made an online request to have my rental furniture picked up. I rented all of my furniture. I was to be contacted to choose a time window. Once I put in the request, I went to take a long shower. I got dressed in a red tank top and black pajama pants. I viewed my phone and this time I had a new message.

Knocking on the door startled me.

As I walked to the door, I realized the message was from Nefer and it made me freeze.

'OMW,' he sent thirty-eight minutes ago.

A sinking feeling developed in my chest. My heart was pounding. I gradually drew closer to the door when I heard another knock and looked through the peephole.

Nefer was present on the other side, wearing a lime green button up shirt and tan colored slacks.

I took a few breaths before I opened the door, immediately stepping aside and gestured for him to come in without peering at his face.

"Morning," he addressed.

"Hi," I answered timorously. I quickly closed the door when he entered and followed him to the couch where he sat down. "Are you... thirsty?"

"Sure. Anything you have."

"Water..." I hastened to the kitchen to grab a bottle from the fridge. When I returned, I joined him on the couch once I handed him the water. Clasping my hands together in my lap, I asked, "So... how was church...?"

"Thanks. It was good. You should come with me sometime."

I thought of the last time I went to church. I knew he wasn't even alive yet. "Maybe."

"What church do you go to now?" He sipped the water.

"I don't."

"Oh. May I ask why?"

Yes, but I won't tell you...

"Well..." My hands were dripping with sweat. "Can we talk about what this is we are doing right now?"

"Just making conversation." He gently replaced the cap on the bottle.

"I mean, the reason you are here. To talk about what this is... between us..." I viscerally swiped my hands on my pants.

He placed the water on the floor, staying silent.

"What I saw, when you touched me..." I resumed, "Did you see it...? The burning eyes..."

"I did," he confirmed. He sat up straight.

"Why don't you care that this is happening? This is not natural."

Not that I'm natural...

"I care," he evenly replied. "That's why I'm here."

"How can you be so calm about this? Do you like seeing me worked up? You're already attractive, so why play these head games?" I was querulous. "I just don't see how you can be so... calm!"

He hunched over, placed his elbows on his knees and held his hands together. He looked at the floor.

"It's hard to put to words," he asserted. "I feel like we've met before. Like, what we saw was a past life. But I never met you 'til a couple of weeks ago. I saw you and... those feelings I felt, what I feel... I just know we're supposed to meet."

"Like... soulmates?" I was flattered by his sappy explanation. I studied his face as he kept his eyes on the floor.

He laughed, sending tremors through me. "I guess. It sounds corny, I know."

"I have to ask... about your wife, Sekima... or your ex..."

"Ok..." His mood changed from excited to undistinguished.

"What is she to you...?"

I sought to ask if she had anything to do with this. I was sure that asking if she was a demon wouldn't be received very well.

"She's my ex." His answer was frank.

"Is that all she is...? I mean, how involved in your life is she...?"

"Not very involved at all. If you're asking because of the job referral thing, that's just to help me out as a friend. She and I haven't been anything more to each other for years."

"She was at your house..."

"Yea, she was. She still has things at my place." He nodded.

"But you two are not together though..." I was incapable of comprehending the situation.

"However it may seem to you, the answer is no." He shrugged, rubbing his hands together.

I believed him, but I wasn't satisfied with how minimal his responses were. "So... then, she—-"

"I gotta be honest," he cut in and admitted, "I don't really wanna talk about Sekima right now."

"Ok..." I wasn't particularly interested in the subject either. I just needed something to lessen my qualms about potentially being misled.

"All I can think about..." He turned to peer directly in my eyes, his enthusiasm restored. "...is what I wanna do to you."

I was ambushed by the puissant emotions. I swallowed anxiously as the line of interrogation I had was in shambles.

"I..." I whispered. "I can't..."

"There's nothing to be afraid of." He rested his hand on my thigh. "Let me show you."

My body implored him to osculate. I placed my hand on top of his and he seized my face with his other hand to lean in for a passionate kiss. As I reclined, he planted kisses on my cheek, my chin, then along my neck. He kissed me another time and slipped his hands under my shirt to caress my breasts. I moaned in contentment before I pulled my shirt over my head. He lightly pinched my nipples between his fingers, pressing his lips on my chest. He started sucking each nipple dotingly, kissing lower to my stomach and then began to pull down my pants. When I stopped him, he looked up at me with expressive thirst. I held his hands securely.

"I wanna kiss you everywhere," he pledged. We maintained eye contact as he kissed beneath my navel.

Breathing heavily, I surrendered to his candor and permitted him to remove my bottoms. The desire mounted as he kissed my hips and inner thighs. My skin tingled from his breath and he adoringly pressed his lips against my lower lips. I began to feel faint as he kissed, sucked, and used his tongue. I whimpered from the incredible sensations. My legs quivered once he slid fingers inside, and he continued pressure with his mouth. My body temperature drastically elevated. I started sweating profusely. Heart throbbing, my sensitivity to his motions heightened. Then, without warning, the sensations peaked and I was bombarded with inexplicable pleasure that sent waves throughout my body. My inner walls convulsed around his fingers.

"Aahh!" I cried out, gripping the couch. I wriggled to withstand the extreme stimulation. I grabbed the back of his head and my legs clamped up. "Oooh... my God...!!"

He gave another affectionate kiss and removed his fingers. He put his hands on my knees in an effort to pry them apart.

"Sorry," I said, breathless and discomfited. "Sorry... I—-"

I unclenched my legs to let him up.

"It's ok," he supportively replied. He came up to my face and kissed me. "I wanna be inside you."

"I..." I tried to stabilize my breath. "I don't know... if I can take anymore..."

He kissed me again. "I'll go slow."

"Ok, yes..." I feverishly needed him to enter me. "Go slow..."

As soon as I approved, he lifted me from the couch and carried me to my bedroom. He laid me on the bed before he undressed, and removed a condom from his pants pocket. He climbed on top of me as he rolled it on.

"Go slow..." I repeated.

"I will..." he promised, caringly kissing as he pushed himself into me.

I moaned with every gentle stroke. I dug my fingers into his back; bit his shoulder softly. It felt so amazing that my responsiveness was declining.

"Can I go faster?" he whispered, his voice a distant echo.

I nodded and closed my eyes, squeezing him. He sped his stride and the room whirled like a carousel.

"Ohh," I gasped, opening my eyes. I threw my head back. "Oooh...f... fuck...!"

The light began to dim as the world fell away. I was gone.

I awoke to being caressed on my lower back. I raised my head to see Nefer, who was naked beside me, lounging and scrolling his phone while rubbing me with his other hand. His touch was exceedingly warm, but it was no longer as overpowering as it had once been.

Daylight passed through the window, indicating I hadn't slept the entire day away. He swiped his screen and put his phone down.

"What time is it...?" I asked, wiping my eyes.

"Four fourteen," he answered. He repositioned himself to his side and propped his head on his fist. "Hi."

I put my head back down. "Hey..."

He smiled and I buried my face in the pillow. I was embarrassed. "Ugh..."

I slept for hours! I thought. *He probably thinks I'm exhausted because of my age...*

He placed his hand on my neck and started massaging it. I felt the tension melt away as he rubbed my neck and shoulder. There was rustling and his lips pressed on my back. Astounded, I rolled over and sat up.

"No, don't," I requested, worriedly. I hugged the covers to my chest.

"Ok," he said.

My reasoning was zipping in multiple directions. It was unclear where this was headed and I was very troubled about it. I wanted to feel comfortable, but I kept thinking about Sekima. I had to know if she was included in some way. Nefer was undisputedly engaged, that much was true. I had to verify that this wasn't a very intricate ploy.

"I..." I guardedly began, "I know that... we were having a conversation before this..."

I paused, in case he wanted to say something. He didn't speak.

"And..." I said, "I have... reservations about what we are doing..."

"Reservations..." he copied.

"Yes, I just..."

"What do you need to know to ease your mind?" He was attentive and serene.

"I just want to know what's going on with you and your ex-wife."

"As I said, nothing." His calm tone endured. "You don't believe me, is that it?"

"No, I believe you," I promptly disagreed. My angst was building. "Does she... feel the same way? That there's nothing between you..."

"Yes."

"How are you so sure?"

"Because, Sekima and I..." His temperament developed minor strife. He sighed and lied down on his back to situate his hands underneath his head as he stared up at the ceiling.

This was the first time I felt any stress from him. I must have hit a nerve. Perhaps this factor would convince me of his involvement in my downfall. It could equally dissolve my internal discord. I speculated profusely, and the period of stillness didn't help.

Suspense is killing me...

"We got married real young," he said at long last. "It was a mistake and... we were stupid."

"How young...?" I queried.

"She was still in high school. We thought we were deep in love, and we were gonna spend the rest of our lives together... The plan was to wait for her to finish school and turn eighteen so she wouldn't disappoint her mom. We had a little over a year to go, when my dad passed. She got this idea that, if she said she was pregnant, her mom would let us get married right away."

"Did you... want a baby...?" I asked, surprised.

"No, actually," he acknowledged. "But I was fine with the plan because I would get her, we would leave town, and find our happiness. I got some money that my dad saved up before he died and was gonna sell the house to get us started. Then, I found out Sekima was really pregnant when we had to get our license..."

"You still married her though..."

"I did. I was in love with her. I wanted to grow old with her." He furrowed his eyebrows, brooding. "So, I changed my mind. I couldn't up and leave after learning that. She was having a baby, and it needed stability. I decided to keep the house. I wanted to be a dad."

He has a kid...?

"Did Sekima want to stay?" I probed.

"Not at all." He shook his head. "She wanted to stick to the plan. She wanted to leave."

"When did she leave...?" I presumed this was what broke them up.

He bit his bottom lip, and with gloom he replied, "After we lost the baby..."

"Oh..." Remorseful, sweat welled in my palms. "We don't have to talk about this anymore..."

"It's alright, I don't wanna make you feel like I'm hiding something from you."

His words resonated with me. I was most definitely hiding something from him. I didn't reply.

"Since I wasn't selling the house," he said, "we stayed. Sekima was unhappy and we fought all the time. One night, we got into a big argument. It was the worst. Screaming, yelling, things got broken... She was like three months, maybe four months pregnant. She was so angry that she left the house. I was pissed off, so I didn't think anything of it until she wasn't back when I woke up in the morning. I called her, texted her, I even called her mom. I called anyone I could think of. I ended up going to the cops. They treated me like I was the reason she ran off by the way they grilled me. So, I said fuck it. I'd find her myself. I searched her school, friends' houses... I was running out of places to look when she showed up a couple days later..."

His grief deepened. "She was... beaten to hell... She said some guy attacked her. He... raped her... Beat her half to death. I took her to the hospital and we found out the... baby was gone."

I wanted to assuage his pain.

He took a deep breath, ire budding as he continued, "She described this guy as tall, white, with green eyes. She kept saying she remembered his eyes because of how green they were. I made her take me to where it happened. I knew it was hard for her, but I wanted to find this guy. I needed to find him... I thought if I found him, I could get closure. The thought kept me out every night, for weeks. Weeks turned into months... I thought I found him once. Some white dude, out at night. He looked out of place. I just knew it was him, so I beat his ass. I almost killed him... Come to find out, he didn't have green eyes. He wasn't even white. I had lost it by that point."

I sensed his indignation had minimized and converted to shame.

"I came home that night and Sekima was gone," he said. "She left a note, saying she was done. She didn't wanna be married anymore, school was over, and she had no reason to stay. Like that was all she was sticking around for... No one knew where she went. She just... disappeared."

"When was this...?" I inquired.

"Uh, almost fourteen years ago now," he responded.

So he's around thirty-something, like I figured...

"She was gone for fourteen years? What made her come back...?" I wondered if she missed him.

"I would think her business. Sometime last year, she reached out to me on social media and said she would be in town for work. She wanted to see me. When we met, I asked her for a divorce. I never thought about it until she contacted me. The divorce was final just earlier this year, but I was done well before that."

"How do you feel about her...? Don't you love her?"

"I don't," he declared. "I care about her, and we will always have history. But, I don't know her. I don't think I ever did. We were young, you know, and it was hard to get to know each other. With what happened... I regret letting her leave that night. I think my chances of knowing her left with her. If I stopped her..."

"You can't blame yourself for things you have no control over," I offered, but I myself was guilty of this. "There's no way of knowing you could've stopped it."

"But I didn't even try," he refuted, repentant. "That night, I let her go and I just called her a dumb bitch."

I shook my head, narrowing my eyes. "Don't blame yourself."

"Yea, well, it's the past now." His frustration was fading. "I have support at church and I prayed over it. She's in a good place. She's done well."

"So she came back to stay here?" I suggested. "And get you a job..."

"Nah, she's here for some work stuff. But, yes, she did help me get a job... I need the money. My dad had a little something saved up before he died, but that was it. Long story short, I'm in deep shit. My old job wasn't paying enough to keep the bills up... she referred me before. I just was too proud to take it."

"You didn't want some of her money? The business seems pretty successful..."

He was affronted. "I'm not depending on her just because she made the right decision by leaving me. My dad has been dead for years. I'm in this hole because I fucked up, not because she left me."

I nodded in appreciation. I imagined he wouldn't ask her for money since he hadn't projected to receive assistance for better employment. I was consoled by how much he shared with me. I was just as despondent, due to my inability to reciprocate the sincerity.

"Does she know what you do with your personal life...?" I asked.

"What do you mean?" he answered.

"I mean... does she know about me? About us...? When she was at your house that day..."

"Oh, no. Well, yea, she knows you because of work, of course."

"She didn't ask why I was at your house? She sounded like she was implying something."

"Nah, she didn't say anything. I doubt she thought we were doing anything... b—-"

"Because?" I interrupted, prickly. "Because I'm old?"

"Old?" He laughed like it was in jest. He looked down at my body as he yanked the covers. He shook his head. "I was gonna say, 'but', I don't give a fuck what she thinks. Why are you so critical...? And why say old? Why not experienced? Or mature..."

"I need a shower," I huffed. I jumped out of the bed and went to the bathroom. I knew he was trying to give me a compliment, but I was offended.

"I'm not joking!" He followed me to the bathroom. "Can I shower with you? It would save water..."

"Um, it's not that big of a shower."

He was at the room's entrance. "You're right... but have you tried? We might fit."

"I think I've had enough of you for now." I activated the faucet for the shower.

"I get it. If you faint in the shower, it could be pretty dangerous." He was being upfront, but I detected a hint of vanity.

"What?" I spun around and went to the door. "On second thought, you can't come in."

I slammed it in his face.

~~ * ~~

In the shower, I replayed the events that came to pass during the morning. I specifically recounted the unbelievable sensations. I hadn't felt anything like them before. I almost still felt Nefer all over me, and in me. The sheer remembrance was effervescent. The pleasures were insurmountable and pervasive. He moved with such skill. There was no way I could handle him.

He can't just be a man, I thought, recalling our conversation where I questioned what he was.

I was positive he had supernatural powers which circumvented my own and prevented me from revealing his authentic wishes. I had met men who thought they were compelling liars. I could see through all of them.

What if he is a demon, and he wants to seduce me like I have done to so many others? Oh, Lord, please... if this is another test... I won't make it. I just won't... I already let him in...

This thought caused me to shudder in amplified fear. I was aware that he came to see me with a condom in his pocket. This was an apparent precautionary measure. I started to ponder how many other women he potentially conquered.

Could he have just wanted to explore some really great sex...? If I ask him, he will tell me...

I dismissed this scheme right away. I scolded myself for even considering it since I shouldn't have cared. I was letting the emotions cloud my view. I shifted my concentration from his sexual endeavors to the visions we both experienced. They came off as a very ambiguous daydream. He had said it was like we were destined to meet. I quickly thought of Sekima and how I was inept at sensing her sentiments. Regardless of his history with her, I grappled with the feeling that she was conniving. She could have a demon who preyed on her ex-lover's new interests. I hadn't met anyone else who was possessed like me.

Here I go again, thinking too much! I put my hands together and closed my eyes. *I pray he is here to release me...*

My entreating was interrupted by knocks on the door. Nefer entered without waiting for admission and hurriedly closed the door. He had his pants on.

I turned off the shower and stepped out, then grabbed my towel to dry off.

"Are you leaving...?" I asked, apprehensive. I wiped down the cloudy mirror.

"No..." he replied. He was puzzled. "Uh... your... cat..."

"My cat?"

"Your cat talked to me..."

I froze. Fright was brewing. "My cat... talked to you..."

"Yea..." His perplexity was augmented by disbelief.

"Cats don't talk." I kept wiping the mirror, yet the fog persisted.

"Uh huh... but this one did..." He was uncertain.

I shook my head and opened the door. I left the bathroom to investigate.

"Yea..." he restated, following me out.

I walked around my room but didn't see her. I pulled out some clothes to get dressed.

"She's in the living room," he reported. He hadn't moved from outside the bathroom.

Shit. Shit, shit...

I found her sitting on the couch. I was panicky, and tried to devise an explanation. I was sure he felt my dread.

Nefer crept up beside me, his eyes wide with confusion.

"Well," my cat purred. She kept her eyes on him. "So he can see me, AND understand me..."

My heart was ready to burst from my chest.

"Uh..." I muttered.

"Uh...??" he parroted. "What is this...?"

Visions don't bother him, but a talking cat is unbelievable??

"I just had to be certain he isn't deceiving you," my cat turned her gaze to me as she spoke. She was thoroughly concerned. "That he isn't succeeding in doing so, but now after talking to him... he has no idea what I am..."

I continually shook my head and I was at a loss for words. My brain scrambled to give him an adequate justification. I remained mute as she vaulted from the couch and trotted off to my room. I felt his eyes on me, drilling a hole. The silence distended for an indefinite amount of time.

"Doris?" he asked.

"Nefer?" I replied, failing to think of a response. I was ill-equipped for this event.

"Say... something, anything! You can't pretend she wasn't talking just now." He was increasingly discouraged.

"I..."

"She wants to make sure I'm not deceiving you?" He moved to stand in front of me.

I avoided him by staring at the couch. I sighed, rubbed my forehead, and inadvertently wiped sweat on it.

He waited.

"I..." I said again. I sidestepped and went to sit on the couch. I felt defensive. "How was I supposed to tell you about her? It's not like the subject came up on her ability to talk..."

"How about just saying, 'she can talk'...?" He scratched the back of his head, staring at the floor.

"Look, I'm sorry, ok? I..." I wrung my clammy hands together. "I'm sorry... I didn't know how to tell you about her. It's just, we have so much already going on... And I'm still trying to figure it out. I wasn't ready to tell you about her..."

After hearing my interpretation out loud, I was even more ashamed. He was nothing but truthful with me from the start.

"Is she doing this to us?" he accused. "Is SHE making you do this to me? Is she the reason we even met?"

"No!" I opposed, earnestly. I stared at my TV. "No... no, she... this has never happened before."

He crossed his arms. "Doris, look at me."

Don't really want to right now...

"Doris..." he said.

"Don't talk to me like I'm a child, ok!?" I balled my hands into fists and dropped them to my sides. I inhaled and exhaled deeply.

"I'm not trying to, alright? I'm not." He came over to sit next to me. "I'm just trying to understand."

I took another breath. "Well, with the visions and how you make me feel, I was waiting for the right time to tell you... I never felt this! Ok? I never saw visions, or experienced what—"

I had an almost uncontrollable urge to confess everything, but I couldn't allow it to direct my words.

"Have you always had your cat?" He was somewhat intrigued.

"Not always..." I responded. "But for a long time..."

"How long?"

"Are you asking my age now?" I was fearful of his reaction if I were to answer.

"I am. Do you wanna know mine?"

"Yes..." I peered at him, and the sensations I once felt were more manageable. I felt the longing expand inside, subtly flowing through me.

"Thirty-four," he answered. "Your turn."

"Right..." I stalled.

"Too late to be shy." He shook his head in disapproval.

"I'm... fifty-five..." I expected him to attach at least twenty years to that for my appearance.

"When did you find the cat?" He didn't bat an eye to my age.

"I was..." I pulled my eyes away. "She found me... I was... thirteen."

"So, what, you just been talking to each other ever since?"

"Not exactly..."

"Ok, I don't know what I gotta ask here to get you to talk to me. What's with you and the cat?" He leaned closer to me.

"I know, I'm sorry." I covered my face with my hands. "I'm really trying to tell you..."

I wrestled a wave of tears.

He started rubbing my back which reduced some of my anxiety.

"She's a demon," I added, my hands still over my face.

His motion slowed as he processed. "A demon..."

I felt the onset of a headache. I swallowed; my mouth was dry.

"Are you a devil worshipper?" He stopped caressing me.

The tears I fought escaped and spilled down my cheeks.

"Did you give yourself to the devil?" His tone was serious.

I broke down in tears and choked out, "I don't know..."

"What happened? How did you meet?"

I uncovered my face to wrap my hands around myself. I took numerous breaths, attempting to reply. "I was... um..."

If I tell him, he is going to run out the door, I told myself. *I know he will run...*

"Tell me what happened," he pushed. His hand rested on my shoulder.

"I was thirteen... and she came to me when I first got my period... My father... she—she helped me... she saved me and my mother..."

"The devil comes in many forms..." He scooted closer and embraced my shoulders with his arm. "He can trick you into doing wrong. Pretend to be what you want most."

"I want to tell you, but I'm just afraid," I blurted, wiping tears. "I don't know... I'm afraid of how it sounds. It won't make sense."

"What do you do for this demon? How do you worship it?"

Worship... I wouldn't call it that...

I sighed. "I... sacrifice..."

"You... kill?" He was uneasy.

"No, I don't kill." I had to elucidate. I did my best to describe it. "SHE does. Or... I... I offer a sacrifice every twenty-eight days. During the final night of my period, I perform a ritual... with my blood and the semen of the chosen. When the ritual is over, the body is gone..."

He removed his arm. "You sacrifice men."

"Yes... I sleep with them during the final act, and I perform the ritual..."

He immediately sprang up.

"Please, don't leave." I felt abashed by the request.

"You just told me you sacrifice men to your demon during sex." His distress smoldered with every word.

"Yes, and I know how it sounds..." I started to get up.

"Not sure you do."

"Yes I do!" New tears formed as I was getting upset. "I've been doing this shit since I was THIRTEEN! Ugh... I don't expect you to want me around. We had sex... I know you must think I'm going to sacrifice you..."

"I'm not gonna lie. I do."

"Please believe me, I'm not. And I don't get to choose like that. She chooses for me... I simply obey."

I initially felt that adding this would bring comfort, but it merely made it appear more possible.

"It's... getting late," he said. He started walking to my bedroom.

"You're leaving..." I pursued him.

"I need to get home now." He gathered the rest of his clothes off the floor to get dressed.

"Good," my cat retorted, laughing. She loafed on my bed, licking herself. "You wore out your welcome hours ago."

He glared at her for a moment, and then looked at me.

"Nefer..." I whispered. I resisted begging him to stay. I wanted so badly for him to.

"I need to go." He walked out.

I whirled around to my cat and furiously pleaded, "Why? Just, why??"

"Eh, he was going to ruin this good thing we have," she responded, composed. "I can't have that."

"Grrr!" I looked up at the ceiling, and screamed. Growing drowsy, I collapsed onto my bed. I thought I could smell Nefer on the covers. I breathed deeply as I drifted off to sleep.

9

At work Monday morning, Nefer wasn't there. I sat at my desk, wondering if it was because of me.

I told him I fuck men and sacrifice them to a demon, I thought. *Would I want to see me after that?*

I nonverbally rebuked my cat. I couldn't gauge why she spoke to him. I presumed she felt threatened enough to confront him. I didn't get an answer from her, as I didn't expect to. I imagined he was so special that it warranted her revealing herself. I wanted to know what she said to him. It made me wonder, was he really just a man? I ran him off, so I supposed I wouldn't find out. I was a devil worshipper.

I mindlessly worked away on my computer when my phone rang. I quickly picked it up in hopes it was Nefer. I didn't recognize the number and assumed it was a robo call, but decided to answer it anyway.

"Hello," I said.

"Hi, I'm calling from Carter's Charters," the caller began, "May I speak with Doris."

"Speaking."

"Hi, good morning. We would like to schedule your furniture pickup. What time are you looking to have them arrive tomorrow?"

"Oh... yes, uh... what's the latest you have...?" I huddled over my phone and stuck my finger in the opposite ear to hear the call better.

"We have... a time window of five P.M. to nine P.M, if that works for you?"

"Yes, perfect."

"Alright, your driver is Robert and he will call you when he's on the way. Thank you for chartering Carter."

"Sure..."

The phone hung up. I felt someone beside me and rotated to see Nefer. I instantaneously straightened up, stunned. I was equally elated.

"Oh..." I uttered. I edgily clicked my mouse and tapped my keyboard.

"Morning," he said, standing by my desk.

"Yes... Hi..."

"Doris, I..." his voice trailed off.

"You don't have to say anything." I resumed clicking random spots on my computer screen.

"Yes, I do." He leaned against my desk and folded his arms. "I want you to come to church with me."

"I don't... do church..." I was sweating.

"You will. Come with me this Sunday. I'm not asking."

I raised an eyebrow. "Demanding..."

"Yea," he agreed, "I'm demanding. You're coming."

He went to his desk.

Church!? I haven't been since my mother... I don't know if my cat will let me... is that what she is fighting against...? He is trying to help me... He IS here to help me, Lord Jesus...

"W—what..." I stuttered, "What do I need to do?"

"Come to church with me," he said a second time. "You will hear His words. You will see that there is a way to help you. To free you from... the weight of your sins."

The weight of my sins, he said. My cat was a sin. He was right.

"I spoke to my pastor," he went on. "Not about... everything. Just about you being in need. He's asked for a one-on-one with you. You can tell him everything. His name is Reverend Mikhael Eriksen. He will guide you."

"I don't know... if I can tell him anything."

"Yes, you can. Trust in His words, the pastor will guide you to understand them." He was doing something on the computer and typing slowly. "Come to my house on Saturday."

"Are you sure you want me at your house?"

"Why not? You've been before."

I shrugged and shook my head.

I don't know if this will be a good time...

"Fine," I replied, accepting his logic. I glanced at the closed door of Gary's office. There was no light underneath. I checked for messages from him but received none. I had no calls from him, either.

"Morning, Nefer," it was Stella, dripping with infatuation. She was alone, which was rare.

"Morning... Sheila..." Nefer greeted, friendly but distracted.

"Stella," she amended, slighted by his inaccuracy. "So... did you have fun on Saturday? I know I did."

I peeked at him from the corner of my eye. I was very focused on his response.

"It was ok." His body language mirrored his answer. He briefly looked at me.

"Want to get some lunch later?" she proposed. Her hunger was clear.

"I'm good, thanks."

I suppressed a satisfied smile.

Thank you, thank you... Now go away.

"Oh, so you could talk to me at the party, but not now?" She felt jilted.

"Just trying to work is all, nothing else." He shook his head.

"Mmhmm. Ok." She scowled at me before walking away and muttered something under her breath.

"No Gary today?" Nefer asked me.

"Hmm?" I craned my neck to look over at him. "I guess not."

"Well, I think I'm hungry after all. Wanna get lunch?"

I regarded the time in the corner of my monitor. I shot him a look. "It's ten forty-five in the morning..."

"I didn't get breakfast."

"Too early for me, honestly..."

"Ok. I can bring you back something." He got up and left.

My cell rang shortly after he was gone. It was Gary.

"Morning," I answered.

"Morning, Doris!" Gary was almost singing. "How was your weekend?"

Exhausting...

"Fine. Are you here today?"

"Yes, but only for a bit. I'm sorry, we were supposed to meet today. It will have to be pushed to next Monday. I need to head out of town for the rest of the week. So, that being said... can you do me a huge, HUGE favor?"

"Yes..."

"I have to catch a flight soon and I forgot my briefcase in the office. Can you please, please bring it down to the parking lot? I am on the way and will be there in ten minutes."

"Sure, I'm doing it now..." I got up to go in his office.

"Thank you! My briefcase is on my chair. I'll see you in a jiffy!" He hung up.

I turned on his light and surveyed the room. I walked through, passing the marble globe on a center shelf. I noticed it had tiny red stickers on its surface. As I stepped closer to get a better look, I heard the ding of Gary's computer. His computer was still on.

He didn't shut down his station or anything! Did he just run out of here...?

When I reached his computer, I saw a new message at the top of his inbox. I recognized the sender's name. It was time stamped at two minutes ago. I lifted his briefcase off the chair to sit down.

"To read, or not to read..." I mumbled, moving the cursor over the message. I was ready to click the exit box, when the message preview that displayed included my name. I kept the cursor hovered to read part of the subject line.

'CONFIDENTIAL: Q4 FORECAST, PHASE III...' the title preview began. The flag denoted urgency.

I skimmed the email and saw my name mentioned more than once. I double clicked to read it.

'Gary,' it addressed, 'We are on track with meeting the quota this quarter. In order to maintain the momentum, please review the attached and use it as a standard for the course of your venture. You will receive your itinerary once you arrive. Report to Dan, who is cc'd on this email.'

I looked at the cc on the message and the address had a government domain.

'I am pleased to hear Doris accepted her new role,' it said. 'Doris must finalize her transition by Wednesday after next. Do everything within your power to see that this occurs. Continue to encourage her to use her abilities, and make sure she is in constant contact with Nefer on a daily basis. Monitor their behavior and record the first sign of change. Since you are away this week, it will allow nature to take its course. Do not interfere while you are absent. I will see that they have the necessary accoutrements during your trip.'

My abilities...?

"'Constant contact...?'" I read aloud.

'Your commitment will not go unrewarded, and expect to see the fruits of our labor prior to the year's end. We will speak soon.'

'Sincerely, Seki.'

The attachment mentioned was named 'Abacus.GR'. I tried to open it, but it asked for a password. I clicked to close the email and an alert message appeared. It said the sender requested confirmation that the email was read.

'Do you want to confirm?' it requested. *'Yes/No'*
Shit.

I clicked 'no' and marked the message as unread. I briskly shut down the computer before I dashed from the office. My head was swimming with fresh theories about Sekima while I rode the elevator to the ground floor. I was so caught up in what developed between Nefer and me the day before that my interactions with her were rather insignificant. I bustled to the parking lot. A dark green luxury car eventually pulled up to the handicapped parking space beside the building's entrance.

"Doris!" Gary called as he hopped out. He eyed the briefcase in gratitude. "Thank you so much. Sorry for the short notice, I promise I will explain everything when I get back."

I nodded, keeping my mouth shut. I sensed he was genuinely relieved and his promise was in good faith. I struggled to steady my hand when I passed him his case.

"I can't be reached until Monday," he said, "but I trust you can handle things? And just like last week, you have the same objective..."

"Yes, training Nefer," I supplied.

"Yup!" He climbed in his car. "Keep training him and we'll discuss on Monday. I'm excited for your new responsibility, Doris! Trust me, you will be great at it!"

I nodded again and smiled. "See you Monday."

Everything he said sounded different to me. His words were bursting with the vibrancy he spoke of. I didn't suspect him of having concealed desires because he didn't show any. Even as he sat in his car, preparing to drive away, his intentions were clear. He closed the door, backed up, and peeled out of the lot. Nefer was approaching along the sidewalk and made a face as the car sped away. He held a plastic bag and a tray of drinks.

"Was that Gary?" he asked when he was within earshot.

"Yes..." I replied, conflicted.

"What's wrong?"

How do I tell you that your ex-wife is using you for some government agenda? I took the tray from him.

"I'm not sure," I answered. I reentered the building as I thought of what Nefer told me about how Sekima disappeared for over a decade.

"Gary must be in a rush. Is he fleeing the country?" He joked.

"He's going out of town, yes. He will be back Monday..."

While in the elevator, I stared at the drink tray.

"You are way more quiet than usual," Nefer observed when we got back to our desks.

"Is that possible?" I replied, deflecting. "I'm not really a talker."

"Ok, I can tell something's up."

Fuck you and your feelings radar.

I sat down as he placed a plastic bowl in front of me. I looked through the lid and saw breaded chicken with red sauce and cheese, on a bed of pasta.

Chicken parmigiana...

He dragged his chair over to sit across from me. He had a corned beef sandwich with fries.

"So," he said, picking up the sandwich. "What's wrong...?"

"Well..." I carefully removed the bowl's lid. "I read something weird... more like really disturbing."

"Disturbing... more disturbing than your cat?" His manner was judgmental.

I felt tension build in my neck, causing me to roll back my shoulders.

"Sorry, I wasn't thinking. How disturbing?" He bit his food.

"To answer your question... yes. More disturbing than her."

He chewed slowly, and I watched his mouth with enthrallment. I was snapped from the trance when he put his hand up.

"What did you read?" He blocked his mouth.

I blinked twice and dug a fork in my food. "That... we met on purpose."

"Where did you read that?"

"Gary's computer."

"So, what did you read?" He put his food back in the container. "I'm asking what you read, exactly. I think we need to work on what it means to answer a question..."

"Huh?" I was thrown off by his lecturing tone.

"I'm saying, whenever I ask you something it's like I gotta figure out what to ask to get what I wanna know."

"I'm telling you exactly what I read."

"On Gary's computer, you read that we met on purpose? And nothing else?" He was skeptical.

I hesitated, staring at my food.

Why is this so hard?

I put my elbow on the desk and rested my chin in my hand. I spun the fork around in the food.

"I'm amazed at how hard it is to get you to talk," he said.

"I honestly don't talk to a lot of people..." I reinforced.

"Yea. I noticed."

"...especially men..." I shifted my eyes to look at him. "I'm sorry..."

He was leaning back in the chair as he stared at me. His pensive expression reminded me of the previous day, and I became aroused.

"Let's stay on point here..." he directed, sitting up straight. "Tell me what you read. Is Gary the reason this is going on between us? Don't answer that, just, what did you read?"

"I read an email to Gary, from Sekima," I answered. "She wrote things that have to do with you and me. She said we have to spend as much time together as we can. And... that if anything changes, he needs to report it."

He furrowed his eyebrows, and his eyes squinted.

"There's no way she got you this job just to help you as a friend," I purported. "I think... I think she knows that we have visions. She knows what we're doing. She has to."

She knows about my cat... my demon.

I contemplated that if she was working with the government, she could know everything about me.

So, the government knows about me...? Why would they care...?

"There was a government email on the message too," I pointed out.

He remained quiet.

"Do you think your ex..." I started. "She left you for years and didn't reach out until recently. A lot can happen in that time..."

I thought of the decades after my mother died. I was homeless for parts of it.

Sekima ran away and found a great job... works for the government...

"Maybe my cat IS the reason we met," I murmured.

His introspective appearance didn't change as he dug in his pocket for his phone. He started swiping and typing.

"What are you doing?" I asked.

He stood up.

"Did you take a picture of this email?" he responded, still peering at his phone and typing.

"No, I didn't think to."

He put his phone to his ear as he headed for the exit. He was talking in a hushed tone to whoever he called.

"Where are you going?" I questioned.

After a few minutes passed, my phone buzzed with a message.

'Going to see Sekima,' Nefer texted.

'And say what?' I replied.

'Ask what the fuck is going on.'

My heart was racing. I put the phone down and tried to eat my lunch. I wanted to leave with Nefer, as I had been hired for reasons I didn't agree to. I reconsidered whether I indeed HAD agreed to this. I pulled my profile up on the management system and reviewed the mounds of documents I signed. I printed these for all new hires and only read them once when I was first employed here. I didn't recall what it said and found nothing unusual about any of it at that time. I was certain that I, along with many people, assumed it was in line with my right to be treated fairly. I browsed the company hiring agreement. In one of the paragraphs, I found a sentence that read:

'Upon completion of six months of employment, I agree and acknowledge that my profile will be reviewed for capability by the Board of Directors and, should they deem necessary, I will be selected to execute duties that may result in a transformation of internal processing.'

The rest of the agreement didn't strike me as out of the ordinary. *Internal processing...*

I navigated to the internet browser and searched for the term. I read that it was about a way of thinking. It referenced how people treat information and had charts but I didn't find this useful. One result mentioned a business method. My phone rang and I snatched it up to answer when I saw it was Nefer.

"Hello," I said.

"Hey," he replied. A long pause followed.

"Hello?" I was nervous.

"Doris," Nefer said, "I spoke to Sekima..."

I waited in anticipation.

"You there?" he asked.

"Yes, you said you talked to Sekima."

"Yea, she says she knows about your cat. She can tell you what's going on with it."

"When?"

The phone hung up. It then buzzed with a text message.

'Lost signal,' he wrote. *'Come to Sekima's house.'*

He sent a link that, when I pressed it, my map reading app opened to display a location forty-four miles away.

I got up and went to Lindsey, the Training and Development Coordinator.

"Lindsey," I addressed.

"Hi, Doris," she greeted, wistful. "What's up? Do we have new hires for orientation?"

"No, I need to take off early. Can you lock up when you leave today?"

"Yea, sure! Oh, I'm leaving at four-thirty..." She frowned, doubtful.

"That's fine. Thank you." I retrieved my things from my desk with Nefer's lunch and left. When I walked by Lindsey, I overheard her gleefully telling people the office was closing early. I got in my car and my cat sat in the passenger seat.

"Are we taking a trip to see Nefer?" she hissed.

"What of it?" I bickered. I flinched as she hissed again and bounded to the back seat.

I drove down an endless number of windy roads. They were narrow and seemed to be one-way. I was thankful it was daytime because I didn't see street lamps. At the destination, the marker was on the exact site where I braked. I didn't notice any paved streets, but a dirt path was evident to my right and I cautiously steered my car to take it. My heart was drumming and I was sweltering because my car's air conditioning decided that today it wanted to blow warm air. The road led through a stone walled gate, and large oak trees with hanging moss lined it beyond. Advancing along the road, it curved before a sizeable white house came into view. It was a plantation home. The road reached a circular gravel driveway at the front of the house. Various flowers adorned the driveway and trees were scattered on the vast land. A dark purplish-blue coupe was parked nearby. I assumed it was Nefer's car and pulled up beside it.

"Whose house is this?" my cat probed. "Sekima, hmm...?"

My shirt stuck to my back as I left my car and ascended the double staircase to the front door. There was a fancy brass knocker designed like a flower on it but no doorbell could be seen.

I anxiously pulled out my phone to text Nefer.

I'm here,' I typed. I heard the locks unhinge as I pressed send.

The door glided open and Sekima stood in the entryway. She wore a white dress decorated with multicolored polka dots. Her hair was fashioned in angled cornrows, a puff of hair to one side.

"Hello, Doris," she welcomed tranquilly. "Come in. Your cat too."

She disappeared into the house and my cat scuttled behind her. I closed my eyes.

Lord, it's me again. I'm still here. If this is wrong, please know I want to be right... I want to be free from this... Please ...

I entered the home and stood under an elaborate chandelier, mollified by the cooler temperature. On the soft golden walls, there hung paintings of scenery. Immediately to the left and right of me were archways that led to a dining room and a sitting area. Straight ahead from the entrance was a kitchen. Sekima was nowhere in sight. The sounds of meowing floated from the sitting room and I went in to find it vacant. There was another doorway on the far wall of the room where I heard the meowing again. Outside the doorway, I discovered a stairwell leading both up and down. The meowing came from below. I warily descended the stairs to enter a den.

The space had three loveseats, a coffee table, a fireplace, a bookcase, and a TV. The room was lit by sun rays sifting through vertical blinds on a set of wall length windows. The meowing was playful rather than hostile. I found my cat tussling on one of the seats with another cat and she stopped as soon as she saw me. She affectionately rubbed her head on the other cat's body. It resembled my cat, but its eyes were a darker gold than hers and its fur a few shades lighter. It had brown stripes along its back and legs, as opposed to my cat's stripes that were all black.

"Have a seat," Sekima's voice came from my rear.

I spun around, stepping back.

"Where's Nefer?" I asked, teetering on hysteria. I felt defenseless against this stranger.

She smirked. She signaled with her eyes towards the loveseats. "Sit."

I knew it was futile, but I strained to read her anyway. I got nothing. My heart palpitations juddered my entire body. I slinked to the center loveseat and sat down. Sweat dripped onto my pants as I placed my hands on my lap.

"Where's Nefer?" My voice trembled.

Sekima sat down in the loveseat on my right and crossed her legs as she rested her arms on the backrest.

"Upstairs," she answered, her voice placid. "You didn't come here for Nefer. You came here for ME."

"What did you do to him?" my voice cracked and I cleared my throat.

"Wouldn't you rather know what was done to YOU?" She narrowed her eyes.

This estimation was precise, but I was tormented with worry that Nefer hadn't beckoned me here. I wanted to be mistaken and would be gladdened if I saw that he was ok.

"You have a cat," I said, looking at the cat seated on the third couch. "Like mine."

She stared without speaking.

"Why did you put me and Nefer together?" I interrogated.

She laughed and looked at the cats. She made smooching noises that captured their attention. The lighter one left its spot and jumped into her lap. It curled up as it closed its eyes.

"Why am I here?" I was beginning to lose my patience.

"Oh, a question I hear so often," she drawled with a smile. "Why do YOU think you are here?"

"My cat," I growled. I glared at my cat as she sat innocent and still. "I'm here because of her... and what I can do for you."

"No." She cocked her head to one side. "I know you saw my email to Gary."

"Yes, so I know you put me and Nefer together," I challenged. "You want me to be a director at your company and you need me to do it soon so you can meet your quota. My abilities are making you good money. You have a cat like me, do you do what I do? Is this a game you play as a servant to the devil!?"

My skin felt ignited because I was so enraged and terrified.

"You think I serve the devil...?" She retained her poise. The cat in her lap slept peacefully.

"Is Nefer your minion? Sent to trick me and win me over?!" My hands clenched to fists. "Do you need money so badly that you would use your ex and worship the devil??"

"Hmm." She patted the cat. "Is that what I wrote in the email? I am certain I did not."

I overlooked her sarcasm. "Why does Nefer need to be around me? What are the visions I saw? You said you did something to me. Is this a government experiment?? Yea, I saw the government on your email!"

"I did not say I did anything to you," she corrected.

"Yes, you did! Earlier, you asked me if I want to know what you did to me. And yea, I do!" I lost my fury and was simply frightened. I wanted to cry.

"Tell me Doris," she said, "When you ask yourself if your life is yours, what is your answer?"

"I..." I shook my head and a tear leaked from my eye.

"Do you feel in control of your life? Do you believe you own your fate?"

I removed the tear from my face. "My fate is with God. This demon cat is keeping me from what God has in store for me. YOU are keeping me from this, by leading me to the devil!"

"Your demon cat..." She glanced at my cat. "Why do you fulfill these exercises to appease this demon...?"

"Because she's an evil demon of lust..." I didn't need to provide any other reason.

"Lust, hmm." She nodded. "That is what you are, right? A sinner... of lust."

"We're all sinners..." I was unsure where she was going with her statement.

"Sinners," she continued. "Is that why you drink blood and semen? For this lust demon?"

I felt disgusting.

"What do you think your God wishes for you, Doris?" she tested.

"'MY' God?" I crinkled my nose.

"Do you think your God wants you to have this... demon...?"

Hearing her refer to Him as 'mine' made me uncomfortable. I was growing upset again. I had no need to defend my beliefs.

Of course not! I just need to get free of it! God helps those who help themselves!

"You told Nefer you know about my cat," I replied. "Are you going to tell me? Or are you trying to hurt me more? Just tell me!"

"I am not here to hurt you," she said. "You want to purge this... demon."

"Yes! Haven't I made that clear already??"

She eyed my cat. "Your cat.... will depart soon. Her purpose is nearing its end."

"You're using me! How can I trust you??"

"You are being used, yes. That will be over as well. Soon..."

"I've had enough." I vaulted up from the loveseat. "Where's Nefer?? I don't need your cryptic bullshit! I thought you wanted to help me and you're just playing games!"

"Nefer intends to take you to his church." She jerked her leg and the cat leapt away. She rose from her seat. "In order for you to receive the... help you need, I suggest you go."

I was disparaged by the conversation. Both of the cats ran out of the room and up the stairs. I went to follow them when Sekima called my name.

"Nefer is not immune to your charms," she commented. "Be... gentle with him. He's determined to accompany you, albeit not solely his choice..."

I climbed the steps as I felt the onset of a headache. Her remark about Nefer's choice triggered a pang of guilt in my chest. I cleared the first flight of stairs and tracked the cat noises to the very top of the staircase. It led to a narrow hall with a few closed doors. I advanced through the hall, calling to him.

"Nefer...?!" I shouted, then louder, "Nefer!! Are you up here??"

"In here," his voice sailed from a door on the right.

I darted to shove it open. It was a bedroom with lavender colored walls. It had a furniture set of cherry wood and Nefer was scooting to a seated position in the canopy bed.

"Hi," I breathed a sigh of relief as I walked over to sit down. I studied his naked upper body. "Are you... ok?"

"I think so," he responded, rubbing his forehead. He was befuddled. "My head is killing me..."

"What happened?" I almost hugged him, but abstained. Sekima's parting words ricocheted in my brain.

"Uh..." He gazed up at the ceiling, as if he searched for the answer. "I came to see Sekima and she said she knew what was going on... she would explain... "

"Then what?" I looked around the room.

"Then... I'm here. And you're here... I can't remember."

I spotted a familiar painting on the wall. It was an embracing couple in multiple tints of blue. I knew I saw it before. I got up from the bed to walk over to it.

"Did Sekima tell you about the cat?" he asked.

"Yes, and no... well, she said it would be gone soon..." I pointed at the picture then looked at him. "This was at your house."

"It was. Sekima came to get it." He had left the bed and stepped up next to me. "Did she say how it would be gone?"

I shook my head, noting the delicate strokes of purple almost hidden in the piece of art. "This is a really nice painting."

"Thanks. It was supposed to be a gift." He started opening drawers on the dresser. "So, how do we get rid of the cat?"

"Wait, did you paint this?" I wasn't trying to change the subject, but I was.

"Yea." He pulled on a shirt he found. "So, how is the cat gonna be dealt with?"

"You're a painter," I confirmed. I had magnified esteem upon discovering his creativity, which mildly distracted me from the fact that he had clothes stored in Sekima's room.

"Yea." He repeated and sounded matter-of-fact. "The cat...? We need to deal with it."

"She didn't say..." I pondered whether the painting was of them. "Did she say anything to you...?"

"I'm not sure..."

I dug in my pocket to check the time on my phone and began mentally reviewing what I had to do ahead of Saturday. I had the impulse to leave. "I should go. I... need to go."

"Me too, actually," he agreed. "I just gotta find my keys..."

I shrugged and then abruptly twirled toward the door to walk out. "Goodbye."

As I made my way to my car, I once again asked myself if I could stop what I had to do. If I could describe the feeling, it would have to be a compulsion. I didn't doubt that. I needed to sacrifice this month, and I needed to prepare for it. I would be meeting the man chosen in two days. I yanked my car door open forcefully.

"Doris!" Nefer was yelling as he ran down the front steps. "Hey!"

I waited at my car for him.

"You're just gonna leave?" He was confused. "You barely told me anything Sekima said to you."

"Yes..." I strived to keep myself calm. I had become frazzled. "I have things to do..."

"For your demon..." he deduced successfully. He sighed. "Come to my place and stay over Saturday. We'll go first thing in the morning."

I got in my car and slammed the door. He knocked on the passenger window, so I rolled it down.

"Is that my lunch?" He motioned at the food on the seat when he leaned in.

"It is."

"Thank you..." He picked it up. "Tell me you're not going back to work."

"Today? No... but I need to find a new job." I started the car.

He laughed. "I'm quitting as of now. I'll find something eventually."

I stared at the steering wheel. I wished I could do the same.

"You should quit too," he added. "I'm sure you wanna."

"Nah, I can't," I reasoned. "I need to find a new job first..."

I need to find a new apartment too...

"Ok, well, I'm gonna go talk to Sekima again before I head out."

"If she wouldn't tell me much, I don't think she'll tell you."

"We'll see." He hadn't moved after a few seconds.

"So... I'm leaving..."

"Text me when you get home." He stood upright to pace back.

"Uh... sure..." I rolled up the window and pulled away.

Lord, I'm going to church. I'm on my way back to you...

10

I stopped by the store to buy some garbage bags and a few other items to stow my possessions. As soon as I got to my apartment, I started packing.

"Did we find a new place yet?" my cat inquired when she saw me stuffing the bags with clothes.

"Do you know Sekima?" I grilled.

"I don't."

"What about the cat? You acted like you reunited with an old friend!" I was peeved.

She sat on my bed with a blank stare. "It certainly felt that way.... An old friend... yes..."

"Do you know the cat?" I snarled.

She stretched and licked her paw. "I don't know any of them. I don't know Sekima. I don't know Nefer... I don't know what came over me. What did she say? I'm on my way out, huh?"

Yes, I thought. *I won't have to sacrifice for you anymore...*

I had packed a suitable amount and decided to take a break to search for an apartment. I called the complex I toured. I learned they no longer had available units but they put me on their waitlist. I was in the middle of browsing other places when I got a text. I already knew who texted since no one else would.

'Did you make it home?' Nefer asked.

'Yes,' I responded.

'Are you going to work tomorrow? I'm not playing when I said I quit.' He sent a second text shortly after. *'If you won't quit, just call out and come over.'*

I took my lunch from earlier and reheated it to eat at the kitchen table. I yearned to do what he suggested, but to say he desired it wasn't accurate. I had hoped he was different from all the others. What he felt for me was what I elicited.

'What did Sekima tell you?' I texted.
'That I should take you to my church.'

It was early when I arrived to work the next morning. I found the office unlocked, which meant Lindsey hadn't locked up. I went straight to my desk and used the computer to continue my hunt for an apartment. I decided to call the place I toured again.

"Hi, Golden Grounds, this is Ken," the person greeted.

"Hi, Ken," I replied, "I'm uh, Doris... I had toured there and was calling you back about your availability...?"

I crossed my fingers.

"Oh, yes ma'am, hello! I wasn't able to hold that suite we toured but I do have one opening up and it will be available for lease on the first. It's a little different than the model, but if you are interested..."

"I definitely am! Thank you..." I wiped sweat off my brow.

"Excellent! We just need you to stop by today, complete some paperwork, and place a deposit of half a month's rent. If you can come in now, it would be fabulous."

"I sure can, sir, yes... uh, what time do you close...? I can come in before you close..."

"We close at four, ma'am."

"Ok, yes, I will be there."

"Great, see you soon! We look forward to having you join the community!"

I was unable to sense emotions across the phone, but I knew he was spurious. I hung up. "Yes... great..."

I won't live out of my car like before, I thought.

~~ * ~~

It was probably just over seven months since I ran away from home. My cat was around, but she didn't speak to me since I was still furious over what transpired with my mother. I had met a few homeless people who had occasionally given me food and one gave me a sweater. I slept in the park and begged for change when my cash had run out. The most money I received was from begging the elderly, which I used to buy food. The sun was setting one day while I solicited a couple for change when a woman approached me. She was short, round and dark, with her hair in rollers covered by a scarf. She wore a blue track suit and white tennis shoes.

"Hello young lady," she addressed warmly. "What are you doing out here?"

"Do you have any spare change?" I pleaded as I held out my hand. "Anything?"

"Poor thing! It's dangerous to be out here asking strangers for money!" She began searching in her purse. "What's your name, sweety?"

"Doris." I waited expectantly.

She stopped fumbling through her purse and looked me over. "Where's your momma, huh? Where's your family, baby? They shouldn't have you out here begging like this..."

I quickly shook my head. "If you have even ten cents, I will take it ma'am."

Her eyes squinted as she studied me a second time. "You know what, how about I just take you to get something to eat, hmm? Come on, girl. This way."

She gestured down the path ahead of us.

I hesitated, but she seemed to want to aid me. I went to the nearby bench to grab my backpack and I followed to her car; a shiny blue four-door sedan.

"*Come on, get in,*" she insisted as she smiled wide. "*I'm gonna make sure your belly is full. There's a place just down the road.*"

As we drove, she introduced herself as Wanda.

"*You can call me Aunt Wanda,*" She grinned. She placed our order at the drive-thru and gave me the bag when we received it. "*Take that burger out. The rest is mine...*"

We continued driving as I happily ate the burger. Eventually, we arrived in the parking lot of a motel. I didn't recognize any of the surroundings.

"*I'm staying here for a few days,*" Wanda revealed. "*Come to my room to get cleaned up. I bet you haven't had a bath in a while, have you?*"

I shook my head.

"*I can tell! That's ok, baby, Auntie Wanda is gonna fix that right now.*" She eased into a parking space. "*I got two beds, and you can get some good sleep too.*"

"*Thank you...*" I mumbled.

"*Uh huh, you're welcome.*"

We entered the motel and it had two beds just as she described. The bedding was a vibrant zigzagged pattern of blue, pink and yellow.

"*Bathroom is back there...*" she pointed, tossing her purse on the bed. She grunted as she kneeled to pull something from under the bed. "*Take a shower and get some rest...*"

"*I don't have... clean clothes...*" I informed her while I stood by the bathroom door.

"*Here...*" She set a suitcase on the bed, then pulled out a big red shirt. "*Borrow mine for now. In the morning, I'll get you some new clothes.*"

I thanked her again and went to take a shower.

Wanda took me to buy new clothes the next day. While we shopped, she told me she was in a motel because her house was being fumigated and it would be a week before she could return home. She fed me again *and bought me a necklace. We then went to a hair salon that she said was her cousin's and I got a new relaxed hairstyle.*

A week passed. Wanda extended the room stay, stating that the exterminators found more problems with her house.

"The thing is," she was saying, "I'm about out of money... Fumigation ain't cheap..."

"Maybe I could get a job at your cousin's salon, Aunt Wanda," I recommended. "I could sweep floors."

"That's an idea," she concurred, nodding her head.

We were idling at a stoplight on our way back to the motel and we had just finished a meal at a local southern comfort restaurant.

"There's a better way to get the cash I need." She picked a crumb off her bright orange shirt and ate it. "And you don't even have to do much..."

"I want to help. I want to thank you." I was willing to repay favor.

"Well... ok..." She shrugged her shoulders. "Ok, sweety. I have a friend who would like to meet you. If you're real nice to him, he'll be real nice to you."

"Yes, ma'am."

We entered the room where she had laid out a glittery pink dress onto the bed. She must have bought it in the course of our shopping trip.

"This will look lovely with your new hairstyle," she smiled and licked her lips, stacking a pair of strapped shoes and stockings on top of the dress. "Go on now, Doris! Get dressed. The nice man will be here soon..."

I obeyed and she placed the pretty necklace around my neck.

"Beautiful," she gasped in revelry.

~~ * ~~

Stella's exasperated complaining snapped me to the present. The workplace occupants were beginning to enter the space.

"The office is fucking dead today!" she griped. "Where is everyone?"

It was not actually empty, but I was aware she referred to specific inhabitants. One in particular was Tiffany, as she was absent once again.

"Where's Nefer?" she questioned, eyeing his vacant desk with forlorn. "He said he'd be here all week..."

"Are you asking ME?" I distastefully replied. "Go do some work."

Irritation level raising, she rolled her tongue around in her mouth. Her tongue ring gleamed when it appeared as she bit her bottom lip. She glared at me sideways.

"Ugh!" She stormed back toward her desk.

I hadn't heard from Nefer while I spent the day applying for new employment. Before I knew it, the time was almost two-thirty P.M. I shut down my station and asked Lindsey to lock up the office when she left for the day.

I received a phone call on my way to my apartment after I finished reserving the new unit. It was Robert, the furniture pickup driver.

"Hello, good afternoon ma'am," he said, "I know it's earlier than the time window, but I was wondering if I could come get your furniture now? I'm in the area."

"Uh, yes," I agreed. "If you give me like fifteen minutes..."

"Ok, thank you ma'am. We'll be there in about thirty minutes."

I hurried into my place and packed up the rest of my things. The driver and his two-man crew rapped on the door seventeen minutes later. Robert was an older white gentleman with ashen hair, a scruffy beard and sideburns. The two men with him were most likely in their early twenties and one may have been a relative. They worked efficiently, completing the job within the hour. Robert presented me with a tablet and asked for my signature. He mentioned the receipt would be emailed to me.

"Alright, looks like we're good to go," he politely assessed with a trace of kindness. He signaled to his crew. "Have a great evening ma'am."

"Yes, you too, thank you," I closed the door behind them.

"Oooh, I LOVE moving!" my cat cheered. She jogged around the bare living room. "New places are always fun."

"Well, you'll love where we're going then," I retorted.

A knock on the door made me check the peephole. I expected to see the movers but it was Nefer. I procrastinated before opening, to allow my initial reaction to pass.

"Hey Doris," he greeted. He wore a royal blue t-shirt and dark denim jeans.

"Nefer," I acknowledged.

"Sorry, I didn't wait for your text. Can I... come in?" His hands were behind him.

"Uh..." I waved for him to enter. "Sure, why not."

He scanned the room as he stepped inside. "You're moving?"

"Yes."

"Is your, uh... cat around?" He bowed his head to peek in the kitchen.

"Not right now... you're safe."

"No, I was just asking." He was timid. "I wanted to give you this." He offered me a bible.

"Oh..." I examined its worn surface. It was soft with dogged corners. 'The New Testament' was imprinted in gold on the front and the pages were so thin, I almost feared tearing them. "Thank you..."

"For Saturday."

"Sunday?" I verified.

"Saturday. You're staying over." He began to leave. "That was all I came for. I gotta get going."

I longed to protest. My heart pounded and I imagined the sensations that had spread through my body as I followed him to the door.

Ask him to stay... I just want to feel him again.

He swung the door open, and halted before exiting. "I'll... I'll text you."

"Yea..." I locked the door behind him.

"Ahem," my cat cleared her throat. "I trust you'll be on your way to the kitchen? Hurry, now! I've waited long enough."

"Consider it your last meal," I derided as I cooked. When she didn't respond, I glanced over my shoulder to see she was gone. I set her food on the table and went to lie down on a blanket and pillow I placed on the floor. After setting my alarm to eleven forty-five P.M., I opened the bible to read.

$$\sim\sim {}^{*} \sim\sim$$

My alarm blared in my ear. I had fallen asleep. I systematically entered my bathroom to remove a vial from my cabinet and perched over the toilet. With the arrival of midnight, blood jetted from me. I captured enough to fill the vial and remained in place until the gushing reduced to a trickle.

Will this be over, Lord? I prayed. *It won't be long now, will it?*

My energy was draining as the blood dripped into the bowl. I cleaned up and hobbled to my room where sleep overwhelmed me when I dropped to the floor.

My phone buzzed and beeped. Its bell blasted. It rang with a phone call. I somnolently reached for it to see the time was fifteen minutes past ten A.M. The missed call was an unsaved number. I also received a text from it.

'Hi Doris, this is Lindsey,' it said, 'Are you coming in today?'

I sighed as I answered, 'Sorry not feeling well. Sorry I didn't call."

'Np. Get well soon,' Lindsey texted.

I got in the shower and then carried all my bags to my car. Nefer sent me a text while I was hauling the final bag.

'Are you at work?' it said.

I can't see him today, I thought. I will see him Saturday...

'No,' I responded.

'You quit?'

'No.'

'Are you sick?'

'No.'

'Ok.'

I had no intentions of being curt, but I needed to concentrate on adhering to the ritual. Until my cat was expunged, I wouldn't be able to resist implementing it. I cleared my apartment and headed to Harriett's door. There was no answer when I knocked. On the second series of knocks, a door opened across the hall.

"She's out of town," a young woman warned.

"Out of town..." I echoed.

"Yea, she left last Tuesday and won't be back till Monday, I think."

"I see..." I slid my key under her door and proceeded to the park.

I had a few hours before six P.M. While in my car at the parking lot, I read more of the bible. I recalled reading excerpts as a child, although I hadn't comprehended any of it and I made no effort to.

"Why are you reading that?" my cat asked. She lazed on my bedding in the back seat. "You don't even understand it."

"Which is why I'm looking things up," I shot back.

"Oh, do you feel smarter now?" She patronized. "Are you understanding those words you read?"

Even though I had the definitions, I didn't fully grasp all the words. I absorbed a few chapters at best.

"Keep reading," she laughed. "Maybe they will make more sense to you."

I ignored her. "I've been lost for so long..."

"Don't be silly. I am here with you. You are not lost."

"Oh? Well, where am I going?" I twisted in my seat to face her. "Huh? Where?"

She glowered at me and her eyes seemed to radiate brighter than usual. We stared at each other without dialogue.

"Nothing to say?" I confronted. I felt my skin growing hot and I had begun to perspire despite the cool air blowing from the car vents.

The sound of ringing cut the staring contest short. Nefer was calling me. The time was five fifty-four P.M.

Shit, I can't talk right now...

"Hello," I panted.

"Hey," he said, "Are you, uh... at home?"

"No."

"Oh, I'm at your door..."

"I don't live there anymore..." I turned my car off.

"Ahh, that's right. So... you moved already...? Where's your, uh, new place? I wanna... stop by." He sounded uneasy.

"Uh..." I climbed out.

"Have you been... reading? I just thought I could come and, you know, talk about... what you read so far."

"I'm... not taking visitors right now..." I slammed my door.

"You're driving. I can call you back..."

"Yea..." I began walking along the cobblestone path toward the park fountain. "I have to go now."

"Just text me when you can talk..."

"Yup." I hung up.

Sunday can't come soon enough... This has to end.

After a short walk, the fountain came into view. Water flowed generously across the three tiers, down into the aquamarine pool below. I arrived and saw the glowing beacon of purplish-blue light emanating from a man seated alone. He was the light skinned man with dreadlocks that lived in the unit across from mine and sat watching the people who passed. As I drew near, his eyes fell on me and he immediately approached. He grabbed my hand and kissed it.

"Sovereign," he venerated, constricting my damp hand. He knelt while holding it. "It felt like an eternity we were apart."

"Ugh," I loathed and wrenched my hand away. "Call me Doris. Speak like you normally would a lover, understand?"

"Yes, my love. I will." He waited on one knee.

Each chosen reacted virtually identical at this encounter. They were overly smitten and praised me exuberantly. They would call me the same thing every time. Until the first taste, they were malleable and I used this time to direct them how I preferred our interactions to go. I developed a set of commands that were succinct. Once the man drinks, any desire for him was dissipated. Any desire from him became mine. He would be bound to me up to the day he was sacrificed.

"You will do as I say," I ordered. "You will come to me only during the times I tell you. Behave as if we never met when we are apart. I will give you a vial. Drink it as soon as I dismiss you. Meet me here tomorrow at the same time with eleven hundred dollars. Acknowledge you heard all and stand up."

"I acknowledge," he validated and got to his feet.

"Kiss me now."

He eagerly kissed me. His lips were as soft as I expected. I felt a current of energy transfer to him. I couldn't help but think about Nefer. I pulled away as soon as the feeling ceased.

"Mmm," he said, staring at me in awe. "Sweet, sweet kisses... Tasty."

"Tomorrow," I reaffirmed. "Don't be late."

"I won't, trust me."

"You're released."

He gulped down the contents of the vial and left the park.

I returned to my car and sat for a while. I was fatigued. I needed to find a place to park for sleep.

"I'm thirsty," my cat purred.

I drove to a nearby strip mall and I took my cat's bowl with me as I used the restroom in a restaurant. I removed my bottoms to fill her bowl and set it down on the toilet lid. As she lapped it up loudly, I heard a toilet flush from another stall, which caused me to flush the toilet. I waited for the person to leave and I washed the bowl before stuffing it into my purse. A woman entered the bathroom, eyes darting around.

"Escuse me ma'am," she said in a thick accent. "We close ver soon. Speshew event."

"I'm leaving," I assured her as I exited. I passed several people entering the restaurant in costumes. I decided I would take a nap.

I was roused from sleep by thudding on my window. As my eyes adjusted, I observed that the sun hadn't risen yet. A disheveled woman stood by the driver side, peering into the car. She waved and knocked again.

"Got room in there for another?" she asked. She began fiddling with the door handle.

I promptly repositioned my seat to start the car, then reversed from the space.

"Hey!" she shouted, tripping backward.

I relocated to my job's parking lot. I slept for three more hours, used the public restroom to freshen up, and changed my clothes. Once I entered the office, I spent the day completing applications. I hadn't gotten a call nor text from Nefer. I was concurrently thankful and displeased.

Since Gary was out of the office, no one stayed past four P.M. I left the office with enough time to meet the man at the designated spot. I failed to learn his name. I decided I would merely accomplish the basic requirements. I brought him to my car where we travelled to a motel and he went in to book a room for us. He reserved three nights, and notified me his daily ATM withdrawal limit was three hundred dollars. He would withdraw the amount requested in portions. I hung the 'Do Not Disturb' sign when we entered and summoned him to the bathroom.

"On your knees," I instructed.

"Anything you command," he responded and got down.

I removed my panties and sat on the toilet seat. I spread my legs, pointing between them, "Take your drink."

"Yes." He was beholden. He slurped and swallowed noisily, moaning.

Tears welled in my eyes as his gulping sounds persisted. I shut them for the remainder of the session, which lasted for over thirty minutes. Then he hoisted up, and I watched him smear my blood across his chin and facial hair when he swiped his arm. He was satiated for the time being.

"Wash up," I demanded. I dwelled on the toilet while he concluded his shower. "Leave and return here tomorrow at six P.M. Don't be late."

He kissed me ardently when he emerged from the bath. "I won't be."

I humbly studied the dirty wall prior to cleaning myself.

Friday morning came and went. I repeated my previous day's activities at work. I met the man and he drank from me until he was filled. Nefer texted me to recommend that I stay over but I rejected his offer. I lodged in the hotel room and read for hours before getting some sleep.

At around nine thirty-seven A.M. on Saturday, Nefer sent me a message saying I could come over any time. I devised to go to him after the man treated himself. I reclined in the queen bed as I read. I was anxious about seeing Nefer. The week was taxing and I knew he would sense it all. I envisioned he would expect to speak on it.

I just want to get this done without having a conversation with him about it, I thought.

Hours had passed. My ringtone played and the name 'Landlord' appeared on the screen.

"Yea," I grunted when I answered.

"Oh, Doris!" Harriett's voice wailed. "I am so glad I got a hold of you!"

"What do you want."

"Well, you left the apartment without a forwarding address, and I have some mail for you. It looks important..."

"I'll come get it then."

"Oh, what's your new addr—"

I hung up and made my way to pick up the mail she spoke of. I banged on her door firmly.

After a minute or so, the door lurched open. An elderly woman in a gown waved at me.

"Oh, hello there!" she greeted excitedly. She pointed into the apartment. "Are you here to watch the shows with me?"

"Uh..." I replied. "The shows...?"

"Mother, that is a former tenant!" Harriett proclaimed, running to the door. "Please go back to the couch."

"Ok, talk to the nice lady about the shows so she can watch." The old woman shuffled away.

"Sorry," Harriett uttered, humiliated. "I just got back from up north and she is getting used to the area—"

"My mail?" I interjected.

She shoved her glasses up her nose, blinking with a dazed expression.

"My mail?" I held out my hand. "Where is it."

"Right, yes..." She disappeared and reemerged with two envelopes. Her hand wobbled as she awkwardly handed them over. "Here you go..."

I ripped one open and turned to leave.

"So, what's your forwarding address...?" she asked.

I waved my hand dismissively and went to my car. The mail was about refinancing my loan. I sat and stared at the apartment complex. I had wasted my time. I now had a little over an hour to meet the man. Starting my car in frustration, I returned to the motel room.

Back at the motel, I heard the lock unhinge fifteen minutes later. The man was in the room.

"You're early," I remarked.

"Yes," he corresponded with fervor. "I couldn't wait any longer."

He snuggled me when I began walking to the bathroom. He kissed the back of my neck and squashed his nose against my head before inhaling deeply.

"I can't get your smell out of my mind," he whispered. His hold tightened.

I peeled his arms off and led him to the bathroom.

I sent a text to Nefer.

'Address?' I wrote.

A response with a link showed almost instantly. It was a forty-minute drive. My heart was playing drums when the navigation displayed that his location was less than ten minutes away. I parked behind his car when I arrived, which left me jutting out onto the sidewalk. I cut off the engine and stared at his house.

Ok, I thought. *I'm going to get help... I will be back on my path... I will be right again...*

His front door opened and he waved when he stepped out.

Fuck.

I grabbed my backpack from the passenger seat before I exited. My back stiffened as I walked around toward him.

"Evening, Doris," he addressed. His exhilaration was so obvious, he might as well have brandished a sign.

"Hey..." I looked down at his feet. "So, I'm here..."

"Yea, I see that." He laughed and hugged me.

I was going to faint. I sorely missed his touch and it had only been a week. To experience it again was overpowering. I pined for it to be his own unbridled attraction. Pressure absolved from my shoulders but it wasn't much. I temporarily squeezed him back and dropped my hands to my sides.

"You're so tense..." He let go then gripped my shoulders.

A relaxing sensation flowed from the spot of contact and I reacted by shrugging. I stepped away and threw the backpack on my shoulder.

"I'm fine," I averred.

He walked to the house. "Ok, come in."

I trailed behind him.

"So, are we strangers now?" he asked when I was inside.

"No," I answered, looking around. I didn't really evaluate his place when I was here last. I felt like I was seeing it for the first time.

The living room had dark blue walls that were undecorated. The furniture was markedly old. Patches were worn into the armrests of the brown couch and parts of the seat cushions. It appeared to have a reclining section because the bottom of one side was shabby. The gray loveseat bared patches as well but they weren't as prominent. Two round glass end tables resided by the couch and loveseat with a matching round glass coffee table on a dusty purple rug. The table had a noticeable crack. There was a large flat-screen TV on the wall, and it was the singular modern item in the room. A door was situated on either side of it. They may have been a closet and utility room.

"I just figured we were at a more comfortable space now," he commented.

"Why?" I enquired. I paced toward the kitchen. "We don't really know each other..."

I wished I could calm down, but I reserved impatience that wouldn't let me.

"We've gotten pretty close."

I figured he must have hinted to our relations.

"You mean the sex?" I typically regarded it as a trivial engagement, although I shivered from the recollection.

"Among other things..." He sat down on the couch. "Have you been reading?"

My mind was suddenly flooded with notions of how he would view me when my cat was gone. I couldn't distinguish my assumptions from any actualities. I was positive they would be aligned.

Will he see a decaying woman that forced him to sleep with her? Would he regret everything we did?

I swallowed; I felt sick. I kept my eyes on the kitchen doorway, fighting vomit. I swallowed again.

"Do you have it with you?" he asked.

"Yes..." I reached in my pack to pull it out. "It's here."

"Why don't you sit down? I can get you a drink." He rose to head into the kitchen. While inside, he called, "Would you like water? Or maybe...?"

"A stiff drink," I murmured and sat on the loveseat. I caught a tinge of stale odor as I sunk in.

"Maybe... fruit juice?" He didn't hear me.

"Ok."

"To what? Water? Or juice?"

"Whatever." I rubbed my face as if to knead away stress. I set the bible on the table.

"Water it is..." He came and handed me a glass.

"Thanks..." I guzzled half the contents.

He retrieved the book and flipped through the pages. "Where would you like to start?"

"Huh?" I wearily placed the glass on the coffee table. "Uh..."

There was a coaster on one end table that Nefer put under it. I was unsure why he bothered since the thing looked like it took a beating.

"What are your thoughts on what you read?" he clarified.

What I've always thought.

"That we're all sinners." I grabbed the glass and emptied it.

"We are." He sat down next to me.

"Did I make you sin?" I didn't mean for him to answer.

"We... do things that seem right at the time, but what you have can be helped. We can be redeemed."

"What I have..." I inspected the glass.

"It starts with repentance."

Sweat doused my hands. I put the glass on the floor and sighed. If it were so easy to oppose the demon, I would have resisted long before this day.

"My pastor can help," he said. "He is a guide, and you will find the strength to drive out the demon that holds you."

"I just... it's hard to see what is right and wrong sometimes..."

"We're only human." He stood up. "Hungry? I made dinner."

He vanished around the corner and I hopped up to tail him.

"What makes you want to help me?" I inquired. I wanted to gauge how much of his determination stemmed from my influence.

"Should I not wanna help you?" He was making a plate of food from storage containers.

"You don't really know me. You don't know much of anything about me. I could be a murderer. Do you feel like doing some charity?"

"A murderer? No. Your demon on the other hand..." He placed the plate in the microwave. "It's clear we were supposed to meet. Not sure how much more you need to see that."

"I just need something I can understand." I sat at the kitchen table. "I need more than some dreams and feelings. I can't trust those things! I can't trust..."

I grappled with the certainty that his ambitions mirrored my wishes.

He removed the heated plate and put it in front of me. It had two grilled chicken breasts, mashed potatoes, green beans, macaroni with cheese, and a biscuit. He sat down across from me with silverware and his own plate.

"What were you gonna say?" he pressed. "You can't trust me?"

I studied the food. A regretful feeling surfaced with his query.

"You're right," he added. "I don't really know you."

"It's easy..." I mumbled. I cleared my throat and raised my voice. "It's easy to... give my body to you... To men. They don't care what I look like, how I feel, or even know what I've been through..."

"Help me to know. Tell me." He rested his hands on the table.

I craved to feel him caress me with them; to grant me the sensations that pushed the misery away.

"W—what I've... I've been through?" I stammered, my leg bouncing. "What to tell... oh... I don't know..."

"Tell me everything."

"Ok... I..."

"Let's start with where you're from."

"Like you, I've been here all my life." An image of my childhood home flashed in my brain.

"You were born...nineteen sixty... four?"

"Yes," I substantiated.

"What do you remember about your childhood?"

"Not much..." I visualized my father. I had concealed a great deal of my youthful memories.

"What happened to your parents?"

I clasped my hands under the table. "Dead."

"I'm sorry."

I shook my head. My emotions were widely detached from the circumstances. "Hmm..."

"Can you tell me what happened?"

I strained to describe the events that surrounded my father's demise. I mentioned that my father abused me and briefly highlighted the ritual that took his life. I told him my cat emitted a shadow that entered me before consuming the body. I went on to my mother's last day and how I met a woman who sold me to older men. Nefer was soundless, watching me intensely.

"She liked me to call her Aunt Wanda." My throat was dry. "I—I'm ... thirsty..."

He fetched a pitcher and poured me a new glass of water.

"Thank you..." I whispered and drank it. I felt his eyes examining my every move. I fumbled with the pitcher to refill my glass, thanking him again when he supported the bottom.

I told him about Wanda's story and how she convinced me to help her.

"She eventually told me she lost her house to the bank," I explained. "We lived in her car for about five years. She promised that we would leave town if we made enough money. My cat taught me how to sacrifice men, and well... she wanted me to stay, I guess. I think the year was eighty-five... I learned Wanda was lying to me. I can... sense hidden desires. I started to sense them when I found Wanda's stash..."

The memory was fresh and instigated resentment. Despite it being the past, I wished I knew sooner that she misled me.

I took a breath. "She had fifty thousand dollars under the driver's seat. I don't know how I hadn't noticed it. She caught me digging in the bag and she accused me of stealing. I was able to grab a few hundred dollars, but she fought me and drove off. I didn't know what to do. All I could think was to keep doing..."

"Prostitution," he said somberly. "When did that end...?"

"Well..." I dispensed my fourth glass of water. "I met a man... who was different from the others. Yes... he wanted what all the men wanted, but he... he cared. I knew it. In his heart he wanted to save me... He talked about making a life and the future. He took me in. He taught me to drive. I got my GED... started college... got a job at the office where he worked... He—his name was Franklin. He was a teddy bear. He was so sweet..."

I sniffed. I was at the brink of tears. "He's gone now."

"He passed...?"

"Yes, in two-thousand nine. He... I... sacrificed him... My cat chose him...I had to..."

She killed any hope I had of being happy...

Nefer went to put his food back in the microwave. He faced it as the timer wound down.

"These past ten years are much better," I reflected, scooping cold macaroni into my mouth. It was good. "My degree helped me get much better jobs. And I guess... that's it for that... I work where I work now. Till I... find another place..."

He didn't say anything. He was watching the food spin in the machine.

"When your demon chooses... a man..." he said, after about two minutes. He carefully recovered the plate then came back to sit. "... he wouldn't know his feelings aren't his... A man could do things he wouldn't normally do..."

"He would do... whatever I told him to..." I supplemented.

"Do you have a chosen now?"

I attempted to eat my cold chicken.

"I spoke to Reverend Eriksen." He sighed. "I was gonna ask him to come by today but I didn't wanna force you to talk."

"I already said I would."

"Yes, but that's tomorrow." He was troubled. "Your demon affects my feelings then..."

My chest stung.

"I find myself doing things I know I don't do," he apprised. "If your demon is doing this, I get it. I wanna help you. So, I will."

Does he really get it? Or is that me talking?

"I'm sorry, I don't have an appetite anymore." I stood up. "Can I lie down somewhere?"

"Of course."

I grabbed my backpack and flopped onto his bed as soon as I entered the room upstairs.

"Did you wanna take a shower?" He was at the door.

"Not right now," I responded. "I need to lie down..."

"Ok, I'm gonna take one then."

I heard him gather clothes from the dresser and leave. I was curious to see where the bathroom was so I went back to the hall. I saw the closed door on the left had the light on. The sound of a shower came from inside. I decided to find what the other door led to. I pushed the door open and flipped on the light.

It was another bedroom. At the left of the room, the bed was dismantled. Its frame appeared broken and the mattress was rested against the wall beside it. The adjacent wall had a chest of drawers with a mirror and a jewelry box on it. To the right was a skinny wardrobe by a closet and beside that was a hole in the wall. I crossed the room to view the box. A thin layer of dust covered it and the chest of drawers. When I opened it, inside were a set of silver banded rings, a dried petal, a spiral shell, and a folded piece of paper. The rings had three small stones in them. The center stone was a sandy colored cluster. The left stone was sky blue and shiny. The right stone was a deep reddish-purple color. I unfolded the tiny paper.

"For eternity," I read aloud.

"You can use the shower now if you want," Nefer announced as he travelled to his room.

I put the paper back. "Where am I sleeping??"

"My bed." He reappeared with a pillow and blanket. "I got the couch."

"You don't want the bed...?"

"Well, I just figured..." He signaled tentatively to the stairs. "It'd be better."

"Stay."

~~ * ~~

Nefer's alarm sounded like a thousand bells. When he rolled over and sat up to silence it, his phone illuminated a portion of the dark room. I saw his silhouette, almost reaching over to rub his back.

"You up?" he queried.

"Yes," I replied meekly. I left to go in the bathroom so I could get ready.

The bathroom walls were seafoam and had a stand-alone shower with a tub beside it. The toilet was off in a tiny room at one corner. Turquoise rugs were in front of the double sink and the tub. I was pleased that everything looked clean and fairly new. I wasn't certain the time, but Nefer tapped on the door to tell me we would be going to the church in about one hour. This news made me even more uptight. I withdrew from the bathroom while Nefer was walking up the stairs.

"You want breakfast?" he asked. "I made waffles."

"Sure," I responded. I brought my pack down with me.

There was a prepared plate with waffles, sausage, eggs, and hash browns. Some strawberries were in a bowl. I ate a few strawberries, then finished the plate before dropping my bag into my car. Daylight was just peeking over the horizon. I gazed at the tiny church across the street.

"Ready?" Nefer was coming out of the house. He slipped his hand into mine when he was alongside me. "C'mon."

As we walked, I could have filled buckets with the amount of perspiration I developed. I was mortified that Nefer held my hand but he didn't complain. He grabbed the door handle once we arrived and propped the door open for me.

I dithered, then entered the church warily. I felt no different than when I was outside. Tall, arched stained-glass windows lined the walls to my left and my right. There was purple carpet along the center aisle between two columns of pews. We advanced through the aisle and directly ahead was a podium, with a large box at its base labeled 'Tithe', standing upon a stage. Behind it was another huge stained-glass window. We went to a room off to the left of the stage. Inside, there were two purple loveseats facing each other. A man sat at a desk.

"Good morning, Reverend," Nefer greeted.

Reverend Eriksen peered up and smiled warmly as he got to his feet. "Brother Nefer, good morning!"

He walked over to clasp hands and they hugged. He was a gray-haired older black man, dressed in a white shirt and cerulean-blue tie. His slacks matched.

"How are you this morning, sir?" Nefer asked.

"Living, breathing and healthy! God is good." He nodded energetically.

"Yes, He is." Nefer gestured to me. "This is Doris."

"Sister Doris, pleasure to finally meet you." He stepped closer and embraced me firmly.

"Yes, hello," I mumbled.

"Brother Nefer told me what ails you." He released me and sat down on one loveseat. "Brother Nefer...?"

Nefer nodded and left the room, closing the door behind him.

"Please have a seat, sister," the reverend waved at the opposing loveseat.

I nervously stacked my hands on my lap when I did as I was directed.

"He tells me you are afflicted," he continued, his dignity swelling. "He tells me you are in need of guidance."

"Yes..." I cleared my throat. "I need help..."

"God's light will heal you when you let it." He leaned toward me in earnest.

"I want to... let it heal me..."

"Tell me about your affliction."

"Well..." I wrung my hands together. "My demon forces me to... have relations with a lot of men..."

He nodded as he listened.

"I've had hundreds." I scratched my chin. "I can't stop... I hope I can end it soon..."

"You feel like you have no control," he said with compassion.

I debated telling him what I was doing. He didn't seem to take it literally.

"I don't have control," I answered.

"Instead of giving control to this demon, give it to God."

Lord, you know I want to.

"Wh—what do... what do I do...?" My eyes filled with water.

"Let Him in." He stood up and when I did the same, he reached for my hands. They were warm, like his demeanor. "Join us this morning, sister Doris. Listen to His words."

"I will... yes..."

"I would like to see you privately. We will review His words together. Your relationship with God will be healed through Jesus Christ." He opened the door. "Come to me after worship."

I was reassured by his acceptance. I planned to tell him everything. I left the office and found Nefer seated in the first row of benches beside an elderly couple. He was easy to identify; most of the attendants appeared closer to my age than to his.

He instantly jumped up to hold me and kiss my forehead. I shuddered as I hugged him back, then joined him to attend the service.

It began with prayer and hymns. Reverend Eriksen introduced himself and welcomed all newcomers to the church by name, including myself. The congregation strode through the pews and I was greeted by them all. I wasn't accustomed to their friendly communication, but their veritable hospitality fortified my assimilation. The reverend's sermon came after.

"When we must do away with our old selves," he was saying, "we must kill the impurity in our souls. We must kill, so that we can be reborn through the light of our Lord Jesus Christ, Amen... The Colossians, Chapter three, Verse five..."

I opened to the passage as he read the text. While he preached, I felt as if he spoke directly to me.

"Inordinate affection!" he shouted. "Evil... concupiscence! You must kill it, Amen..."

The reverend tirelessly expressed that trusting in the light would dispel the darkness. When he gave his closing remarks and led the final prayer, I went to him after. We arranged to meet each evening of the week for study at seven thirty P.M.

"Sister Doris," he said, "we are on this journey together, but only you can reconfirm your belief. Only you can accept the healing powers of Jesus Christ and be washed of your sins."

Nefer and I walked hand in hand back to his house. As soon as we were by my car, I hurried to leave.

"You're not coming in?" he asked, somewhat dejected. He opened his front door and awaited my response.

"No..." I replied. "I'll... I need to go... Thank you..."

I rushed off to the motel room before he could oppose.

11

I went to work Monday and confronted Gary. I questioned what I was really doing at the company. He told me he was to monitor and encourage my talents, that Nefer was to enhance this. He was inefficient at giving much detail on the reason why.

"So, Nefer is, what?" I asked. "Was he sent to make me do whatever I'm asked?"

"I only know what I need to," he conceded as he held his hands up. "I'm sorry, Doris. I can't tell you that part..."

We were standing in his office.

"What can you tell me then?" I persisted. "Nefer quit. What is real? Am I working, or is this all just a front?"

"It's real. Today, I am to show you what your duties are as Office Director. If you allow the training, I promise it will all make sense at the end." He pointed to the arm chair. "Sit, please."

I dropped into the chair. I expected to learn more from him, but he genuinely had minimal information to impart.

"I need to show you what we do with the interviewees." He sat at his desk. "The process for picking them, scheduling them, et cetera... Then I need to show you who our clients are."

Over the course of the week, Gary outlined the main goal of the company as I observed him.

It was a third-party organization, often contracted by public and private firms to assess candidates for various exploits. The exploits required no advanced training which was why most, if not all, were elected for the positions. The activities needed test subjects. They were physically, mentally, and emotionally challenged. Their responses were documented. It was preferable that the results were natural. Candidates were accepted, particularly after I denied them. It was because I sensed their desires and could determine their interests in the role they applied for. Candidates with higher levels of apathy were the most desirable.

About four months ago, Gary took me on a trip to Charleston for a job fair. We interviewed around forty people. I denied each one and Gary hired them. The following day, he told me that none of them showed up to start. This was true according to Gary, but he later learned that the candidates did show up as assigned. They were dispensed to a unique client that required a select ethnic group to test an experimental procedure involving radiation. They were comparing the effects on the body, mainly behavioral. They staged their experiment every four years. Upon reported success, they renewed their contract with the company.

A majority of the customers were concentrating in areas of manufacturing, media and entertainment, beauty and healthcare, transportation, energy, finance, science and technology. A fraction were research institutions, focusing on developmental sciences. The public sector was a frequent user as well.

Any candidate I approved had been designated for special projects. Gary didn't know what those were, only that they were few and far between. I had probably approved a handful.

I contemplated what he was telling me, and was concerned for the people I denied. I submitted them for experimentation without their knowledge.

"So, these people have no idea what it is they are interviewing for..." I murmured. "We're lying to them."

"No, no!" he disputed, waving his finger in the air. "Not lying. We put all that is required in plain text. We have to."

"Come on, Gary! There's no way you tell them if they are applying to be exposed to harmful chemicals!"

He smiled. "We don't unwittingly expose them to anything. We hire them for our clients and all terms are spelled out in the agreements."

I shook my head.

I spent my days with Gary and my nights with Reverend Eriksen. At six P.M., I met with my sacrifice for his drink. Nefer asked that I stop by after my sessions with the reverend, and I would stay for around thirty minutes at most. I communicated what I learned from Gary and inquired on Sekima's whereabouts.

"She's out of town," he had replied. "She won't answer my calls."

My cat was generally absent. I would catch a glimpse of her from the corner of my eye. I thought I heard her meowing in the darkness when I was in bed. She wouldn't show herself to me directly. It was as if she was weakening.

It was Friday evening, and Nefer invited me to spend the night. He made pizza for dinner.

"How was your week?" he queried, putting slices in the oven to reheat.

"Good, I think," I responded. "I am really just trying to stay focused…"

I am on my way to you, Lord, I thought. *I will be in your light again soon…*

"I haven't seen your… cat lately…" Nefer placed a piping hot pizza slice in front of me.

"Thanks… me neither…"

"Have you… sacrificed another man…?" He reeked of discomfort.

"No…" I blew on the piece, growing dizzy.

"You will, though…"

I didn't reply.

"I just…" He sat down and crossed his arms. "I thought we were working on this demon. So that you won't have to do that."

"I can't. I can't NOT do it… I—I don't have a choice…" My heart pounded.

"What do you do exactly? Are you sleeping with this guy?" he was inquisitive.

I knew he would ask again. I was vague with my version of the ritual.

"N—no..." I stuttered. "Not sleeping with him..."

"You will when you kill him, won't you?"

I bit my lower lip upon hearing him say that I kill.

"When?" he pushed.

"Four days..." I divulged.

"No, you won't. The demon will be gone before then."

Lord, give me the strength...

The next morning, I entered the church to see the pastor for an entire day of lessons.

"Sister Doris," he said after we finished, "Are you ready to confess your sins?"

"Yes, pastor," my speech trembled. I confided in Reverend Eriksen about my demon, and the sacrifice I would make on the twenty-ninth. I was in tears as I spelled out my routine in detail. I came clean about the money I coerced men into splurging for my expenses. I described my fourteen-day menstrual cycle that came thirteen times a year, the feeding of blood, the swapping of fluids and what occurred after the intercourse ended. I disclosed that the shadow ripped the man apart during consumption.

"Sister, you have never been baptized." Reverend Eriksen commiserated. "I will baptize you. You will receive His gift, and be healed, reborn in the light of God."

He was unfazed by my avowal. He may have believed I was hallucinating. His sympathy was exalted by propriety.

"Prepare to receive His blessing tomorrow morning," he instructed. "Come here at seven A.M. sharp."

"But... I am... on my cycle..." I reminded him.

"It matters none." He hugged me. "Seven A.M. sharp."

I headed to Nefer's. He hadn't said much to me since our conversation the previous night. I waited at his door for several minutes before he answered. He wore tattered red sweatpants and a gray t-shirt with a dull green logo. He stepped aside for me to come in.

"You look... relaxed," I stated as I scanned his appearance. I stayed outside.

"You don't like my sweats?" he enquired. He looked down at them and shrugged.

"I am... being baptized tomorrow."

"I'll be there. The ceremony is at eight." He motioned for me to enter.

"You already know? Reverend Eriksen just talked to me today."

"He called me. Everyone will be there as witnesses." He signaled again for me to go inside.

"No, I'm tired..." I readjusted my purse on my shoulder. "That's all I wanted to say. Can I... come by later?"

"Yea, I should be awake. If I don't come to the door, just call me."

I travelled straight to the motel to meet the man. Once that was over, I returned to Nefer.

He made dinner for us and we watched a movie about a reformed black ex-convict. He was uncommonly silent the whole night. It was late, so we retired to the bedroom.

"I don't usually do this," Nefer muttered as we lay in the dark. He was perturbed.

"Do what?" I queried.

"This. What we're doing. I don't... have women at my house, in my bed... What we did... I don't do that."

I had my back to him, but rotated around.

"I've been thinking a lot about this," he resumed. "About all this. I just... needed to tell you, this is not me."

"We both are doing things out of our control..." I corroborated.

"Yea, but it's getting harder to tell when it IS my control." His anxiety worsened. "Until you're free, I don't know what I really feel about... any of this. I don't... know what I'm trying to say right now..."

"I understand..." I empathized with dismal.

"It doesn't help that I know what you're feeling."

"Maybe I should go..."

"But that's what I'm saying, it won't matter. If you're here or not, I feel it like you're right next to me." He sighed and placed his hand on my cheek. "I'm just thinking out loud. I know you want this to end."

I held his wrist and kissed his palm.

"You're beautiful, Doris," he spoke softly. "I hope you know that."

I had an arduous time getting sleep. I woke up around four A.M. and stared at the ceiling, listening to Nefer breathe. He was positioned on his back. I lightly rested my hand on his chest and felt a small burst of warm energy glide through me which caused me to tug away. I gingerly climbed out of bed and left the room. As I descended the stairs, I heard meowing.

"Doris," my cat hissed from the kitchen.

Her eyes glowed in the center of the room, but dissipated when I switched on the light.

"You can't be saved." Her voice exuded from the walls.

"Where are you?" I beckoned. "Too afraid of me now?"

The fact that she remained missing boosted my assurance. I was in such a good mood, that I opted to make Nefer breakfast for a change. I found a book of handwritten recipes after I rifled through his cabinets and drawers.

"Ooh, pancakes," I uttered. "Looks easy enough..."

I prepared the food with the instructions. They came out thin, lumpy and charred. By the time I made the last two, the smoke alarm was triggered. I frantically fanned the detector with a kitchen towel, but I was too late to stifle the screeching siren. Nefer came barreling down the stairs.

"It's ok!" I yelled. "I'm just cooking!"

The alarm stopped.

"Morning..." Nefer strained to see with one eye open.

"Yes, hello." I flipped the pancake in the pan. "I'm making pancakes."

"I smell it..." He turned on the sink. "Let me help."

I transferred the blackened pancake to the plate and grabbed the eggs from the kitchen table. Nefer swiftly retrieved the carton from me. He then lifted the container of milk I left out to put back in the fridge. He set the eggs by the stove.

"I'll make the eggs," he declared.

"Ok, sure." I put away the other ingredients on the table and deposited the plate of pancakes in the middle.

Nefer poured scrambled eggs onto two plates and brought them over. I jubilantly gave him pancakes. He eyed the misshapen black patties, holding a bottle of syrup.

"Are you gonna eat?" I asked, bubbly.

"Yea," he replied, hesitant. "But don't be mad if I don't eat the... pancake."

I bit my pancake and spit it back out. "Bleh, I won't be mad. It's not good..."

After breakfast, we got ready for church. I coped with the angst brewing in me. We entered the church a few minutes prior to seven A.M. and found Reverend Eriksen on stage behind the podium, preparing a cross-shaped baptistery built into the floor. It was underneath a mat that he had pulled away. When the time hit eight A.M., the church was already full. I had climbed on stage with the reverend, stepping down into the baptistery beside him. He held my hand tightly.

"Good morning, family," he pronounced. "We are here to witness our sister Doris reconfirm her faith in Jesus Christ."

I quivered and clutched his hand fearfully.

"Sister Doris," the reverend addressed me.

"Yes, reverend," I said, looking in his eyes.

"Do you believe Jesus is Christ?"

"Yes, I believe Jesus is Christ."

"Do you accept Him as your Lord and Savior?"

"Yes, I accept Him as my Lord and Savior." I quaked in the luke warm water.

"I now baptize you, in the name of the Father, in the name of the Son, and in the name of the Holy Spirit." He let go of my hand and repositioned to support me.

I held my nose and shut my eyes as he guided me back into the water. I was under for a couple of seconds, when his hands slipped away. I felt the temperature of the water aggrandize dramatically. Once I gained my footing, I shoved myself to a standing position and broke the surface gasping for air. Screams filled the church as I wiped my eyes to look around.

The church was incredibly dark. Shadows appeared to cover the windows. Reverend Eriksen was crawling away from the baptistery toward the wall. People were running to the exit, but the door wouldn't open, so they banged and rammed. Their terrified cries continued.

The simmering liquid in the baptistery grew murky and thick. I waded to the stairs of the bath, scanning the area for Nefer. I spotted him mounting the stage. He assisted me while I climbed the stairs and called for the pastor.

"Reverend Eriksen?!" he hollered.

The reverend huddled against the corner, shaking his head wildly. He was petrified.

"You didn't listen to me," a voice boomed. I recognized it.

The terrified crowd was scampering toward the stage now, attempting to scale it.

"Reverend?!" Nefer shouted again.

He monitored us in revulsion and mouthed words.

"I told you," my cat bellowed, "You can't be saved. None of you can."

The group had joined Reverend Eriksen at the wall. Down the aisle, my cat's eyes floated as they increased in size and brightness. A pale violet-blue light shone from above, flooding over her. She tramped in our direction as she transformed. Her shadowy figure took on the shape of a female, her claws elongated and her tail extended well above her head. Her eyes flared as she glowered at me.

"You can't escape," she growled.

A flaming sensation seared through my chest and drove me to my knees. Nefer helped me rise again as sunlight suddenly passed through the windows. My pain had faded along with my cat. The yelping died down and was replaced with murmurs as the people watched us, appalled. Reverend Eriksen elbowed his way through to the front of the mass.

"Brother Nefer," he sputtered, his breath heavy. "I don't know what manner of evil this is you brought into our house, but you need to take it out!"

The crowd expressed agreement with the reverend's words.

I bit my lip as my eyes watered. I was in shock.

"Reverend, but—" Nefer objected.

"NOW!" he exclaimed. His valor rematerialized with the group's approval of his order.

I glared at the reverend and pointed in reproach.

"You..." I snarled, gritting my teeth. "You... COWARD! Y—you... you... ALL of you!"

I oscillated my finger across the entire assembly. My skin blistered with wrath. I was useless at articulating anything else but choleric sounds.

"Doris," Nefer urged. He took hold of my hand and sensitively tugged. "Doris, it's ok..."

"No... it's not..." I grimaced. My consternation deteriorated by a few degrees as I cried.

"C'mon, let's go." He steered me to the exit.

As we treaded down the aisle, my feet felt like bricks. Nefer heaved the door open while keeping me close. Outside, a limousine was parked just at the curb where a black man and woman were standing beside it talking, but concluded when we stumbled from the church. The man was tall, and probably in his late forties. He was dressed in a dark gray suit. He quickly opened the rear passenger door of the vehicle.

"Good morning," the woman was Sekima; hair in full afro. Her lavender dress ruffled in the slight breeze. She tilted her head at the open door. "Ride with me."

I huffed in exasperation.

She smirked. "I believe our last conversation was prematurely terminated."

"Sekima," Nefer said, flustered. "What is all this?"

"Ride with me," she reiterated.

I clamped Nefer's hand firmer but didn't move. I wrangled with more tears while I thought of the frightened people in the church.

"Tell us what all this is." Nefer stepped toward the car.

"In." She entered the vehicle. "Now."

Nefer looked at me.

I followed Sekima into the limousine with Nefer right behind. The man closed the door and got into the driver's seat.

Sekima's gaze shifted between the two of us as the car pulled out of the lot.

"Save your tears, Doris," she evenly advised when I wiped them from my face. "Those you weep for are sheltered from the cause."

"What cause is that?" I contested, sniffling.

"The interminable and unfeasible quest for control." She studied my soaked clothes. "Your baptism... Did you think it would admit you veiled aptitude to vanquish your... demon?"

I had no verification, but her tone seemed condescending. I was insulted.

"Sekima, that's enough," Nefer ordered, with minor impatience. "If you have something to say, just say it. You're stringing us along like puppets. We already know you've got something to do with this."

She laughed. "Yes, my dear. You are puppets. You are all puppets..."

Lord, what must I do to end this??

"Doris, I asked you if you think your God wants this for you," Sekima said. "If the answer is yes, you will have to extrapolate what that signifies."

"I don't..." I muttered. "I don't know..."

"Lucas," she called, "Please pull over here."

The driver slowed down and we parked on the street of a busy intersection. The buildings towered over the sidewalks that were bustling with people.

"Look at all these individuals," she peered out the window. "All these puppets... Oblivious to the artificial structure of their lives."

I watched a man aimlessly walk into the street while immersed in his phone. He was alerted to his surroundings when a car horn blared. His eyes fluttered in confusion but he was otherwise unresponsive. A woman paced the center island of the street holding a sign that asked for money to feed her three terminally ill children. She twitched and scratched her head rigorously when the cars began passing through the traffic light that changed to green. A nearby coffee shop had a line of people out the door.

"You told me that your fate is with your God," Sekima veered her eyes from the window. "Your belief is a part of this contrived scheme."

I shook my head. "I..."

"Where do you think your sacred texts are derived from?" She raised an eyebrow. "Do you suppose their sanctity prevents them from adaptation? Do you have faith that you receive the unconcealed accountings of the Creator?"

A headache brewed. Even though the car wasn't moving, I felt like it was and it made me nauseous.

"Do consider the story of Adam and Eve," she went on, "To review it as an allegory, what would you envision? Would you view Adam as the earth, and Eve as humanity? In the story of their fall, would you perceive the snake as transcendence of the consciousness, and not the devil? What if the seed that is spoken of is actually legacy, rather than offspring? Ponder upon the narrative of their first children, Cain and Abel. What would you say if I told you they were the separation of what is measured good and evil, which is the opposing force of what is desired and what is required for supremacy in one's own mind? Cain murders Abel. Would you question the reason as to why Cain himself becomes an unsettled vagrant or that the reprisal for his death would be multiplied seven times?"

Nefer tried the handle on the door. He sighed heavily. "Let me out."

"Not just yet, Nefer, sweety," she crooned. "You can't run every time you hear something you don't like."

"I don't understand..." I repeatedly shook my head.

She turned her head to the driver. "Lucas, please proceed..."

The car started and we were on the road again.

"You pray for freedom, Doris." Sekima pointed at my attire. "You seek the answer. I will tell you that in order to achieve this, you must destroy the system that binds you; the system that binds your world. Otherwise, your prayers will never be answered."

"The... artificial structure of our lives?" My heart pounded.

"Yes. The structure your leaders label civilization. It will be the devastation of this world and everything in it." She examined Nefer, who was tapping the arm rest on the door. "What do you think your purpose is here?"

He shrugged and resumed tapping while staring out the window.

"Both of you want to escape, do you not?" she directed her inquiry at me. "To be liberated from the demon...?"

"Yes..." I whispered.

She watched us as we sat in silence. "Your society prevents the dominion you yearn for. To obtain this, it takes sacrifice..."

I quavered at the word. I wouldn't be able to stop myself from the one I had to make in two days.

"Doris," Sekima's tone was smooth. "Humanity is on the brink of annihilation. It may appear that the world is progressing but I will tell you it is not. The advancements boasted are derived from powers beyond this world. Powers including the... demon you have. They are implanted in your populace to manage the declination, but not to prevent it. The erosion is merely being delayed for the core objective of ascension."

The car slowed down as we turned onto the dirt road leading to Sekima's home.

"My demon..." I swallowed and rubbed my sweaty hands together.

"It is a manifestation that has lost its connection to the source," she replied. "Due to this severance, it is corrupted by unconscionable abuse. It exists as a fiend in physical form and feeds on the depravity to survive. Its ambition is to devour, but at one time it was a mediator. You have tendered hundreds to it. You will offer another and would continue along this path. I expressed that I am not here to harm you. You retain a gift that transmuted into a curse by humanity. Your next offering will be your last."

My last sacrifice...

When we were stationed at the front of her house, the driver opened the door.

"Hold on—hold on now," Nefer protested. "You said... ascension?"

"That is what your leaders entitle it, yes," Sekima lightly slid across the seat toward the door. "Akin to the structure you live by, it is ersatz. While the general public toils away in the pits, your leaders prepare their expedition to the world afar. I am sure you have heard occasional reports regarding the planet Mars. They are modest and do not reveal the extent of this voyage's prominence."

"I—I'm confused..." My head throbbed.

The driver stood patiently by the door.

"I am saying to you, that your world is dying." Her eyes could have cut through me. "Your leaders, the men and women who influence the order, are preparing to syphon the remaining energies to complete their withdrawal in four months. The reason I am telling you this is because you possess one of the keys to salvation for all of mankind. Your Reverend Eriksen counseled you, and you are aware of the sacrifice to justify the sins of man. In order to accept deliverance, to complete true ascension, all the sins of man must be harnessed. You regard your cat as a demon of lust. This lust demon stems from a configuration that had several divisions. The deadly sins that plague your world generated from this. I imagine that what

I communicate sounds absurd. I must converse in a manner you understand, until your understanding allows the truth. Everything you are doing in this world is a diversion; your occupations, your obligations, your culture. You and those in your category are bred for compliancy and overindulgence. Both of these are needed for the organization to persevere and for the beneficiaries to accomplish their aspirations. Anyone who discovers this assembly is either converted or exterminated. Others who have become aware of its possible presence simply resume in their postings. The contemporary names of this system are extraneous to your function, but know that they involve the expropriation of control by all means. I cannot tarry any longer with this. I must tend to the others and we will speak again. For now, Doris, Gary will help you glean some comprehension. Ask him about the Abacus. Lucas, please take them home."

She nimbly exited the vehicle as she gave the order to the driver and he punctually shut the door.

There was no conversation through the ride back to Nefer's house. I gaped out the window, watching the puffy clouds in the sky as I tried to gather my thoughts. Lucas pulled the passenger door open once we arrived.

"Out," he instructed in a heavy bass voice.

The limousine headed off immediately after we did so. Nefer let me in the house and I all but ran to get my things. I had a splitting headache and I didn't know where to begin deliberating my morning. I could scarcely digest it. I felt like I was in a haze. My purse was in his bedroom and he had followed me upstairs. He blocked the doorway.

"Where are you going?" his tone was somewhat authoritative. He didn't appear to want an answer. "We need to take care of whatever this is with Sekima. Now. I'm gonna go to her house. Come with me."

"I have to leave..." I checked my phone uneasily. It was about to be eleven-thirty A.M. I wanted to be away from the area. "I need to..."

"You're gonna kill that guy." He folded his arms, assertive.

We stared at each other. The familiar longing for him gnawed at my thoughts.

After a few more seconds, I advanced toward the door. He didn't try to stop me from going, but it was apparent he wanted to. A small percentage of my anxiety dispersed when I stepped outside. I sat in my car and stared at the church in the rear-view mirror. Cars filled the parking lot. I was wounded by their reproving and debated returning to them. I instead drove to the motel, my mind running in all directions. One main notion was that this could be my last sacrifice.

I don't have any reason to believe her...

Hours later, the man met me as scheduled and he had been steadily increasing his intake of me. This caused my fatigue to worsen when he would finish. I fell back onto the bed as he left the room. I thought of the day and wondered if my cat was around.

"Where are you?!" I yelled to the ceiling. "I know you're still here!"

My phone hummed with a text.

'Sekima told me how I'll help you,' Nefer texted.

I anticipated more but he didn't send anything, so I responded with *'???'*

He called me.

Ugh, I don't want to talk...

"Yes," I answered.

"Doris, after you..." His voice dangled.

"Hello?"

"I'm here. I know you can't stop it, so... after you... do the thing... on Tuesday, come to my house."

"I... can't." I shut my eyes.

"Why not?"

"I just can't. I won't be able to go anywhere for a while."

"I'll come get you."

I wrestled with replying. "... I won't be awake."

"Where are you right now? At your new place?"

"No... I'm at a motel..."

"Tell me where. I'll pick you up."

I preferred for him to let me handle this and get it over with. I was uncertain how he would react after this was over. He needed to have his own feelings but I couldn't refute my worries.

If my cat goes away after this last sacrifice... he will see me as I really am.

"What are you going to do?" I queried. "To... help me."

"So, I talked to Sekima. She said your sacrifice drains you and that you need to, uh, replenish or whatever. I'm gonna help you and make sure that happens."

"How...?"

"Alright, so she said get you plenty of fluids. Like, water. Also, you need food. I think I gotta make sure you get enough sleep and stuff too..."

"Ok..." my voice was just above a whisper.

"Tell me where you are."

I gave him the motel I was staying at and informed him that there was little time before I lost consciousness. It was arranged for him to await my text.

We spoke briefly on what Sekima presented to us. We both agreed that it was a great deal to absorb. Sekima had not illustrated the ascension to him, nor elaborated on her remark about civilization.

After our call ended, I did a search on my browser for space travel. I read editorials and viewed photographs taken by robots.

There were designs to fly a vehicle to Mars next year, but nothing involving humans yet. I jumped from website to website, and read for hours. They plotted for people to travel to the moon in the near future and reach Mars in another decade.

Is there really a plan for Mars next year?

I then explored the company I worked for. It appeared to be established in eighteen seventy-seven and changed its original name in the early nineteen fifties. It was once called Aurora's Proletariat Partners. There was little information on the company aside from a one paragraph description of its hiring services and a mention of offices in several countries. Sekima became the CEO three years ago. This was all I could find.

~~ * ~~

I went directly to Gary's office on Monday morning.

"Does this company help with the mission to space?!" I spat out. "To Mars?!"

He was puzzled as he sat at his desk. "Um, close my door...?"

I kicked the door to shut it. "Are the clients a part of the mission?"

"Uhh..." He shook his head, stupefied.

"What is the Abacus?"

This question garnered the desired response and he realized what I was asking.

He grinned in accordance. "Ok, THAT is something I can answer! Geez, Doris, um, good morning? Let me pull it up..."

He typed, then clicked away on his computer as he indicated that I come to his side of the desk.

"I was planning to show you this today," he was ecstatic. "This is how we make sure to meet our clients' expectations. Fill the chart and you will be good to go. Sekima put this together, if that helps."

I leaned over his shoulder to review the chart. It seemed to track an array of demographics. Various numbers were inside the cells of each column and the information had an extensive scrollbar. He slid the screen to the bottom of the chart where two rows were separated. The upper row was titled 'Aggregate Preferment Levels'. There were seven color-coded boxes in the row and each box was filled with a three-digit number and a letter, except the last one. It was a deep blue box with the number three and the letters 'GR'. The lower row was titled 'Faculty ID' beside a gray box and had a description to enter each new hire's ID number.

"What's this?" I pointed to the colored blocks.

"Don't worry about that," he waved his hand. "Those numbers generate on their own. All you have to do is put the New Hire IDs in the shaded box."

I squinted my eyes.

"Easy, right?" His grin was expansive.

"Gary, how are you ok with hiring these people for things that could be illegal?" I was surprised by his attitude.

"It's not illegal. We have authorization and follow all guidelines. No one is asked to do anything without their explicit consent. They must sign this agreement for our elite clients..." He pulled up a form that had small font and was two pages long.

"I can barely read that!" I skimmed the document and noted the intricacy of the language. "You expect them to read all this??"

"Well, they should, yea." He shrugged. "They sign it, so, yes I do."

My mouth gaped as I blinked several times, stunned by his confident manner. I nearly argued against its complexity but withheld.

"So, we just randomly pick people?" I asked. "Or do we go by the numbers...?"

"No, we don't discriminate." He adamantly enforced. "We just enter in the New Hire ID. The chart does the rest."

"Well, what were you doing before I got here?"

"You were hired a week after this office opened here. I came from another location and trained under their Office Director."

"Now you're going to a new office..."

"Yes." He gleefully grabbed a pile of papers from his desk and stood up. "We actually have some interviewees today to practice on! When we get through these and hire them, we will put them in the chart so you can see how the numbers work their magic!"

I deferred in following him to the door.

"We are doing this for a reason," he assured as he opened it. "It looks unrelated, but it is important. You'll see."

I believed him. I analyzed the candidates and accepted them all despite my senses revealing lack of interest in the positions. Either way, they would be put to the chart in one form or another. I felt guilty because a few of the candidates were teeming with desperation.

This doesn't feel right, I thought. *But, if the terms are all there, why do I feel bad? They should be reading the documents, so that means they are, right?*

Gary showed me the system he retrieved their IDs from, which were assigned during the online application process. He explained that it randomly nominated the applicants who were then scheduled for interviews. We entered each ID into the chart. While the numbers on the chart fluctuated in various columns, the numbers in the color-coded boxes at the bottom didn't change. Once we finished, Gary emailed the chart to Sekima.

At four-thirty P.M., Gary dismissed me.

"I think we had enough fun today!" he laughed, but swiftly became serious. "Doris, I hope that what I showed you today makes at least a little sense. Tomorrow, we'll get a detailed look at the client list!"

Nefer called me as I was leaving the office to ask if I wanted to stop by for dinner. I declined. I would be too exhausted.

The man was at the motel before I arrived. He sprang up from the bed when I entered.

"I j-just..." he stuttered. "I just needed t-t-to see you again. I-I need another taste... I know you told me six, but I... I can't wait..."

His behavior was unusual, although I didn't typically deprive the men of attention while they were chosen. He failed to be sated after an hour. I was close to comatose when he concluded around eight P.M. He left the room and I climbed into the tub where I passed out.

The tub was stained with my blood when I awoke. I blearily rose up and turned on the shower. As I washed, I heard muffled sounds of mewing that caused my heart to palpitate. The noises spurred me to hasten out of the bathroom and I checked my phone once I was dressed. The time was seven forty-nine A.M.

Gary was delighted to see me when I dragged into work, with no qualms about showing it.

"I'm so happy for you!" he was saying. "You're a natural."

"Why are you doing this?" I asked. "All these people... why?"

"We are helping all these people," he replied, certain. "When Sekima hired me, she showed me that what we're doing is for the good of all. I believe her. She's... incredible, inspirational."

His admiration resounded.

I queried what he saw in her, but he was unable to describe the reasoning behind his fondness.

"I wish I had words," he answered, chortling. "You'll have to see it for yourself. She's beautiful. Inside and out."

At four P.M. I left the office and Gary didn't dissent. I stopped at a liquor store in advance of going to the motel. Once again, the man was present in the room prior to my arrival. The time was just four fifty-one P.M. He was fretfully wandering the space and relief washed over him upon seeing me.

"Sovereign," he bolted toward me and seized my hands. He kissed them erratically. "I'm sorry, I'm sorry! I—I don't know who I am without you."

My instruction on his behavior during absences must have dispelled. It held no bearing at this point; tonight, was his last night.

He removed his clothing and I directed him to lie on the bed. He reached his hands out to me, in sincere reception. I stripped as he watched, my heart thumping.

"Come here," he begged.

Not long after I straddled him, was he ready to finish. I subsequently conducted the ritual and heard soft crying from the walls, which exacerbated my apprehension. My cat hurdled onto the bed, wailing. Her mouth gaped wide for the shadow to spill out, and the room's temperature skyrocketed. Her shining eyes dimmed as the darkness swirled around the area, then she collapsed beside the man in a heap. The shadow rapidly invaded my body, disabling me. The stinging coursed through me until the darkness expelled again. When I could finally breathe, I staggered off the bed. The shadow engulfed the man without pause and gradually hefted him into the air. Tiny pockets of light flashed like static electricity. His body shredded and every torn piece of him disintegrated. A high-pitched scream filled the air. I covered my ears but this did nothing to staunch the piercing sound.

I lumbered to the bathroom, laboring to wash up quickly. The shrieking changed to ringing in my ears and diminished when I opened the door. I threw on a sweatshirt and jeans, and saw the room was empty. I solemnly sent a text to Nefer after I gathered all of our things. He struck the door moments later.

"Hi," he greeted, dressed in a light blue long-sleeved thermal shirt and black jeans with a black skull cap on his head. His attitude appeared unaffected and I didn't sense any negative feelings.

Is she gone? That sacrifice was different... She never did that before... I was reminded of the church and the dialogue with Sekima. I peeked up at the ceiling. *Do you want this for me, Lord?*

"Are you ready?" Nefer inquired, scanning the room momentarily. "We can get your car in the morning."

Inside his car, it smelled like a garden. As we held hands on the way to his house, the lethargy I usually suffered had not occurred, but it arose when I left the vehicle at his home. I grew shaky upon closing the car door. He aided me in entering his house and jagged aching shot through my stomach when we ascended the stairs. I crumpled to the floor at the top. I glimpsed a large red spot broadening between my legs.

"I got you," Nefer escorted me to the bathroom. "C'mon, get in the shower."

I shed the soiled articles, disconcerted by the excessive amount of blood. I cautiously stepped inside the shower when he turned it on. Crimson streams flowed down my legs and into the drain. I shuddered as I began to rinse off. After some time, the color was cleansed away. I exited to Nefer who waited with a towel and he gave me a large purple t-shirt as we went to the bed.

"How do you feel?" he asked when he brought me a glass of water, concerned.

"Cold..." my teeth chattered. I drank the water in four swallows then passed it back to him.

"Ok, I'll turn up the heat." He disappeared.

I curled up under the covers, shivering violently. It was as if he cranked the air conditioner to full blast.

"Is that better?" He peered in the doorway.

"No..." I draped the comforter over my head like a hood.

He entered with another blanket and climbed in the bed behind me. He placed it over us and slid his arms around my waist to cuddle me. The chills dwindled as his warmth surrounded me. I progressively grew aroused. My heart rate strengthened.

Please, no, I thought, sweating copiously. *Please, no...*

"Doris," he whispered, squeezing me tighter.

I couldn't block the emotions from flourishing. I pulled one of his hands up and pressed his palm against my chest, then leisurely twisted around to face him. It was hopeless to resist my body's pleas. I succumbed to the calling and kissed him fervidly. He responded with zeal, acquiescing my advances and we soon found ourselves intertwined. I struggled to maintain my grip on reality as he grabbed the headboard for support and rapidly thrust into me. It was difficult to affirm the passage of time while the room was spinning in slow motion. I shut my eyes and clutched the bedspread.

I sensed his body become more rigid as he reached climax. The unexpected expansion of sensations caused me to cry out in uninhibited satisfaction. He grunted and kissed me passionately, performing soft strokes before coming to a complete stop. He pecked my neck, then my chest while he pulled out and fell face down on the bed.

The room felt like a sauna. The light that passed through the windows had reduced. As I sat up and gazed around, I saw darkness creeping across the floor. I shook Nefer.

"Nefer," I called, alarmed.

He didn't react and seemed to be unconscious.

"Nefer!" I attempted to wake him. "Get up."

The shadow scaled the walls and snuffed out any remaining radiance as it spanned the ceiling. Purplish blue light crackled on the floor. The darkness slid up onto the bed and rolled over Nefer.

"Nefer!!" I screamed. "NO!!"

An invisible force pushed me on my back. It weighed on my chest and I was helpless as the shadow invaded my every orifice. My skin was scalding from the contact. I gagged and began to asphyxiate while the darkness bore into me, receding from the surfaces. Light gradationally returned to the room once it was inside. I was released from constraint and immediately drew breath. My skin continued to singe, like tiny needles were stabbing me. Blisters formed on my flesh. I howled in agony as they burst and yellowish-green pus oozed from the sores. My throat was constricted when the secretion filled my mouth. The fluid hardened to encase me and I was once again immobilized. The knifing pain was torment as I slipped into nothingness.

12

I must have been dreaming. My eyes opened to a white space and I was suspended. Bright colorful lights swished around me at varying speeds and sizes.

"Doris," a series of voices whispered. "Consummate..."

"Hello...?" I replied.

"You must... consummate..." they seemed to be ubiquitous. "Do not falter..."

"What is this?!"

"You will be tested... do not falter... You will be questioned... remain... resolute..."

"Where am I?!" I tried to focus on a yellow quarter-sized dot that floated by.

"You will be affrighted..." the lights spun wildly around me. "Seek... consummation..."

They landed on my arms like tiny insects. The warmth of them spread along my body. The heat began to burn as the lights seeped into my skin. The space settled to darkness once the illumination was completely absorbed, then a pale blue glow developed in front of me. It expanded and a shadow morphed at the center. Two gleaming golden eyes opened, blazing menacingly.

"Doris," a voice rumbled.

"You..." I gasped. I heard my cat. "You're..."

"Wake up."

"I..." I shook my head, confounded.

"Wake up. Wake up now."

"But... I don't—"

"Wake up, NOW!!" the shadow swelled and lunged at me.

~~ * ~~

"AAAHH!!" I screamed. My eyes shot open to more darkness. I abruptly sat up, short of breath and my heart pounding. My vision acclimated and I was in Nefer's bed. I felt like I was wearing something on my head. I reached up to touch it. My hair was thick and springy.

"Huh?" my voice rasped.

The light clicked on, and I shielded my eyes while squinting from the glare.

"Doris...?" Nefer warily said.

I immediately noticed my hands. My long nails were healthy looking. My brown skin was smooth and soft.

"I—I'm young," I mumbled, aghast. I peered down at my body. "I'm naked..."

My breasts sat supple with pert nipples. A fluffy patch of black hair was nestled between my thighs. I ran my hands along my legs and inspected my toes. The toenails were almost as long as my fingernails.

Lord, am I still dreaming? I thought. I glanced at Nefer, who stood in the doorway.

"I wasn't sure how long you'd be like that," he said, slowly walking over.

"Forever?" I caressed my arms.

"I wasn't sure how long you'd be asleep," He sat on the bed carefully.

"What time is it? What's today?" I rubbed my plump lips and puckered them.

"It's..." He pulled out his phone. "Uh... ten fourteen P.M. Today's Wednesday."

"Wow..." I patted my hair. "Well, I usually sleep for about twelve hours... so it's been a day."

"No... today's the sixth. You've been asleep for a week."

"The sixth..." I tried to comprehend. I had an engagement scheduled. "My new apartment..."

"Hmm?" He eyed my thighs as he spoke. "What apartment?"

I sighed and fell back. "I... put a deposit on a place. I was supposed to move in on Friday... last Friday now..."

"Maybe you can call them tomorrow? And I, uh, brought your car here..." He was weary.

"My car..." I nodded. "Right..."

I remembered the filthy crust that enveloped me.

"I'm clean," I noted.

"Yea." He was studying my feet. "It washed right off like Sekima said..."

"Is she here? Sekima..." I speculated whether she instigated what had occurred.

"No, but..." He pointed at my toes. "I can give you clippers for this."

"I would really like some clothes?" I shuddered and touched the goosebumps on my arms.

He went to the dresser and collected a set of clothing. He hesitated. "Actually. I'll get those clippers first..."

I began cutting my fingernails when I obtained the nail trimmers. "Where's Sekima?"

"She'll be here in the morning." He watched me drop nails all over the bed.

"So... what happened? I just remember..." A memory of Nefer's glistening body flickered through my mind.

"Well..." He lifted a trash can from the corner of the room and casually swept the nails into it. He set the can by the bed, then leaned against the wall by the door.

I continued trimming my nails and he didn't speak for a time. The sound of cutting was the only noise.

"Doris," he eventually said awkwardly, "What we did... I..."

I stopped clipping. "What."

"I'm just confused, I guess." His reluctance amplified.

"About what." I was almost finished snipping.

"I thought that after what you did... this would be done. That your cat would be done and I could..."

I peeked up from my toes.

He was shaking his head in bewilderment. "Like I said, I can't tell what's real anymore. This is not me, it's not how I am."

"I don't know what's supposed to happen." I brushed the remaining trimmings into the trash. "I just know that I'm young... and my cat..."

"She was here." He handed me the clothes and waited as I got dressed.

"My cat? What did Sekima say..." I started to perspire.

"She'll be here in the morning," he restated.

Sekima said that was my last sacrifice... but my cat is still here... She could have nothing to do with any of this, and might be using us...

"Do you believe what she's told us...?" I stood up and pulled on the pants. "That stuff about ascension... and about the world dying? What if she's just messing with our heads?"

"Well..." He surveyed my body. "She didn't tell me much, except how to help you..."

"You said my cat was here."

"Just before you woke up, she sat right on your chest." He was agitated. "She said you weren't gonna get rid of her..."

"Hmm..."

"You're probably hungry."

I had no appetite whatsoever. "No... I'm not."

"Alright. I'm glad you're awake, but now I'm tired." He turned to leave.

"Where are you going?"

"To the couch." He was in the doorway with his back to me.

"And why?"

A solid thirty seconds passed before he undecidedly answered, "I just think I should..."

"For what? You can sleep in your own bed."

"Because, how I feel right now..." He sighed. "Goodnight."

He left the room and it was as if all the warmth drained with him. This compelled me to follow him and when I ran downstairs, he was setting up the couch by stretching a sheet over it. He unfolded a blanket to lay it down.

"So, you're just going to avoid me now?" I demanded, irked.

I had no desire to torture him, but his decision to leave incited my reaction.

"I don't know..." he replied. "I'm not trying to make you angry. I just need to clear my head..."

"I'm not angry!" I rescinded that assessment. "I mean... yes, a little, but you shouldn't have to sleep on the couch."

"Your demon told me everything I feel belongs to her." He was exasperated. He dropped the pillow and sat on the couch.

I joined him, ashamed. "I'm sorry... my cat, she's still affecting us..."

"Nothing I feel is me. Ever. Like, now... I can't tell what is really me, or you, or..."

I gently placed my hand on his back and was hit with a sudden flurry of emotions. The wind was knocked out of me.

"I felt that." He hopped to his feet.

"What was that?" I panted.

"I'll be back..." He dashed to the door at the right of the TV that was a closet. He pulled a coat out to put on. He slid on shoes.

"But—"

He yanked the front door open and repeated, "I'll be back."

It slammed loudly behind him. I sped to the window in time to watch him drive away. My heart was pounding as I searched for my phone, beginning in his living room. My bag was in the closet and I found my phone under an opened bottle of vodka. I plugged the phone to the charger since it had just under twelve percent battery. There were several missed calls and three voicemails. None of them were from Gary.

I guess I shouldn't be surprised...

The voicemails were all from the Golden Grounds apartment complex. The first message was from Thursday requesting a confirmation to my contingent move date on the first. The second was on Friday morning, asking that I bring the second half of the deposit by the end of day and complete the lease signing. The last one was on Monday morning, stating that my deposit would be lost.

"We'd love for you to join our community," the woman said, "but due to our reservation policy, we can't hold the apartment past twenty-four hours without the full deposit and a signed lease agreement. Unfortunately, we'll have to release it unless you bring the remaining balance by this afternoon—-"

I hung up. I brooded over where Nefer went. It made me anxious.

What did he feel? Where did he go? Did he go to Sekima? When will he be back? Should I text him?

"Stop fussing," I muttered to myself. I slumped onto the couch and turned on the TV. I flipped channels and settled on a movie that was halfway over. The scene had a woman running down a dark, endless hall. I checked the time. It was ten minutes to midnight and had been an entire hour that Nefer was gone.

Infomercials were starting to play when my phone rang. He was calling at two A.M.

I inhaled and exhaled deeply.

"Hi," I addressed, antsy.

"Hey..." he replied. He paused for a few seconds. "I'm... I'll be back in the morning."

"Ok..." I turned the TV off. "So... where are you...?"

"I'm at Sekima's house. I'm gonna sleep here—"

"I see..." I clicked off the lights and walked upstairs.

"—then be there in a few hours." He concluded.

"What time...?" I entered his room to return to the bed.

"Probably ten or so..."

"Hmm... ok..." I was disappointed.

"Just thought I'd call and let you know."

"Right. Ok. I'm... hanging up now."

"...Goodnight, Doris."

I tossed my phone aside and slithered under the covers. My opinions were scurrying off with the idea that he went to Sekima for comfort. I stared at the ceiling, attempting to push my postulations aside.

$$\sim\sim\,^*\,\sim\sim$$

The daylight beamed on my eyelids, drawing me from slumber. I stretched and went to the bathroom. Studying my face in the mirror, I was amazed by my youth. I unclothed and twirled to look at my backside. I caressed my shapely thighs, pinched my soft skin. In the reflection, I caught sight of Nefer standing in the doorway. I spun toward him.

He didn't say anything as his eyes grazed over my body.

"Are you getting in the shower...?" He was visibly tense.

I was delighted to see him, but discouraged by his disposition.

"Yes..." I responded and proceeded to enter it.

"Sekima's here." He stood by the shower as I washed. "I'm gonna go to the store. I'll be back..."

He brusquely departed without letting me reply.

I took a long shower. I didn't want to get out.

Sekima's here, I thought. *What were they doing all night? He's acting really strange... I shouldn't jump to conclusions! He hasn't lied to me, why would he start now?*

I recollected the sensations that kindled between us. I then contemplated his conflict with the authenticity of them, which wrought remorse. I induced hundreds to yield to me, and bemoaned it more each time. I was overly chagrined by my effect on Nefer because I craved his feelings to be genuine. I needed my cat to be gone. If Sekima had the answers, I needed to talk with her.

I rifled through Nefer's drawers to find a white A-shirt and pair of green plaid pajama pants. I trudged downstairs to the living room.

"I see things went well," her voice originated from the kitchen. She casually emerged, dressed in a burnt orange turtleneck sweater and dark gray wool skirt with auburn high heeled boots. Her hair was tied in a curly mass that sprouted from the top of her head.

I instantly became stressed.

A smile formed on her face as she viewed my outfit. She walked past me to the couch. "Come now, sit."

I restlessly sat on the loveseat, wiping my hands.

"I'm sure you have something you want to say." Her complacent tone intimidated me. She reclined in the seat. "Out with it."

"M—my... cat," I babbled.

"Yes, your cat."

"Nefer... said she—he... he saw her..." I strained to respond.

Where is he? When will he be back? What did he go to the store for?

She observed me quietly.

"I thought..." I continued, "that she would be gone, after this last sacrifice... You said it was the last..."

"Where is she now?" she inquired.

"I don't know..." I gulped dryly.

"Call her."

"Call... her?" I was baffled.

"Yes. Call her."

Call her? I've never called her a day in my life...

"How...?" I shook my head.

Sekima raised an eyebrow. "The same way you call anyone. By her name."

What she instructed made sense, except I didn't ever call my cat by any name. I realized I had no idea what her name was.

"I..." Tears were creeping into my eyes.

"Are you going to call her, or what?" She sounded impatient.

"I—I... can't... I don't know her name..."

She narrowed her eyes. "You know her name."

"No, I don't..."

"You gave it to her." She pushed the footrest back into the couch.

I tried to remember. "I... never called her anything..."

Suddenly, a named appeared in my mind and I had no question whether it was hers.

"Edna," I announced.

She came trotting from the kitchen and leapt onto the coffee table, licking her paw.

"There you are," I said, shaken. I glanced at Sekima, who was clearly amused. "Edna..."

Sekima stood up. "Send her away."

"Uh, I..." I couldn't believe she listened to me.

Sekima glared at Edna, who immediately sprinted away back around the corner to the kitchen. She stepped over to the window and peered out. "You want her gone, but do you know why she is here?"

"You said she..." I made an attempt to recollect Sekima's words. "Feeds on... depravity... a manifestation..."

"Your demon... was conceived to regulate power that is destructive due to its potency." She revolved to look at me. "It seems you don't recognize your importance in what must be done."

"I'm going to save everyone..." I deliberated how to respond.

"You are envisioning frivolous motives to remove your burdens. This... demon is a mere inconvenience for you, is it not?"

"I don't know what you want me to say..."

"Once Edna is extracted, what do you expect to ensue?"

My eyes were trained on a worn patch in the sofa. I thought of Nefer.

"All that you must attain endorses a commitment far beyond private fancies," she added.

"So, what am I doing?" Frustrated, I garnered strength to be confrontational. "You tell me I'm part of a 'system called civilization', and I must 'destroy it' or the world will die. Then you talked about some 'ascension' and some other nonsense about Mars..."

I was making air quotes as I ranted. "You had this big long speech about people being oblivious or whatever to this 'artificial structure' and that humanity is not progressing, that some powers are behind all this, but look around! People are living their lives and technology is advancing us every day! Oh, and Mars? I saw the mission. They are sending some car, not people. They think in like fifteen years humans will be trying to get there. Women are going to the moon in a few years, and I didn't see anything about going to Mars anytime soon."

The corner of her mouth turned up slyly.

"I don't see a problem with going to space," I went on, sustaining my vigor. "They want to see what's out there so we can better ourselves and..."

"'They'?" she cut in. "Not you? Not the people you see, 'living their lives'?"

She seemed to mock me by using quotation mark gestures.

I lost my steam.

"Have you not asked yourself if you are capable of more than the mundanity you are subjected to?" she asked. "For such an 'advanced race', you sum your lives up to an arrangement that is fostered from repetitive, endless, and vapid sequences. It is astonishing that humans aspire to be unrestricted when in actuality they are requesting a larger sty. Oh, I'm sorry, you have variety ... hmm? That gives you distinctiveness... I must ask if you can attain the serenity you pursue in this limited capacity? You are born into a system that orchestrates every aspect of your existence according to a common principle. Do you infer that your intellect is intended to conform to predictive behaviors, for the duty of feeding an engine that is ultimately insatiable? If this is the case, why do you have it?"

"You said the powers are why we are advanced..." I said. "What do you mean..."

"What is civilization, Doris?" she answered with a question.

Please, Lord, if she is about to test my knowledge...

"Cities, languages ... labor, economic, social classes..." She looked intently at me. "Organized religion, centralized government. Art and culture... The pieces constructed to form civilizations of this planet are founded on a system meant for conquering the earth and its subordinate creatures. Your leaders have molded this system to mechanize humans and have birthed the impossibility for equality or true freedom."

"Freedom isn't impossible here. We can choose how we want our lives to be and we have a chance for happiness..."

"Choose? Freedom of choice is not freedom."

"Are you about to say we're all slaves? I don't want to hear it..." I was irritated.

"You are focusing on my dialect, and not on my message."

"And what is your message? Why are you saying so much, but saying nothing at all??"

"As I have informed you, I must speak in a style you can understand. You are at the cusp of insight but in order for you to reach it, you must let go of what you believe your motivation is for being alive. I asked you what civilization is. And I ask you why you think humans adapted it to live here."

I shrugged and decided it wasn't worth responding.

"When humans are to... advance... it is with the target of reaching ascension." She sat on the couch again. "That is, to leave this earth and realize destiny granted by the Creator. Ascension is a natural evolution that humans are designed to achieve, but this generation has circumvented the process and remains here on earth. The growth requires propensities that must be disciplined through passion and virtue. Instead, they dwell here and are used to keep an engineered organization persistent in fueling a synthetic ascension. You regard generations as your children and children's children. I will tell you; this is the third generation of humans to ascend, and the only one that has accepted the tools without the resolve. This is because your leaders have decided it was not an achievement worthy of the many, but the few. Humans constantly alter themselves to appease the peculiar rationale of dominance. This idealistic belief that flawlessness is how to reach ascension has caused permanent damage, for humans were already made in the image of the Creator. These cravings for alteration are encouraged because they allow exploitation of the desires driving them, and this corruption is required to dissuade you from the reason they are manipulated. Do you know where I am going with this?"

"I..."

"The desires include your cat, or your demon... Lust, and the other six desires that your nation identifies as sins. They are a distraction." She stolidly crossed her legs. "They are all a distraction, woven into your social practices, your education, your information, media and entertainment. They are sophisticated enough to simultaneously condemn and inspire you. A significant infraction is the very loyalty you have to your God, and the lack thereof. As two sides of the same coin, this is why your God wants this for you just as much as your Devil. They are one and the same."

I shook my head. "No."

"Yes. You pray to your God; the same deity that wished your demon upon you. That deity is human."

My skin was enflamed. "You think I can believe anything you say to me?!"

"Have I lied to you Doris?" She tilted her head to the side.

"How would I even know? I have no proof of-—of ANYTHING you say!" I trembled with anger.

"Hmm, you require something you can see, correct? Something you can feel?" She rose from the couch and grabbed my face.

$$\sim\sim\ ^{*}\ \sim\sim$$

There was blackness. There was no sound, and weight on my face gave me the sensation of being suffocated. Air sharply flooded my lungs and my eyes opened as I gasped. Bright, hot luminosity nearly blinded me. I couldn't fix my eyes to see anything. I was in some kind of tube of light.

A loud whirring noise vibrated the shaft before I was thrust downward at a dizzying speed. I travelled for an interminable period. I was at the edge of fainting when I unexpectedly halted. The light around me disappeared and I fell.

A brief flash of light caused me to blink and I was by a group of about ten people standing in a field. The temperature was chilly. I must have been in a different dream. The group seemed to be arguing in a foreign language with their backs to me. A shadowy being was lying on the ground beside them, trying to crawl away. It was an entity I had witnessed once before.

The ground violently shook while the group seized the arms of the being and hauled it to its feet. It turned its head to look at me, and I saw a shining golden eye on its forehead. This caused the group to direct their attention to me.

My heart pounded wildly; I was frozen with terror. One of the men yelled something at me, but it was incoherent. Another man called to me. Two women and one man started to approach me with daunting expressions. I stepped back in fear.

The captive being let loose a deafening scream. The group cringed from the noise and I had the instinct to escape. I spun around and almost tripped over a man lying face down in a pool of blood. As I ran, snow began falling at an exponential rate.

I shivered from the immense cold that gusted through me.

"What—" I wheezed, hugging myself. "What—"

"I don't expect you to have perspicacity nor confidence in what I showed you," Sekima calmly folded her arms. "But know it was the fall of this generation."

"You..." I whispered. "You made me see those visions..."

She didn't reply.

"Why?" I was nauseous.

"Doris, the reason humans will not ascend is because they refuse to abandon mendacity. They cannot do this because it is engraved in society. Despite the nature of man, this fact will not allow you to reach your full potential. You are currently on the path to reset your nature, to remove the detriments forced upon you by the errs of humanity."

"What is my potential...? Why am I here?"

She smiled. "You asked me this, why you are here... remember? What did you tell me, hmm? That... you are here because of your cat. And what did I tell you?"

I didn't retain what she had said.

"Did Gary show you the Abacus?" she asked.

"Yes... So, your company helps humans that you say are killing the planet to reach ascension. How can I believe you when you are doing what you say I am supposed to stop?"

"We must keep the series of events going. In this world, one cannot stand on a mountain to scream 'the end is nigh' and expect your ears to hear it."

"'We'?" I squinted my eyes. "As in you and I? I don't even know the series of events."

"We, as in myself and those who ascended before you."

"You mean that... you...?" My head pulsed. "You ascended...?"

"No. I am but an emissary. Did Gary explain what the preferment levels are?"

I shook my head as the word rang a bell. "The colorful blocks at the bottom...?"

"They are a measurement of your sins." She exhaled heavily. "They are needed to complete the final sacrifice..."

"What is the final sacrifice? Is it my demon? You mentioned before that there are others... The other sins...?"

"Your demon... is involved in the process, yes..."

Nefer hadn't returned yet and it had been some time since he left.

"Doris," Sekima alerted. "the sins I speak of, I need you to know that your demon, is not a demon."

"Oh, because my human God gave it to me?" I retorted.

"No, your God did not give it to you."

"You said my God gave this to me."

"I did not."

I reconsidered whether she had.

"Your cat will be dealt with today," she stated. She collectedly walked to the closet and removed her coat. "You are to be dressed and ready by nine P.M. Goodbye."

"Wait, where's Nefer?" I asked her, bounding up from the loveseat. "He said he went to the store and he'd be back..."

"Then he'll be back." She left.

I entered the kitchen, searching for my cat. The room was empty.

"Edna," I declared.

"Mrowr..." she mewed as she climbed on the table. "Well, hello."

I was astounded by her subservience. "You're here..."

"Yes, where else would I be?" she laughed.

"Gone." My heart palpitated and I balled my hands into fists. "I'm getting rid of you."

"Ha! You think so?" She cocked her head, her golden eyes lustrous. "Why? Because that woman says so? Who cares what she says? You just met her! She may have some kind of effect on me, that's true... but she can't do anything to send me away. I've been with you a long time. We will be together until the end..."

"Go away!" I was livid. When I blinked, she had vanished.

"Fine," she whispered from the walls. "I'll go for now..."

I heard the front door open. I headed to the living room to see Nefer bringing in plastic shopping bags. I went to help carry them, took one bag from his hand and looked inside.

"What's all this?" I asked.

There were paintbrushes and a small container of spackling paste.

"I need to do some... home repairs," he answered. "Thanks..."

He exited again and came back with paint buckets.

I assumed the items were going upstairs so I brought them to the spare bedroom. Nefer arrived to the room with several more bags. Once he set them on the floor, he held one out in front of me. It was a department store gift bag.

"I got you something," He wouldn't look me in my eyes.

"Thank you..." I cautiously accepted it. I peeked in to see articles of clothing.

He bought me clothes... I thought of the trash bags filled with clothes in the trunk of my car.

"Welcome." He began unloading the contents of the bags. He then left to go downstairs.

I went into his room and excitedly dumped all the clothes onto the bed. There were two tops, a skirt, a pair of slacks, a set of flannel pajamas, and four pairs of panties. Two of the panties were thongs, one was lacy.

"Hmm..." I lifted the lacy thong to examine it.

"The lady at the store said it was popular," Nefer was at the door. "I, uh... didn't know your size. And I got confused by the bras, so I didn't get any..."

I giggled and picked up one of the tops. "Thanks..."

"I just figure you'd wanna wear something else besides all my clothes."

I beamed, feeling adulated.

He didn't have to buy me these.

I turned to respond, but realized he wasn't at the door anymore. I tried on the top and the skirt, then went to the other room.

"It fits," I informed him.

"Ok, good." He was repairing the hole in the wall. He glanced at me temporarily then resumed what he was doing.

"Nefer..." I stepped closer to him. I was rueful.

"Yea?" He meticulously scraped the wall with a metal spatula.

"I'm sorry..."

"Huh?" He stopped the action.

"I said, that... I'm sorry. For making you feel this way. For... how you feel. I'm sorry that I do this to you..."

He put the tool down. "It's really not your fault, Doris. Besides, your cat won't be here for much longer."

"Sekima told you?"

"Yea..." He crossed the room to move the mattress to a different spot, revealing another hole in the wall.

"Well, what else did you... talk to her about...?" I attempted to be calm.

He went over to a toolbox that was on the mirrored chest of drawers to dig in it.

"When you touched me last night..." He pulled nails from the box, "I felt like... like you were in my head. I don't know how to explain it... I heard your voice. While you were sleeping, Sekima told me you would be changing. I had to go to her because I felt something different."

He held a hammer and knelt beside the bedframe.

"If I touch you now, what will happen?" I questioned.

I sought his contact at that moment. I was delighted that he bought me something and wished to be in his arms. I disregarded the circumstance that his feelings weren't his own. I needed the comfort of his embrace.

The loud banging of the hammer made me flinch. He continued to repair the bed without answering. His silence was agonizing.

I retreated to his bedroom and grabbed my phone. It was almost one P.M. when I called the apartment complex.

"Hello ma'am," the woman said, "We don't have anything at this present time, but I can add you to the waiting list. What's your name?"

"I think I was on the list already," I replied. "I put down a deposit to move in at the beginning of the month, and got a call on uh, Monday that I would lose my reservation... my name's Doris..."

"Oh, yes ma'am. We have placed you back on the list. Sorry, we can't refund the deposit..."

"Uh huh..." I bit my lower lip anxiously as I strode through the room.

"So, you're all set and we will call when we have something available."

I looked out the window, then hung up. I tossed my phone on the bed.

Nefer lingered in the doorway, staring at me. When he stepped in the room, I could feel the temperature rising. I swallowed and sweat formed in my armpits.

"Your cat will be gone tonight." His gaze didn't calm me. He was disturbed. "I don't wanna hurt your feelings. I just need to know that what I feel is real. Until she's gone, I..."

"I understand."

I was fearful of what would come to pass. I aimed to eliminate Edna, but was equally concerned over how things would change. I enjoyed the way it felt to have Nefer treat me like a person with unconditional affection. I preferred that it didn't end, but I knew that it could. I also didn't quite comprehend the events Sekima conveyed to me.

How will getting rid of her destroy civilization? How will it bring an ascension? Will I really be saving people? Lord, am I being deceived? I am confused...

Nefer retrieved clothes from his dresser, then walked out. "I need a shower..."

What I wouldn't give to join you...

I exited the room and idled at the bathroom door, listening to the sound of the water running. I was tempted to open the door, but instead I descended the steps to the living room and turned on the TV.

A talk show was on. Three men were sitting on a couch discussing their drug addiction experiences with the host. The bottom of the screen had a headline that read: *Rehabilitation Miracles.*

"The treatment really changed my life," one man was saying, tearfully. "The doctors were so helpful, the entire staff."

The audience clapped and cheered.

I sure feel addicted to Nefer. How he makes me feel, I need it...

In mere hours, I would discover his true emotions.

Sekima arrived fifteen minutes to nine P.M. As soon as she entered the house, she went directly upstairs.

I sat on the couch nervously waiting. I got up to stand at the window and peeked through the blinds to see rain pattering. The rhythm was calming and I imagined the water washing over me. I envisaged it rinsing away my despair, then replacing it with the sensations Nefer provided. I heard Sekima's voice upstairs. She was talking to him.

"—go through it," she was saying. Her feet drummed the steps as she came back down. She held her hand out to me. "Take this and put it on."

It was a ring, with three stones in it. I did as she advised and my finger tingled. The prickling moved through my arm. It was like my arm was falling asleep.

"Let's go." She opened the front door and raised her umbrella when she stepped out.

I followed her into the rain, and we walked across the street. I stopped, realizing she was leading me to the church.

Why are we going here...? I don't think I'm welcome... Is Reverend Eriksen a part of this?

"Let's go!" she yelled over the rain. She resumed toward the entrance. She tugged the door, then held it ajar. "Come inside, now!"

The door slammed behind me as I warily made my way down the center aisle with her. The church was empty. Dim light filtered through the windows.

"Remove all of your clothes," Sekima commanded when we reached the baptistery on stage. "Get inside."

I timidly undressed to enter the baptistery.

She knelt down beside it. "Call her."

I was freezing. Peering up at the ceiling, I exhaled noisily. I recalled the people fleeing in horror and the reverend shrinking in the corner.

"Edna." I bade firmly.

Edna emerged from the shadows. She jogged to the steps of the baptistery and sat down.

"Call her to you." Sekima was unwrapping a cloth on the floor.

"Edna, come here." I pointed in front of me and Edna obeyed.

"Pick her up." She extended her arm out to me. She was holding a red handled knife by its blade.

I observed it uncomfortably.

"Pick her up," she repeated sternly.

I lifted Edna into my arms. I could feel her tiny heart beating rapidly.

"What are you doing?" she queried in dread. Her eyes darted from the dagger to me.

What AM I doing? Am I supposed to stab her? I've never hurt her...

My hand quaked as I wrapped my fingers around the knife's handle to obtain it. It had substantial weight, but no distinctive details otherwise.

"What do you expect to do with that??" Edna quivered.

"Kneel," Sekima said.

I got down on one knee.

"Don't do this," Edna pleaded. She dug her claws into my chest, causing me to let go of her and she landed on the floor, frozen in place. She looked at Sekima. "You can't do this. Please..."

"Wh—what am I doing?" I asked Sekima. I gripped the blade tightly, fear rising.

"Pierce her neck," she answered. She tapped her neck. "Insert it here and do not retract it."

"Ok... ok..." I nodded. I took hold of the back of Edna's neck to haul her up again. I pressed the knife's edge to her throat.

"Please..." Edna begged. "No..."

I pushed harder.

I promptly began to sweat. The room was roasting, and the minimal light from the windows evaporated. Soft blue illumination casted over us from above.

"Dori," a voice sighed.

I gazed up to see ghostly figures surrounding the baptistery. Sekima was nowhere in sight.

"Dori," the male voice whispered a second time. One of the shapes moved to the stairs. Its body became visible in the light overhead and the face was revealed.

"Daddy...?" I was incredulous.

"Baby," he descended the steps. "Don't do it. Please..."

I shook my head, tears welling. "No..."

"Don't kill her..." he continued. "Don't kill... us..."

"You're not dead...?" I watched him as he stood right in front of me.

"No, Doris," another voice responded. "We are here with you. We always were..."

Franklin came down the steps and stood by my father.

"Franklin..." I was overwhelmed with grief. "I'm so... so sorry..."

"It's ok, honey," he placated. "I feel no pain."

I peered at Edna; whose eyes were wide with panic. I maintained the blade at her neck.

"Don't do this to us," she implored.

"Doris," my father said, "I'm so sorry for what I did to you. I was sick. But Edna... she saved me. She saved us all..."

The shadows around the baptistery began to bare faces. They were all the men I sacrificed. They were naked, and must have filled the entire church.

"I..." I choked out, tears rolling down my face.

"They aren't dead," Edna's speech wavered. "They are here with us. Here with YOU."

My grip on the knife weakened.

"She took our sickness away," Franklin assured. "She healed us... We are free."

I saw their bodies rip apart! How can they be alive?

"You're free," I restated. "If you're free, then why are you still here?"

"We need to complete the ritual," Edna answered. "We need to, please. That woman is lying! If you do this, all of them will die..."

"You... you've been nothing but cruel to me!" I accused. "You hurt me, forced me to do terrible things! How can I believe you now??"

It was strenuous to determine her motives. She could have been trying to save herself.

"Please, I'm telling you the truth!" she cried. She flailed her arms to grab at me and connected. "I'm like this because it's my nature. I'm telling you the truth, please..."

"You could have told me this already! You haven't told me anything!" I was infuriated.

"I can't tell you what I don't fully know!" Her claws were digging into my arm. "I just know that you are doing this to complete the ritual so they can be free... I'm sorry that I didn't say this before. Please... I'm a wild beast. I'm attracted to the delicious energy! I don't mean to do this... I don't know any other way to be!"

Blood dribbled from the wounds she made on my arm.

Is she being honest, or just afraid to die?

"How can you believe that woman over me!??" she screamed. "She met you only weeks ago! I've been with you your entire life! I showed myself to you when you called, but I saw you born! I'm here for you, BECAUSE of you! Don't kill me, please!"

"Wha—" my words were caught.

"Dori," my father placed a hand on mine that held the knife. His touch was warm, like he was living and his skin glowed with the reflection of the blue light. "Give me the knife, baby."

"Daddy..." I felt like a little girl again. I wanted to oblige.

"Doris," Sekima's voice drifted from my left. "Pierce her neck."

I turned my head in her direction, but only saw the men who hovered nearby. "Where are you?"

"I'm here," she replied. "I haven't moved."

"I can't see you..."

"What do you see?"

"A... bunch of... all the sacrifices I've made..." I peered up at Franklin. "They're all around..."

"It's an illusion, Doris," Sekima asserted. "They aren't here."

"But... one is touching me." I looked at my father's hand. "I can feel it..."

"I'm not an illusion," Franklin disagreed. "We are all here."

I shuddered, and my heart thumped raucously. I gradually lost strength in my arm.

"Doris, focus." Sekima's voice echoed. "I am here. No one else is here but the three of us."

"I BEG you!" Edna squealed.

I renewed my hold on the knife and applied pressure to her neck.

"You must break the flesh," Sekima guided.

I pushed into her body and severe pain coursed through my neck. I flinched.

"Ah!" I shouted. "What was that??"

"Fight through it. It will hurt."

"I felt like I stabbed myself!" I swallowed hesitantly.

"You did. Keep going."

"I'm a part of you!" Edna wailed. "Please, don't trust her! She's trying to kill us!"

"It hurts..." I murmured. "This can't be right... Lord, this can't be..."

"Doris, I am telling you," Sekima calmly said, "Focus. Edna will say anything, show anything to deter you from what must be done. It is her defense. She does not want to be extricated. Do not give in to her."

"I..." I stared into Edna's terrified eyes.

"It will hurt," she continued. "You will share the pain."

I thought of Nefer. I would release him from the spell and I needed to let him go. I wouldn't be obligated to sacrifice another man. I decided then that I would have to finish this. I stabbed her neck forcefully.

"AAHHH!" she yowled.

I hunched over in excruciating pain. My airways were constrained as I lowered Edna to the floor. I gritted my teeth and shoved the knife deeper. Edna's screams changed to gurgling. As specks appeared in my eyes, I closed them. My lungs burned.

"Quickly, take this," Sekima ordered.

I pried my eyes open to see all the specters were gone. Sekima was beside me, holding a small mason jar out. It took all my strength to reach for it.

"Drain her blood into it, hurry," she urged.

I dragged Edna over the top of the jar and removed the knife.

Her blood gushed into the jar. With her gaze fixed on me, the glow of her eyes slowly faded.

I could breathe again when the light completely disbanded. My head was ready to explode. I was disoriented and nauseous. I touched my neck, expecting to feel a gash but nothing was there. I laid Edna by the jar when the blood flow ceased. Sekima deftly wrapped her body in the cloth. She placed a lid on the jar and picked it up.

"Give me the knife," she said. She climbed out of the baptistery as soon as I handed it to her.

A dull pain initiated in my stomach when I stood up. It increased and became crippling. I dropped back to my knees.

"My stomach..." I griped. I tried to stand again.

"Stay down," Sekima directed.

"What's happening?" I fell down on my hands and knees.

There was a strong pull between my legs. Dark blood whooshed from me and splashed into the baptistery. It poured like a tub faucet. The sensation of intense heat charged through my entire body. I struggled to rise again.

"Stay down."

The heated blood flowed over me as the area filled. When it reached my chin, I held my breath and closed my eyes, becoming submerged in the liquid. Once again, I attempted to get up and failed. It was impossible to withstand the pressure on my chest from holding my breath. I exhaled and blood rushed into my mouth. When it entered my nose, I anticipated drowning, but I was able to breathe. I inhaled the substance and it penetrated me for several minutes. It eventually stopped, allowing me to open my eyes. The bath was empty. The blue glow from above faded and the church was dark.

"Get dressed." Sekima handed me my clothes. "Quickly."

The rain had ended. As we left the church, my headache worsened. I sluggishly followed Sekima back to Nefer's house. I stumbled through his living room and she led me up to his bed. I didn't see Nefer.

"Undress and lie down," she instructed.

I did so, and my eyelids felt heavy.

"Listen to me very carefully." She held the mason jar up. "Beginning tomorrow, drink two ounces of this for five days. Do not drink more, do not drink less. Drink it before noon, and on the fifth day, have Nefer call me. I will place this in his fridge. Do not remove that ring."

"What isssit...?" I slurred, raising my hand to view it.

"Stones that you need. Aragonite, hecatolite and alexandrite. Do not remove that ring." She switched off the light and shut the door.

"But... weh..." I wanted to ask her to delay her exit, but my eyes would not stay open.

Where's Nefer? Doesn't he want to see me? I should shower... I feel filthy...

I sat up and the room swayed. I fell backward.

I sat upright, screaming. My stomach was knotted. It pulsated and felt like barbed wire. I fell out of the bed, writhing in anguish. The room was baking; it must have been over one hundred degrees. I rolled onto my front and crawled toward the door. I barely inched ahead before I lost awareness again.

13

The morning fast approached and I awoke with a hasty beating heart. I was in bed. My arms were weak as I pushed myself to a seated position. I searched around for my phone to see the time. I deduced that it was probably downstairs and exited the room, noticing the other two doors in the hall were closed.

Maybe he's in the room sleeping? I thought.

I tiptoed to the stairs and went down to the kitchen. I found the time on the microwave. It was ten thirty-seven A.M. I opened the fridge and immediately saw the jar of Edna's blood. I stared at it, coming to terms with what I had accomplished.

I killed her. She's really gone...

I didn't know where Sekima took Edna's body. I pulled the jar from the fridge and delicately set it on the table. I searched the drawers for measuring cups. I didn't remember how to convert ounces so I recommenced my hunt for my phone. I found my backpack and purse in Nefer's closet.

The walk-in closet smelled like mothballs and had women's clothing hanging on one side. The items were draped with dust.

Sekima's clothes.

I returned to the kitchen and found a tablespoon in a drawer, then sat at the table.

"Ok," I sighed, unscrewing the lid. I scooped up the thick fluid. I was uncertain what would happen should I ignore instructions, but I had no plans of finding out.

I drank the blood. It had a slightly chalky texture with a mix of sweet and sour flavor. The aftertaste was vaguely bitter. The second tablespoon was salty. The third was also sour and the fourth tasted like a juicy steak. I considered the fact that I was naked and sitting all over Nefer's furniture.

I should wash...

As I placed the jar back in the fridge, I began to feel queasy. My finger itched. I scratched at it, and noticed my nails had grown. The skin around the ring I wore had fused to it. Stunned, I almost vomited. I lethargically made my way to the bathroom and took a shower. When I was drying off, I could hear movement outside the door. I paused in disquiet, waiting for the noises to pass.

I'm scared to see him, but does he want to see me? Does he still have feelings for me? If he did, he would say so...

I opened the door when all was quiet again. The hall was empty and the door across the way was closed. I sighed in relief and snuck to his room. The door creaked loudly while I closed it. My headache manifested again, and I fell into bed.

I grabbed my chest as I stirred. I had dreamt someone was crushing me with a large metal plate. The sun was still out. I reached for my phone, and discovered it was the next day. It was Saturday; the time was nine forty-three A.M. I got up to drink.

It became a routine. I would drink the solution before twelve, become ill and languid, then sleep the rest of the day. I didn't bother putting on clothes. I was comfortable without them. Nefer remained in the guest room. I never saw him when he was out. It was as if he intentionally postponed until I was incapacitated.

On Tuesday, I woke up at seven fifty-five A.M. I elected to get dressed, since Sekima was to be called after I drank the final two ounces. I wore the pajamas Nefer bought me. I worked up the nerve to go to the guest room. I loitered at the door for a while, listening for any commotion inside. No sound could be heard. I balled my sweaty hand into a fist.

Is he sleeping? It's kind of early... I don't want to wake him, but I need him...

I knocked on the door and concentrated again on sounds inside. Creaking from the bed signaled he was getting up. I awkwardly stepped back.

"Yea, I'm here," Nefer announced. He didn't open the door.

"Uh... hi..." I wheezed. "I... uh..."

"Hey... you ready for me to call Sekima...?" He was guarded.

"Yes..." My perspiration expanded. I paced closer to the door and tried the knob. It was locked. "Are you... coming out...?"

"Yea, a little later." He sounded farther away from the door.

"Ok..." I skulked, trying to think of what to say.

When? I haven't seen you in days! Don't you want to see me?

"Fine..." I mumbled.

I entered the kitchen to swallow the last of the jar's contents. My hand stung, then grew very hot and I watched the ring seep into my skin. The site drastically turned cold. It traveled up my arm and through my body. I quavered as the room started to spin. I staggered from the kitchen and up to Nefer's room. My vision blurred while I climbed into the bed, energy draining from me.

I couldn't determine when I fell asleep, but it was dark when my eyes opened. My sight had not cleared. A terrible ache erupted from my abdomen. It felt like my insides were being torn apart. I curled into a fetal position and started to cry.

"Endure," someone whispered.

I lifted my head to look around. I couldn't adjust to the surroundings, but the minimal light inside the room showed no one with me.

Is someone here?

"Sit up," the voice prodded.

I put my head back down, squirming in torment.

"Sit up."

"I can't," I sniveled.

"Sit up... now..."

I grunted laboriously as I pushed myself up. I screamed and swung my legs over the edge.

"Open the window..." the whisper said.

I shook my head, breathing heavily. "I... it hurts... I can't... I..."

"Open it, now..."

I forced myself from the bed and landed on the floor. I shuffled along to reach the window and clutched the sill as I hauled to a seated position. Fumbling with the string of the blinds, I eventually yanked it down. I shoved the window open and the pain was gone. I inhaled the cold night air.

The moon shined full and bright in the sky. A few stars twinkled. I heard soft voices whispering as I stared.

"Are you talking to me...?" I murmured to the moon.

A cool breeze blew over my face, followed by a warmth that showered me. Numbness generated in my toes and crept up my legs.

Images of the church flashed through my mind. I couldn't help but question if I did the right thing by killing Edna. Did I kill all of those men too? Were they waiting for me to complete the ritual? Was this ritual the final sacrifice? I had no reason to speculate. Edna was already gone.

I felt energized and got to my feet. I needed to know what changed with Nefer. He was evading me and I was doing the same. I mustered courage to speak with him as I stood at the guest room's door.

He's in this room with the door locked. He'd better open it for me, or I'm breaking it down. We can't avoid each other anymore. If things are different... I just need to know...

When I gripped the doorknob, it twisted without resistance; the door was unlocked. I pushed it and it swung open with a dull creak. I heard the sound of the bed inside the dark room as he stirred. My heart was ready to burst from my chest. I almost returned to the other room.

"Doris," he called. "Are you... alright?"

The sincerity was unmistakable.

"I..." I croaked, on the verge of tears.

"Come here."

I charily crossed the room toward his words. I touched the bed and could faintly see him sitting up. I sat on the edge.

"Are you alright...?" he asked again.

"I... think so..." I felt his hand rest on mine. "...I..."

The sensation was welcoming and I erupted in tears. I pulled my hand away to cover my face.

"Come here." He embraced me powerfully.

I continued to weep as I hugged him back.

"I'm sorry," he shakily whispered.

I swallowed. "W... Why?"

"I've... I haven't been good to you," he admitted. He kissed my neck. "All you've been through. I've just been so selfish. I'm sorry..."

I stopped crying. "You've been good to me..."

"No, I haven't. I've been selfish. Now that your cat is gone... I see everything much more clearly."

"Yes, she's gone..." I sniffled.

"She told me my feelings were from her. She was right." He released me. "Doris, you've been used your whole life, even by me. I'm so sorry. Please, forgive me."

"Well..." I wiped my tears. "Yes, I do. I mean... You didn't have a choice..."

"No, I didn't, but now I do. And how I was to you, is not who I am. I wanted to help you so we could... spend more time together. I needed to help you. Ever since we met, you were all I could think about. It got worse every day after. I heard your body calling to me.

You told me everything you wanted, and I wanted to do everything you asked..."

"You didn't have a choice, Nefer..."

"You've tested my will... my faith..." He sighed. "Sekima tested everything..."

"I... you have control now. We can find out what this all means."

"Yes, we can. Before... I didn't actually care."

"But... but you helped me." I defended. "You said you wanted to do everything I asked..."

"I did all those things to free you from that demon, so that I could make you happy."

"Sekima told you how to help me. She said that I would save everyone..."

"Anytime I went to her, it was to find out what I needed to do to get rid of the cat. Sekima told me I couldn't do it, that you had to do it..." He scooted off the bed. "It was harder to tell the difference between what I wanted and what you wanted. I keep replaying in my head... over and over... when you told me about your childhood... about your father... and that woman. About all those years you were... selling your body. It's horrible. But, at the time when you told me I only thought of how that demon made you give yourself to other men. I only thought of how you needed to be free... you WANTED to be free. So, you and I could come together..."

He was pacing the room apprehensively. "But... then I learn that I'm not controlling these feelings. An—and I just, I didn't know what was real. I didn't feel like myself... I'm sorry, I really am..."

"Just, stop," I ordered. I rose from the bed. "Stop."

He halted. "Sorry."

"And stop saying sorry!" I flicked on the light. "And it's too dark in here!! Shit."

I squinted against the brightness.

"I'm feeling really bad about this whole thing." He muttered. "I can't help saying it right now."

The undershirt he wore was ragged and he obviously hadn't been shaving.

"You don't need to say it," I responded. "I can... sense it and I know how you feel. I just... I was scared your feelings would die with Edna..."

"Edna...?"

"My... cat."

He stared at me, opening his mouth to reply.

"If you say you're sorry, I'm going to slap you," I warned.

He smiled and came over to kiss my forehead, grazing me with his prickly facial hair.

"So... Sekima... she said to call her..." I took hold of his hands.

"We'll see her in the morning," he said, then sighed heavily. "I'm tired as shit. I haven't been getting much sleep..."

"Ok... bed then." I switched off the light.

"My bed, though..." He shoved me out of the room and we went to his.

$$\sim\sim * \sim\sim$$

We arrived at Sekima's house a little after eleven thirty A.M. on Wednesday morning.

Usually, my menstrual cycle would have entered at midnight. The event did not occur. I was free from Edna, the blood cycle, and the sacrifices.

Since Nefer was no longer being controlled, he informed me that he was still conflicted by what transpired between us and that

Sekima was the only other woman he had been with. He vowed to retain his abstinence.

I strove to respect his wishes, but more so I yearned for him to be inside of me again.

Nefer used the knocker on the front door. A few minutes passed before Sekima answered. She wore a cream-colored cable knit sweater and dark denim jeans. Her hair was cornrowed with a braided bun.

"Come," she beckoned. She walked away from the door. "Outside."

We followed her downstairs and through the den to a paved patio out back. Patio furniture was positioned around an ignited fire pit. There was a stone path through the yard beyond that had vast vegetation. Sekima sat in one of the chaise lounges, pointing at another chair as she looked at me.

I anxiously sat down.

"Nefer," she said composedly, "The items we spoke of, please go get them."

He reentered the house without replying.

"So..." Sekima began with a grin, "here we are again. You can ask me anything you wish, but know what must be done, will be done. If you are to gain cognizance of it before the time comes... I suggest you choose your words wisely."

"Civilization," I answered. "You said that it was artificial and that our leaders are using it to complete ascension. You said that... I am going to destroy it. That, my... God... is human..."

Lord, that isn't true, is it? I gulped and trembled.

"Is that your question?" she inquired, arching an eyebrow.

"Huh? I..." I endeavored to ask her one.

"Your civilization depends on your trust and obedience. It encourages you to relinquish your determination in exchange for boundless dependency. You accept this because it is presented as a customary benefit. They have called it... outsourcing, or any delineation of this term. Fundamentally, you waive your competency under the impression that you are ameliorating while saving time and effort. You submit yourself to a mammon system that maintains no opulence at all. You labor for equality, under the misconception that this means you are the same. Your sins... they are nourished by every aspect of your society and I must stress the fact that they are interferences."

"You said my demon is not a demon," I pointed out.

"It is not." She shook her head, glancing down the path through the back yard. "It is a superior airborne protozoan that was constructed to monitor the chemical discrepancies that affect behavior. The initial creation was to aid with ascension by identifying, isolating, and extracting abnormalities. The microorganism was discovered along with the monitors for it. Instead of using it as intended, the eukaryote has corrupted and become a malignant parasite. Its cells were designed to bond with specific blood types. In order to take physical form, the parasite fused with a feline and gained sanction with you. The shadow you viewed is the parasite. The other microorganisms are currently in the possession of your leaders. Each one targets the chemical stimulants and neurotransmitters that form all manners of sin."

"The others... the ones you spoke of...?" I envisioned other parasites that ingested people.

She slowly turned to look at me. "Yes. They have been conditioned to complete the final sacrifice for ascension. Despite the discovery of the microorganism, it is still unknown by your leaders how to apply it. Which is why they collaborate with me."

"Your company..."

"What do you know about the Golden Ratio, Doris?" She lightly thumped her left index finger on the lounge's armrest.

"The what?"

"The Golden Ratio. It is also called the Golden Spiral."

"I don't... know what that is." I shrugged.

"It has been used to attain what is considered perfect symmetry... an equation with a sequence of numbers. I will not outline the details to you, but know it is the formula for natural ascension."

"I thought that you would tell me all I am doing..."

"I will." She nodded in affirmation. "I don't need to explain your nature to you, though. You will be as you are without clarification, once your reversion is complete. The Abacus provides the integers for ascension."

"How are... my leaders going to complete the man-made ascension?"

"This man-made ascension... To achieve this, it requires the elements buried in this earth and the living creatures that inhabit it to contribute until desolation." She raised her finger to the sky. "The mass investments in climate change and space travel are disputed as bogus on many accounts. The atmosphere is being studied and replicated through data gained from all efforts toward the environment. Spacecrafts have been built to carry your leaders and their chosen. It is believed that the accumulation of capital is to disguise illicit activities for world domination by your country. They maneuver the tendencies of funds and goods through an exchange market. Not to discredit the accusations, but I will say that it is not the main goal. The pursuit of centralization is vital to ensure that all supply lines are available to support their synthetic mission. The ascendants informed humans of the devastating effects, and have provided aid in correcting the matter. Unfortunately, it is not enough to merely amend the path. Your leaders obtained the instruments for improvement and over time they have used them to separate those decided to be unworthy of the truth. The most recent method of doing so is by reconstructing society to run on automation."

"So, why not just destroy everyone?" I tried to understand. "Why are you using this... golden ratio?"

"The intemperance of your population will cause humanity to expire." She clasped her hands together on her lap. "Death would be the typical course of resetting the cycle, except humans are decimating the earth. The earth is like a crib, and humans are its children. The ascendants are not here to murder children of the Creator. They are in need of guidance. The reason for intervention is to prevent the earth from obliteration before the damage is irreparable. This was home to the ascendants once and is home to every generation after. That is the cycle."

"The Creator..."

"Your God, is a concept that your leaders crafted for you," she responded evenly. "You pray to your God, but the Creator holds your fate."

"Then I've been reading a lie..." I visualized Reverend Eriksen.

"Not necessarily. The words are masked and reveal themselves to those who decipher the language. It deliberately has many interpretations. Although, certain details have been reformed so that individual peoples find them relatable to their circumstances."

"You keep saying my leaders... do you mean like the president and government and all that?"

She laughed. "Hmm... Your country's government acts on behalf of your leaders and they receive their priorities from these principal committees. The Committees of Ascension."

"I doubt they'd let you stop their plans... And if they're above the government, they have to know what you're doing."

"Your leaders and I have come to a mutual agreement on conservation."

"All those men I sacrificed..." My head began aching. "...did they die for nothing?"

"No, not for nothing..." She looked back out at the yard. "You received instructions from a fragmented source. Edna, as you named her, directed you on a sacrifice that you were yet to make. You primed the men by feeding them your blood. The parasite consumed those men to collect their elements, but their potency is so nominal that it stipulated an offering on the schedule you tolerated for forty-two years. The parasite thrived on the sensations, and that led to the hundreds who perished."

"They're dead..." I was repentant.

I understood that Edna's pleas were to avoid death, but a part of me hoped I didn't also kill all of those men.

"They are dead," she confirmed, "yet their essence remains. You will complete the final sacrifice, and they will inherently be free. All of mankind will."

"Why did I have to do that for so long? I sacrificed so many..."

"It had to occur..." She kept her eyes on the backyard.

"But all those men... it's not right that they died. They didn't even know what they were dying for. I didn't even know..."

"I know you are remorseful, Doris, but the concept of right and wrong is a matter of oversight. I cannot say anything to support the circumstances ... but we could not disrupt the sequence of actions. Casualties are a result of inaccuracy. There is a great deal of that in this world."

"Edna is gone now. So how is this going to bring ascension?"

"Edna was a shell that carried the parasite in her blood. The parasite was meant to unite with you and it has successfully done so. Ascension will occur after the final sacrifice. Your body is preparing for this. It needs continuous preparation, for time has caused mass injury to your physiology." She rose up from the lounge. "You will need to consume a supplement for the next three weeks. Nefer should have finished loading the containers in his car. You will finish one gallon each day..."

"Wait, you didn't tell me how I will bring ascension." I stood up.

"As I said, with the final sacrifice."

Nefer came walking out of the house almost immediately after she completed her sentence.

"Hey, sorry I took so long," he said.

"It's alright, my dear Nefer," Sekima replied. She and I stared at each other. "We have no more words to trade at this time..."

I started to sweat.

"Ok, so I put those jugs in my car..." he stated.

"Thank you." She nodded.

"I'll... be in the car...?" He was indecisive.

"Yes," Sekima agreed. "Doris will be right behind you."

He nodded and left again.

I pointed at the house. "He...??"

Sekima squinted her eyes at me.

"What is Nefer to all this...?" I felt sick. "Why did you even marry him?"

"I must first tell you," she answered slowly, "Nefer and I were never married."

"But you were pregnant," I objected. "He said you... lost the baby..."

"Nefer has never been married. He never conceived children."

How could Nefer have lied to me? I would have sensed it!

"But... he said..."

"What Nefer told you is a memory from his father," she notified.

"Huh..."

"Nefer is not my husband. He is my son."

"Your... son..."

"All of Nefer's memories are a reproduction of his father's. Some of his father's experiences retained their congruity during his conduction. They were so powerful that they embedded as recollections."

"His father... you're his mother..."

"Nefer's father, as his father before him, and so on, bequeathed his genetic code."

"Why...?"

"To preserve his blood."

"He's like Edna...? So, he's just a blood sac then??"

She chuckled, but I didn't find it humorous. "No. He is not just a 'blood sac'. He was meant to interact with you. This should be evident by now."

"What about the visions we had?" I recalled the creature present in them.

"Splintered memories and a secondary outcome."

"I saw something with three eyes..."

"Yes..."

"Was it... the Creator...?"

"The Creator is not an 'it'... and no. You did not see the Creator." She began to enter the house. "Nefer is waiting for you..."

"But—"

She was inside before I could dispute.

I ran behind her, but she seemed to disappear. I exited her home and met Nefer out front. He was in his car, listening to music I didn't recognize. I opened the passenger side door and he turned the music down when I didn't get in.

"Hey, you ready?" he asked.

"No..." I responded.

"What's wrong?"

"Sekima... told me some... things."

"Well, I put a bunch of gallons in the trunk... some stuff you're supposed to drink that'll help with the after effects of your cat... or something like that. We gotta refrigerate them."

"Not about that... about you."

"Like what?"

"She said you were never married."

He frowned, perplexed. "Why would she tell you that?"

"I don't know..." I muttered.

"Huh? I can't hear you. Are you gonna get in?"

Why is it so hard to tell him?

"I said, I don't know..." I sat down in the car. "She also told me you were made for me, pretty much..."

He laughed.

"That's funny?" I was surprised.

"Yea, it is. Well, that's how it's felt anyway." He shrugged. "Even now that your cat is gone. I feel the same."

I gulped restlessly.

"Woman, speak," he ordered, smiling.

I stared at the windshield. I felt him watching me. "I think... you should talk to Sekima..."

"About what?"

"I..." My face grew hot and I felt a pain in my chest. "She told me something..."

"Babe, it's ok... Just tell me." He placed his hand on mine, and a tingling sensation went through me. He pulled away. "Hmm, you shocked me."

"Sorry..." I rubbed my hands together. "Not sure why it's so hard to talk..."

"We both know you don't talk much." He laughed again. He touched my hand and this time there was only warmth. "Whatever it is, we'll deal with it."

I was sweating. "Sekima said... you're not her ex. You're her son."

"Her son..." he narrowed his eyes.

"She said you... your memories are from your father. They aren't yours."

"But..." he was shaking his head. He turned off the car.

"What do you remember about your life? I mean... really remember?" My heart hammered.

"I remember plenty." He was confident. "I've lived in the same house all my life, same town. My dad raised me. My mother..."

"What happened to your mother?"

"She died... when I was a baby." He answered with uncertainty.

"You grew up in town... what school did you go to?" I asked. "You told me your dad passed away. Do you remember how?"

He didn't reply.

"How did you meet Sekima?" I continued. "When did you meet her? She was still in school, right? What school? Do you remember your birthday?"

"I did..." He stated slowly. "I do remember... I remember my birthday..."

"What's your dad's name? Your mother's? Do you remember what you were doing before Sekima came back?"

"This makes no sense..." He was growing alarmed. "I know those things. I... know them. I just can't remember..."

"If Sekima is your mother... None of what you remember will be true."

"Why would... why would she not tell me this?!" He yanked his keys from the ignition.

"What do you remember, Nefer?"

He got out of the car.

"Ok, then..." I climbed out and shut the door.

He was already at the front door, banging forcefully. Sekima opened it with a smile.

"Nefer," she said, "You seem upset."

"You're my mother?" he demanded, combative.

She glanced at me. "I am."

I felt dizzy.

"Why did you let me think you were my ex-wife?!" His hands were fists.

"Come in." She stepped aside. "You're letting the heat out."

She led us to the sitting room and sat on the pale green couch. She pointed to matching armchairs by the loveseat.

"Why didn't you tell me?" Nefer asked. He was in the doorway and I stood behind him.

The room was rocking, so I pushed past him to sit on the loveseat.

"Sit down," Sekima responded.

He complied, sitting beside me.

"I did tell you, my dear," she said smoothly, crossing her legs. "You declined to hear it."

"No," he rebutted. "I'd remember this."

"You would not. You do not."

He stared at the floor, shaking his head.

"Humans spend so much of their lives working against time," She watched Nefer. "Chasing age-reversing techniques, such as transforming their bodies, sampling experimental pharmaceuticals, consuming genetically modified foods and supplements... cloning... Scientific inventions allow for a wide assortment of procedures to try to stave its progression. The fact remains that time will inevitably prevail over organic creatures... with impatience it is an enemy... but used wisely, it is an ally."

She's going somewhere with this... I narrowed my eyes.

"My point is," she resumed, "it was not time for you to digest the information..."

"His father," I remarked. "Who is he? How old is Nefer...?"

"I answered this. Nefer is his father. To maintain integrity, he has been reborn, and he is currently thirty-four years old."

"How old are you?" I stared at her face, wondering if there were wrinkles that I hadn't identified.

She laughed. "Doris, do you think I'm immortal?"

"You said you're not an ascendant. Are you human?"

"I am human. I cannot tell you my age. The recording of such measurement is not applicable."

"How many times has he been reborn?"

"He has been reborn fifty-nine times."

I looked at Nefer, who sat speechless. He glanced at me, and opened his mouth to speak. He quickly closed it and stared at the wall.

"The final sacrifice, what is it?" I wanted to throw up.

"Doris, it is crucial that your sentiments do not obscure your judgment. The final sacrifice is necessary for true vindication by the Creator. To correct the imbalance and to reveal humanity's purpose."

"Which is...?"

"What you ask, you are not prepared for."

"How is she getting prepared?" Nefer spoke.

"With the supplement," she answered.

"Then she's not free from the cat..." he was upset. "And neither am I..."

"You are," Sekima assured. "Edna's influence over you has been contained. You react all on your own."

"What do I gotta do? Since I'm not in control of myself..." He stood up.

"You are, Nefer..." I lightly held his hand.

"She will need your support," Sekima advised. "The process will not agree with her."

"I'm..." He briefly squeezed my hand. "I'll be in the car, Doris."

I got up. "Wait, Nefer..."

He left.

"Let him go." Sekima said. "All is as it will be."

"I'm trying to ask you what it will be and you won't tell me." My head was pounding.

"Drink one gallon each day. Your mind has been conditioned by an unnatural system and it will not be comprehended. Do you trust me, Doris?"

I hadn't considered how much until she'd asked, but I did. This unnerved me.

"Yes." I acknowledged.

"I have not provided any substantial evidence, this I know. I do apologize." She was staring at the doorway. "Ingest the supplement so that you may fathom perceptions..."

I left her house once more. Nefer was in the car, blasting music. He pulled off as soon as I entered the car. He sped the entire way, which incited panic while we zipped down the narrow roads. His motions had extra effort, and when we arrived at his house, he could have broken the gear shift with the way he handled it.

I got out, but he stayed inside the car. After a few seconds, I walked to the driver side window and knocked. He eventually lowered it, keeping the music loud.

"Can you open your trunk!?" I shouted. "You can sit there, just open the trunk!"

He turned off the car.

I went to the back and waited. The trunk popped open and he rushed around.

"I got it," he attested. He gave me his keys.

"Fine..." I grabbed one of the gallons from a crate then opened his front door. I left it open for him and headed straight to the kitchen. My phone vibrated in my pocket.

It was Harriett.

"What," I replied.

"Doris...?" she said. "May I speak to Doris?"

"This is Doris, Harriett."

"Oh, hello! I wasn't sure. You sound different..."

"Ok."

"Uh, I am calling because I think I have some more mail for you. It's been a little while and you still haven't given me a forwarding address... but this looks important. I am sure of it."

"Uh huh." I placed the gallon on the table and removed the lid to smell the contents. It was flowery.

"I think you may want to come get it—"

"Open it." I grabbed a glass and poured the liquid into it. It was watery and brown.

Nefer arrived with a crate.

"Open it?" she asked.

"Yes."

"But it's your mail..."

"Open it... please..."

"Ok." She sounded a little excited. There was silence. "It says... that... your automatic payment failed to process for your October loan statement... and that, uh... 'please send payment by November fifteenth to avoid further penalties'... Whoa, that's a lot of money..."

I watched Nefer stacking the crates by the fridge. "Ok..."

He stopped what he was doing to look at me.

"Do you want to come get this?" she queried.

"No."

"Oh... but... well, yikes... that's a lot of money..."

"Got it, thanks." I hung up.

"Everything good?" Nefer asked.

"Yes..." I put my phone on the table and sat down. "Did... Sekima tell you what's in this stuff...?"

He was readjusting the shelves in the fridge, but sighed when I mentioned her name. He nodded and shrugged.

"Yea..." he replied, agitated. "She said... a mix of extracts from... Nympho—something. I can't... remember..."

This seemed to anger him. He shoved a gallon into the fridge.

"Ok..." I whispered, lifting the glass to study the liquid. Tiny dark flakes swam around.

Nefer finished putting the containers away and sat at the table with me.

"What Sekima said..." he began, eyeing the glass, "I'm her son..."

"Yes..."

"She... slept with me, with her son..."

"Uh..." I shifted in the seat and cleared my throat. "You actually haven't slept with anyone, but me..."

He pointed at the cup. "You should drink that."

"I should..." I poured a little into my mouth. I quickly put it down, almost spitting. "Bleck! It's gross!"

It had an incredibly bitter medicinal taste.

He bent forward and sniffed it. "Smells like flowers."

"Yes, but it tastes disgusting! There's no way I can drink this for three weeks!"

"Maybe drink it fast...?" He pushed the gallon closer to me. "Straight out the jug?"

"Ugh..." I grabbed the handle, sickened. "Maybe..."

He stared at me for a time, before he said with regret, "I'm being insensitive..."

"Well, I have to drink this. I get your suggestion."

"No, what I said before. About my... about Sekima. Her sleeping with her son..."

"Huh? Ohh..." I heard my father's voice in my head, telling me he was saved. "Don't start apologizing. Not today. I'm not thinking of it like that. Sekima said she's your mother. You're allowed to be shocked.... And, plus... my father is gone... I'm still here. I'm ok. What happened to me... That doesn't make me who I am. Please, just... be yourself to me. It's fine. Whatever, ok?"

He appeared deep in thought. After a few seconds, he said, "You told me about what you've been through, but I still don't know you.

You know, like, what you like to do. What do you like? I know how you feel... but when I bought those things for you, I didn't know what to get you. I had to ask a woman at the store."

I smiled. "Ok, but can we talk after I drink this...? It's hard enough as it is..."

I needed time to answer his question. I had spent very little energy on what I liked.

What do I like...?

"Sure." He leaned back and crossed his arms.

I hastily tilted the gallon and the fluid swished into my mouth. I gulped, gagging. "Bleh..."

Nefer watched me, making a sour face.

"Nefer, go away," I covered my mouth, nauseous. "You're distracting me..."

"I'll be in the living room..." He left the room.

"Ugh." I drank more and eventually could tolerate the flavor to empty the container. I rinsed my mouth with water and as I exited the kitchen, my head started to pulse. I walked over to Nefer, growing sick.

"Hey, how do you feel?" he asked, standing up.

"Well..." I sat on the couch. My mouth was overly salivated. "I feel like I'm going to throw up."

"Oh..." He pulled a blanket from the back of the couch and draped it around me. "Lie down."

"Yea..." I fell over onto my side. "I'm going to throw up... I think..."

"The bathroom is right there by the stairs." He pointed to the door at the left of the TV.

I closed my eyes. "Ok..."

Just close your eyes... it'll pass... please don't throw up on yourself...

The room swayed. When I opened my eyes, Nefer was gone. I saw Edna sitting on the coffee table.

"Wha—" I breathed, swallowing back spit and vomit.

"Hello there, you," she addressed. Her eyes glowed like neon signs, rocking with the room.

I wiped my sweaty forehead. "How..."

"I missed you," she purred. She floated to the arm of the couch. "Did you miss me?"

"No..." My limbs shook as I propped onto my elbow.

"No? How rude."

"You can't be here..." I shook my head. "Ugh..."

Nefer was walking downstairs with a trash can. He came to the side of the coffee table, directly by Edna.

I pointed at her with a wavering finger as he placed the can in front of the couch.

"What?" he asked, turning to look at the wall.

He doesn't see her. She's not here... Lord, she can't be...

"Still calling on your Lord?" Edna asked, slanting her head. "Forever faithful, you are being heard..."

"I..." I reached for the can. "I need... that..."

He held it up for me and I shoved my face inside as I heaved. I hiccupped, retched and choked.

He sat on the coffee table, keeping the can steady. "If it makes you feel any better, it still smells like flowers."

"It doesn't." I threw up again, snatching the can. "Go away..."

The urge passed and I set the can on the floor. I shivered from an icy breeze that flowed through the room. I shut my eyes and felt heat on my forehead. My eyes snapped open to see Nefer was pressing the back of his hand to it. The sensation was pleasant.

"Mmm..." I moaned. I tried to touch him. "You... feels... good... sssooo..."

My speech was slurred. I felt inebriated. I spotted Edna, levitating by the TV. I pointed. I laughed.

"Doris," Nefer's voice echoed, "Try to sleep..."

"But..." Drool spilled out and ran along my cheek. I attempted to rub it away. "Ew..."

I was beginning to feel queasy.

Nefer swiped a cloth across my face.

"Hey!" I shouted. I swung my arm to repel him, but slapped myself in the face. "Ow..."

"Doris, rest." He sounded like he was in my ear.

"Hey... ssstop... yelling..." I blinked slowly. "Ugh..."

I threw up.

$$\sim\sim\ ^*\sim\sim$$

I woke up groggy with a splitting headache. The living room was drowned in black. I rose to a seated position and discovered my shirt was missing.

"Oh..." I mumbled.

"Hey..." Nefer was there.

"Oh, hell! Nefer, what the fuck! You... you're just sitting in the dark??"

"I wanted to make sure you were good through the night..." He got up and turned the light on.

"My shirt..." I had my eyes closed.

"It got dirty."

"I threw up on it."

"Yea..."

I looked around. "Where else...?"

"Just your shirt and the blanket..." He indicated the new one that covered me. "No real harm. And it didn't stink..."

I shook my head. "I can't drink that for three weeks..."

"It may not be like that the whole time. Maybe..." He walked over to me, my phone in his hand. "Your phone rang a bunch of times. It was your landlord, so I answered it."

"My... landlord...?" I was slow to realize. "Oh..."

"Uh, Harrietta? She said she needs a forwarding address for mail. She told me you had a loan that was a lot of money... don't know why she told me that, actually..."

"Ugh..." I massaged my temple.

"Do you have a forwarding address...?"

"Please don't tell me you gave her yours..."

He laughed. "No, no, I didn't... but... do you have a place?"

I sighed. "I don't..."

I know where this is going...

"You can stay here as long as you need," he offered.

"I'm already here like it's my place..." I remarked. I took my phone. The time was ten fifty-one P.M.

"Which is fine. I think you should stay."

I know.

I checked my email. I ruminated over all we were doing. I was young again. My cat, or, the vessel that held the parasite, was gone. I wasn't bleeding, which was a huge relief. Was the end that Sekima spoke of an actual event? Were we really part of a plan that needed us to stay ignorant? I couldn't explain why I deemed her words as truth.

Why would she lie about being Nefer's mother? Why would she put him through all this? How did she make me see that vision? She helped me. She knew how to help me.

"Will you stay?" Nefer questioned.

I had almost forgotten the subject of our conversation.

"Not really a lot of options here..." I responded.

"How do you feel? Better?"

"A little…" I laughed sheepishly. I'd never had anyone ask me how I felt so many times in my entire life. I was embarrassed that he'd seen all manner of fluids come out of my body.

"Sounds promising. Three weeks may not be so bad."

14

Nefer's prediction of my condition over the next three weeks wasn't far off. For the first week, I vomited every day after drinking the gallon. My instincts impelled me to bear it and by the next week I simply felt nauseated. By the middle of that second week, Edna no longer appeared to me and I didn't grow as fatigued. The taste wasn't affected by this improvement. I repeatedly struggled through half the contents before it became acceptable. Nefer recalled the word Sekima told him about the drink. It was Nymphaeaceae.

During this time, Nefer and I conversed more on my interests. I had very little. This spurred him to include me in his routines, since I was now living with him. When I was able, we began each morning with early exercise, which I wasn't entirely enthused about. There was a gym he frequented close to town. I would drag through his workout and complain about its intensity. He helped me with my form and his energy encouraged me to keep at it. It was almost fun. Once a week, Nefer would go for a jog. I opted out of this action.

He liked to go to the local farmers market on Saturdays, so that was what we did on the second weekend. The vibe of the market was pleasant and people were sincerely excited to trade their wares. He made meals and attempted to get me involved. I had no hunger for anything. I was tasked with whatever didn't require the stove or oven. Surprisingly, I participated. It was established that my skills were poor, but it didn't prevent me from an occasional potato peeling or cheese grating.

We didn't speak much on the events of the church until that Sunday. It was the twenty-fourth. I asked him if he found another church to attend. He hadn't and he didn't plan to. I could tell this was disturbing him.

"What I saw..." he had told me that morning, "it's hard to describe..."

I was there... I thought. I knew it was more of an impact for him.

"Have you spoken to Reverend Eriksen?" I asked. I sensed his unease without hearing his response.

We reclined on the couch and he was massaging my feet.

"Yea..." He squeezed my foot and started to rub my ankle.

He was running for his life when I last saw him.

"What did he say...?"

He shrugged and shook his head. "It's not really what he said... I just..."

"What is it? Did he do something?"

"Well, yea... but I just keep thinking about all that's happened. I know we don't talk about it, but..."

"I didn't want to make you talk if you're not ready..."

He stopped caressing me while his discomfort increased. "I feel like I'm on a roller coaster. Everything is happening at once and I don't fully understand any of it. Before all this, I was sure of my life. I was sure of myself before..."

Before me.

"You were sure before you met me," I proposed. I sat up and repositioned to tuck my feet underneath me. "I know."

"Yes... but not because of you. Sekima..." He paused and bit his bottom lip in agitation.

"Sorry, I didn't mean to bring this up..."

"No, it's alright." He leaned forward and tapped my knee. "Gimme your feet..."

Nefer had called Sekima a few days prior. He was upset with her, but it passed. The majority of his memories were not his. What he told me about his relationship with Sekima was a blend of those memories and his own imagination.

"Sekima almost lost a baby," he explained, "it was a long time ago. There was no guy with green eyes, but I remember the eyes like it was yesterday..."

Sekima revealed that he had grown up at the house we were in and so did his father. She bought the house in nineteen fifty-one. She lived in the plantation home since its construction in eighteen thirty-four and inherited it upon the original owner's death. The title deed was currently in Nefer's name. She came to America sometime during the early seventeenth century.

I asked him how it was possible that he couldn't remember the particulars of his childhood.

"According to Sekima, they were replaced," he replied, shaken. "When my father died, I forgot most of my real memories."

"How and when did he die...?"

"Don't know. She just said it wasn't an accident."

"That's not very reassuring..."

"Well, could be natural causes...?"

"Like of old age...? I don't think so..." I frowned.

Nefer was bothered by this and began complaining. I eventually had to tell him to stop despairing about theories of the past.

"We're here now," I said. "Making real memories."

Sekima was on travel and not answering any calls.

On Monday, we cleaned his house and donated all the women's clothes in the main bedroom closet. I moved my clothes out of my car.

I was straightening up the guest room while he vacuumed downstairs. Inside the closet, I found art supplies. Containers with paint and brushes were on the upper shelf. A few canvases sat on the floor. The first two were blank and the one in the back had various triangles painted in shades of purple and looked unfinished. I grabbed it and went to Nefer.

"What's this?" I queried, pointing at it.

He switched off the vacuum and set it upright. He squinted at the canvas, stumped.

"It looks like a bunch of triangles," he answered. "Where'd you find that?"

"In the guest room closet. Did you paint this?"

"I guess... but I don't know what it is..." He was about to start the vacuum again.

"Why don't you paint anymore?" I quickly asked before he turned it on.

He shrugged casually. "I don't feel like it. It probably wasn't me anyway..."

This had become his approach to anything related to his habits or memory.

"Don't you even start. Damn it, Nefer, you can't mope around the house forever!" I was growing irritated with his attitude. "I feel all that and it makes me depressed!"

He stared at me.

"Look, I know how you feel, just like you know how I feel." I set the painting down against the wall and crossed my arms. "I feel your doubt, ok? And I have it too... I don't know what to think of all this. I was told I've been praying to a human. Are people going to Mars? Is there an ascension? Is the world ending? I don't know, maybe? Maybe not? How would we know? We went out to that market and people were happy. I just... I look at myself and I still can't believe I'm young... My... the thing that I've been doing most of my life is over. Sekima..."

He still didn't speak. His shoulders tensed and he peered at the painting on the floor.

"She hasn't lied to us, has she?" I asked. "I feel... strongly about what she says. I don't know, I think she's telling us the truth..."

He walked over and picked up the canvas.

"She said something that I've been thinking a lot about," he replied, running his finger along one of the triangles. "About ascension. About harnessing our sins..."

My heart was pounding.

He furrowed his eyebrows. "I think of the sacrifice made for our sins..."

"There is a final sacrifice," I answered, "but she wouldn't tell me what it is."

I was afraid that I already knew.

He sighed. "I'm really trying not to be in a bad mood."

We finished cleaning up the house.

Nefer's temperament improved by the following day and he wanted to go to the supermarket on Wednesday morning for some reason.

"Come with me," he said.

He was getting dressed while I sat on his bed.

"Uh..." I traced a pattern on the bedspread.

"I know you hate shopping, but you did so good at the market. I just gotta get something..."

"What?"

"Just something." He carefully pulled socks from the dresser drawer.

I raised an eyebrow in suspicion.

He turned toward me. "I wanna make dinner. Thanksgiving dinner."

"Ohh... uhh..."

I had observed the town was decorated for the season. I was so absorbed in the little world we made in the house that I disregarded the holidays approaching.

"I just wanna do something..." He paused. "Something... normal."

"I'll get dressed..."

Nefer had gathered ingredients when we went to the market but needed other items that weren't available during our trip. I had no intention of eating any of what he planned to prepare. My appetite remained absent. We headed to the supermarket.

We were in the frozen foods aisle and Nefer browsed whipped cream containers when a woman called his name.

"Is that you?" she called, eager and amazed.

Stella strolled over, holding a half-filled shopping basket. Her smile slowly faded when her eyes glided from him to me. A small amount of aggression formed inside of her.

"Hello," he greeted, pulling his selection from the freezer, "Sta... Stacey."

"Wow, you still don't know my name? It's Stella." She glared at him, offended. "Is that why you don't call me, text me, or anything?"

"No..." He disagreed. "I... I'm not trying to be rude, Stella. If I led you on, I'm sorry. It's just, I'm with my lady right now and we're trying to shop."

He motioned at me with his free hand.

"Your LADY?" Her hostility deepened as she looked me over in disgust.

I studied her face. She wore an excessive amount of makeup that gave her the appearance of a doll. The foundation was noticeably lighter than the natural complexion of her neck. Her eyebrows were thick stenciled arches. Her long false eyelashes sprouted from a liberal amount of eyeliner. She had bright pink lipstick on her lips.

She was dressed in a fuchsia sweater and light blue jeans under an unbuttoned taupe trench coat. Her nails were like cat claws and she ran one hand down through her straight hair, as if to smooth it out. She impatiently rolled her tongue in her mouth and gazed at my hair.

I watched her silently. I was rapidly overwhelmed with the impression of our station in society. I sensed her swelling anger towards me, and it was clear she believed I took something that belonged to her. I found her resentment misplaced and the very conversation meaningless.

"Yea," he confirmed, "And—"

"So, what, you like all-natural women," Stella cut her eyes at him, "Is that it?"

"It's not that..." he stated. "I mean, do you. It's your body."

"Damn right it's my body!" She rolled her eyes. "Fuck you, Nefer!"

She stomped away shortly after.

Nefer was embarrassed. "I..."

I shook my head.

"I have nothing against her looks..." he assured me.

"Doesn't matter," I answered, continuing to shake my head.

"I do like your looks, though..." He put his arm around my shoulders and kissed my forehead.

I smiled with appreciation but couldn't dismiss the feeling that arose from the encounter. It persisted as I observed the other people shopping in the store.

As soon as we returned to the house, Nefer began cooking. I sat at the kitchen table, peeling sweet potatoes.

"I know I said I wanted to do something normal," He was at the stove, "but normally I'd be doing this for church..."

"If you want to, we still can," I suggested.

"Well... we can bring them the extra food..." He sighed. "I... I'm just thinking out loud. I... have a new perspective on everything."

"What perspective is that...?"

He moved to the sink and washed his hands. "A perspective from the top, instead of the bottom..."

I started to chop the potatoes. "Hmm..."

"I need to run back to the store real quick. I'll be back." He exited the kitchen.

I decided to lie down in bed after I finished cutting the food. I closed my eyes for a while and opened them upon hearing Nefer's voice.

"Your phone is off," he remarked. "Is it dead?"

"No," I answered, sitting up. "I haven't paid the bill."

My phone service had sent me a message warning of the disconnection and I overlooked it.

"How many bills haven't you paid...?" He stepped over to the bed.

"Uh... just a couple. I don't have many." I picked up my phone from beside me. I must have slept for an hour.

"Your loan?"

My missed loan payment was another notice I neglected. I was convinced that I didn't need to agonize over what I owed any longer. I was either going to be right, or I would have some really terrible credit by the end of all this and debt collectors after me.

"My loan sucks." I tossed my phone back onto the bed.

"Here." He pulled a card out of his wallet. "Pay your phone, though. I wanna be able to call you."

"You don't have to..."

"It's fine, take it." He placed it down at the foot of the bed. "We need to keep in touch."

He left the room and I went back to sleep. The house smelled like a restaurant when I rose again and reluctantly paid my phone bill.

Since he doesn't like that he can't call me...

I went to the kitchen and saw that Nefer completed the meal. The counters had plates and bowls of food. The dishes were washed and he was preparing a plate. Another plate sat ready on the kitchen table.

"I made you a plate," he said.

"I'm not going to eat," I replied, sitting down. "I'm not hungry."

"Are you gonna throw up?" He came over and sat down with his plate. He picked up a pitcher of tea to fill two glasses.

"No, I do feel nauseous, but I'm just not hungry. I haven't been hungry for weeks."

"Maybe it's that stuff you've been drinking..." He held out his palms to me sincerely. "I wanna say grace..."

We held hands and he blessed the food.

Lord, I know my prayers are being answered.

"What are you thankful for?" Nefer asked. His apprehension was apparent.

I squeezed his hands, with matched anxiety. "I don't know who's pulling the strings here... if it's Sekima, or the government... leaders... or the Creator... or whatever, whoever... but I am thankful for it. For... you..."

Is it you, Creator? Am I on my way to you?

He smiled. "So am I."

"Ok, no more sappy shit." I was close to tears. "You know how I feel."

"I do." He leaned in and kissed my wrist.

This stimulated me.

"Every minute of every day," he added. He kissed my palm.

"You should..." I breathed heavily, "eat your food before it gets cold..."

"I will." He immediately stood up, then came around the table. He pulled me to my feet and grabbed me by my waist.

"Whoa, what are you doing?" I was slightly dizzy from the abrupt motion.

He scooped me into his arms. "I'm gonna eat my food."

He carried me out of the kitchen.

I laughed. "That's not what I meant!"

"I know what you meant."

~~ * ~~

The days were much colder by the end of the month. Nefer had the heat on a schedule and declined to adjust it regardless of my criticisms. He bought me sweaters and cozy socks.

"Icicles are hanging out of my nose," I had embellished.

He bought me a fleece blanket.

It was Tuesday, December third. I drank the final gallon as soon as I woke up that morning. Nefer sat in the living room, watching the morning news. The volume was high enough for me to hear the newscasters reporting on technology that could potentially eliminate the need to see a general practitioner. The development company's diagnostics device had an eighty-six percent accuracy rating on detecting the causes for many common ailments.

"I'll be satisfied when it's one-hundred percent," a female anchor commented with a laugh. "That's my health they're talking about! Fourteen percent is a lot!"

The doorbell rang.

"I think they should work on robots to replace all the people who prepare your food at the drive-thru," another one said. "Even eighty-six percent would be better than what they do now! Every time I say no onions and no mayo, they put it on! Heh, is it so hard? I say no onions, it means no... onions! Easy!"

I exited the kitchen to see what channel Nefer was watching, but stopped when I noticed he was at the front door, talking to Sekima. I instantly became troubled. She glanced at me.

"Good morning, sunshine!" she exclaimed, grinning.

Nefer stepped aside, moderately stressed.

"Oh, Nefer, stop pouting." She entered the house and walked over to me. "Did you drink all of the containers?"

"Yes..." I answered.

"Come with me." She turned to leave. "Both of you."

Nefer dawdled at the open door. He didn't move until I was beside him, then he retrieved our coats from the closet.

"I feel like her pet," he muttered.

"You're her son," I replied. "Not her pet."

"Yea, well, you know the feeling. Following orders and don't know what's really happening."

I didn't have a response.

We sat in Sekima's limousine without speaking for several minutes after the vehicle began moving. Nefer stared out the window and I gazed at the floor.

"You two need to cheer up!" Sekima said.

"Not in the mood," Nefer sighed.

"What are we doing here?" I cautiously peered up at her. "The final sacrifice...?"

Pain developed in my chest.

"Doris, you ask me this, but you already have the answer," she noted calmly.

I gulped back vomit in my throat. "I am asking what it is..."

"You must continue to maintain your trust," She stared at Nefer. "I have not lied to either of you."

"I trust you..." I rubbed my hands together. "I know that what we're doing needs to happen even if I don't fully understand everything... I know..."

"What do you know, Doris?" She watched me.

"I know..." I cleared my throat, "that our civilization goes against our human nature and our time on this earth is temporary. The ones who lead us are higher than our government and they are global. This country is the hub of a plan for synthetic ascension and people like me involuntarily play a part in its success. There are only two classes in society and ours is the largest. I know that Edna was not a talking demon cat... the voice was mine and the parasite I harnessed is part of a series of parasites feeding on the chemicals produced by our rank's sinful behaviors. The other six parasites are with our leaders and they've used them to motivate us to give in to these behaviors. They are all distractions and the system needs to have them. The committees of Ascension use your company for assistance. I know we all hope to reach the Creator, whether we have belief or not. I know that both my blood and Nefer's blood have something to do with this. I know that there is a final sacrifice... and sacrifice is needed for true ascension... I know..."

I know Nefer is going to die.

I nibbled my lower lip and peeked at Nefer. I couldn't conclude what I was saying.

"You know then, that you cannot allow your fear to avert you from what must be done," Sekima nodded. "The final sacrifice will activate the signal to begin ascension. Thus, the earth will receive the means to rebalance the cycle of life. This will absolve humanity."

"What is the signal?" I watched Nefer, who still stared out the window quietly.

"It is the last calculation in the Golden Ratio. The formula determines space, time, and energy. With all that you have accomplished, know it is according to this design. A set of twelve numbers are sequential directives that I have translated for you."

"To rebalance the cycle..."

"Yes. The cycle has become unstable due to the restriction of wisdom. The perception of five key elements that would be liberties for you; time, control, knowledge, understanding, and truth. Your leaders have persuaded you into believing these elements can be owned and through this falsification, you are owned."

"Through the system..."

"Through the system," she reaffirmed. "Your civilization is a value system. Value is meaningless and unquenchable. It is adaptable to conditions in favor of any preferred outcome. Therefore, it cannot acquire true equilibrium. This system goes against nature, and deprives you from honoring the oath of the Creator."

I placed my hand on Nefer's and squeezed. This action soothed a portion of my feelings.

He turned from the window. "What oath...?"

"Upon ascension, all will be revealed." She kept her eyes on me.

"Why?" I questioned. "Why me? Why am I here? I asked you before and you didn't give me a straight answer..."

"With all that you know, you still ask me why?" She squinted her eyes.

I was sweating profusely. "My... blood..."

A smile gradually appeared on her face. "What is present in your blood, Doris?"

"Instructions..."

The car slowed down to turn onto a familiar dirt road and the driver opened the door for us when we arrived.

"You will have to listen to me and remain patient." Sekima began to climb out. "Let's go."

She led us around to the back of her home. When we entered the garden beyond the patio, it was noticeably warmer as we walked along the stone path. We passed a pavilion and a small pond. There was a large area of what appeared to be recently disturbed dirt. Six fresh mounds of soil were in a row, with one hole.

"Doris, undress and enter the earth," Sekima directed.

I fearfully looked at Nefer as I slowly removed all my clothes. He took hold of my hand and we stepped up to the hole. He assisted me while I lowered myself inside and kissed my hand, which magnified my fright.

"Please don't..." I whimpered.

"I'm sorry," he replied, doleful.

"What did I say about that sorry shit?"

He laughed, but was filled with poignancy. "I'm not sorry."

"Lie down, Doris." Sekima held a shovel out to him. "Nefer, cover her."

Once I did so, the warm dirt seemed to cling to me. I watched Nefer pour the soil over me. He stopped at my neck.

"Cover her completely," Sekima ordered.

I shut my eyes and felt the dirt fall onto my face. I held my breath.

"Relax, Doris..."

I began to panic as the weight of the dirt increased. It started to get hot. I exhaled when I couldn't hold my breath any longer. As I breathed in, I smelled flowers and steadily grew fatigued.

"Relax..." Sekima's voice echoed.

I drifted off to sleep.

I wasn't certain whether my eyes were open or closed, nor if I was even awake. I heard subtle humming in darkness. Pressure increased in my ears and became painful.

"Doris," Edna's voice, sang to me. "Oh, Doris!"

The pain subsided upon hearing her, but I remained blind.

"Doris, what have you gotten us into?" she asked. She sounded like she was directly in my ear.

I couldn't answer.

"Well," she went on, "I didn't expect to be around after you and that woman killed me, but... since I'm a part of you, where else would I go? I know you miss seeing me. I can tell..."

I had the sensation of dangling in the air. My feet touched a smooth, warm surface that allowed me to stand in the black space.

"Do you hear that...?" she said.

I didn't hear anything but the faint buzzing. It strengthened before converting into squeaky grinding. The noise blared as a tiny white dot formed in front of me. When the dot expanded, through it I could see Sekima's garden. I was pulled toward it and my eyes opened.

The daylight sun beamed down on me. I had something pressed against my mouth. A liquid that tasted sweet and salty trickled into it. I gasped and grabbed at the object as I shut my eyes. I clutched it to swallow the delectable drink. Moaning in pleasure, I opened my eyes again to see I was suckling from a wrist with an open wound. I peered to my right and realized it was Nefer.

He was lying on the ground beside me, his eyes closed.

I felt a pang in my chest. Although I tried to stop drinking, it was too good to stop.

Stop! I advised myself. *Stop! Let him go!*

The craving to drink abruptly ceased and I released him. I quickly sat up to shake him.

"Nefer..." I implored breathlessly. I unsuccessfully attempted to find his pulse. Terrified, I looked around.

He must have pulled me out of the hole. The other six mounds were also empty.

"Help!" I cried. "Please!"

I turned him over onto his back and pressed my ear to his chest. I was relieved to feel his heart beating. His chest moved from shallow breathing. I kissed his forehead lovingly.

"Don't you fucking die!" I begged, wiping tears. "Help me!!"

I caught sight of movement to my left. When I glanced over, I saw Sekima's driver walking up.

"Oh..." I was suddenly insecure about being naked.

He approached me aggressively. Without saying a word, he grabbed my arm and yanked me to my feet.

"Ow!" I shouted, mostly from shock.

He lifted me to deftly toss me over his shoulder. He whirled around and went toward the house.

"What the fuck!" I squirmed, kicked. I looked at Nefer in despair.

He's just going to leave him??

"Put me down!" I ordered and continued to cry. "Don't... leave him there! N—no!"

He ignored me. He walked around to the front. We were headed to the driveway. We went to the limousine and he opened the door before setting me down, then grasped my wrist to force me inside.

I resisted. "I can do it! Stop!"

"In," he demanded. His voice vibrated my bones.

I entered the car and he slammed the door shut. A sharp pain shot through my abdomen as the car began moving. I gripped my stomach and fell over. It was a very uncomfortable ride. With each bump, I felt closer to vomiting. I spent the drive lamenting over all that I had done up to this point.

After some time, we halted. The driver exited the car and when he opened the passenger door, cold air breezed inside, causing me to shiver. I gazed up at him, and presumed he waited for me to get out.

"It's cold," I stated, tearfully. "I don't have any clothes."

No response.

We were in what seemed to be a densely wooded area. I sighed and left the car. I didn't see any paved roads nearby, but a dirt path before me led through the trees.

He pointed down the path.

"It's cold, dammit." I rubbed my arms in an effort to warm up. I ventured forward when it was obvious that he didn't care. I sensed his concentration on the direction he gave. "Ok... I'm going..."

I followed the long path through the forest, cautiously watching the ground. I periodically glanced up at my surroundings, listening to the rustling leaves and the birds chirping. The temperature rose the deeper I trekked. I heard the sounds of water and eventually arrived to a small beach. I could see someone standing at the shore. I knew it was Sekima as I despondently approached.

"Come beside me, Doris," she said, while she continued facing the water.

"Nefer..." I stumbled over, fighting against my emotions. I could barely stand when I reached her.

She held out her hand to me and revealed a ring inside. "Put this on."

The ring was a gold band with a cloudy crystal. I collected it from her hand and slid it onto my trembling finger. The spot burned.

"Step into the water." Her tone was even.

"Nefer..." I repeated, distraught. "I..."

She soundlessly viewed the waves rolling over the sand. Even though I couldn't determine her desires, it was clear she wouldn't engage me in conversation.

I walked into the water, bawling uncontrollably. The freezing waves crashed against my midsection. My hand swiftly stung. The stinging travelled up my arm, then while flaring through my entire body, the color of my skin started to turn a dark purplish-blue. As if I was being controlled, my arms stiffly went to my sides. My head turned upward and I was prevented from moving. I noticed the moon hovering in the daytime sky, unusually close. My eyes were fixated on it.

A full moon...

My mouth forced open. I stood frozen as a dark shadow slowly wafted out. The parasite cloud escaped me, and my skin was scorching. It increased in size upon floating. I couldn't determine how my body was reacting due to the insufferable pain. The smog gained speed and began to spread. It dispensed from me for hours as the day became night.

The moon above appeared to shine brighter. Faint whispers commenced and increased in volume, but sustained incoherence. There was a flash that resembled a camera just before the moon disappeared. I could finally move moments later, and the fog made its way across the sky. I plummeted forward into the water. The waves were set to pull me farther toward the ocean when I was snatched by my arm back ashore.

The driver held me firmly, guiding me to safety. I combed my mind for his name while he pulled me through the forest.

"Uh, Lincoln?!" I blurted, unsure. "L—Lucas! Where are we going??"

Is Nefer waiting for me? Is he ok? Where is he? Did I kill him?

Once again, he didn't answer. He fostered no reaction but the diligence to bring me to the vehicle. At the car, he prepared to shove me inside but I pleaded with him and he allowed me to enter unaided.

Lucas periodically glared at me through the rear-view mirror during the trip. My senses assured me he didn't study my body with lust, but I covered my breasts anyway. He was also void of anger, so I deduced it was simply his expression. We ended up at an airfield and drove along the runway to a large shed. He parked inside next to a small, sleek plane and continued to stare as he cut off the engine. I stared back, trying to open the door.

Of course, it's locked... I peered through the window and spotted Sekima beside the plane.

"Doris!" she shouted once Lucas opened the door. She approached holding folded clothes and shoes.

My nausea crept up, followed by sorrow as soon as I saw she was alone. I exited the vehicle, biting my lip to avoid tears.

She handed me the clothes and beckoned me to leave the shed with her. I quickly put on the clothing to follow her. I glanced up at the blackness overhead, convinced that the air had gotten warmer.

Lucas began to wheel the plane out of the shed. He opened the door and Sekima climbed into the back. I cautiously entered behind her and picked up a headset that sat on the seat. Lucas got into the front and shut the door. He donned a headset prior to interacting effortlessly with the dashboard. A few seconds later, the propeller on the front started to spin.

"Put those on," Sekima pointed at the headphones I held. She was already wearing a set.

"Nefer..." I mumbled. I put on the headset when she didn't speak. "Where are we going...?"

The plane lurched forward.

"To my office."

"I am the only one
You play me twice, and when you're done
You hear three contradicting sounds
Once all the cat's lives have been found"

Don't miss out!

Visit the website below and you can sign up to receive emails whenever Lauren Jiggetts publishes a new book. There's no charge and no obligation.

https://books2read.com/r/B-A-HGSO-TFQOB

BOOKS 2 READ

Connecting independent readers to independent writers.

About the Author

Lauren Jiggetts was born in Queens, New York and has been writing ever since she was young. Despite how long she's been writing, she has only recently released her work to the world. When she isn't working, she enjoys spending time with family, reading, playing video games, and watching shows. Some of her favorite genres are science fiction, fantasy, horror, and drama. Her family encouraged her to share her writings and her hope is that others find them an interesting read. She plans to have more writings in the near future.